D1374705

30130502065334

God's wounds, but it was another fight. And Anna was sure she could guess what the cause was, too.

As if theatre life was not already unpredictable enough, Anna thought wryly. Robert Alden could always be relied upon to liven things up.

And that was why she was such a fool. She finally had her life orderly again, after the end of a most ill-advised marriage and a blessed widowhood. She helped her father with his many businesses, especially the White Heron, and she loved the challenge of it all. She had no more use for the perils of romance—especially with an *actor*.

But when she looked at Rob Alden she felt like a silly girl again. A blushing, giggling clot-pole of a girl—just like all the legions of ladies who only came to the theatre to watch him on stage.

He was a handsome, tempting devil indeed. One with the magical gift of poetry in addition to his azure eyes and tight backside. Anna refused to be tempted. Her task was only to lure plays from him—those wondrous tales that drew vast crowds and great profits.

But there would be no beautiful words if he killed himself in a brawl…

THE TAMING OF THE ROGUE

Amanda McCabe

First published in Great Britain 2012
by Mills & Boon, an imprint of Harlequin (UK) Limited.
Large Print edition 2012
Harlequin (UK) Limited, Eton House, 18-24 Paradise Road,
Richmond, Surrey TW9 1SR

© Ammanda McCabe 2012

ISBN: 978 0 263 23698 9

Harlequin (UK) policy is to use papers that are natural,
renewable and recyclable products and made from wood grown in
sustainable forests. The logging and manufacturing process conform
to the legal environmental regulations of the country of origin.

Printed and bound in Great Britain
by CPI Antony Rowe, Chippenham, Wiltshire

Amanda McCabe wrote her first romance at the age of sixteen—a vast epic, starring all her friends as the characters, written secretly during algebra class.

She's never since used algebra, but her books have been nominated for many awards, including the RITA®, *RT Book Reviews* Reviewers' Choice Award, the Booksellers Best, the National Readers' Choice Award, and the Holt Medallion. She lives in Oklahoma, with a menagerie of two cats, a pug and a bossy miniature poodle, and loves dance classes, collecting cheesy travel souvenirs, and watching the Food Network—even though she doesn't cook.

Visit her at http://ammandamccabe.tripod.com and http://www.riskyregencies.blogspot.com

Previous novels by the same author:

TO CATCH A ROGUE*
TO DECEIVE A DUKE*
TO KISS A COUNT*
CHARLOTTE AND THE WICKED LORD
 (in *Regency Summer Scandals*)
A NOTORIOUS WOMAN†
A SINFUL ALLIANCE†
HIGH SEAS STOWAWAY†
THE WINTER QUEEN
 (in *Christmas Betrothals*)
THE SHY DUCHESS
SNOWBOUND AND SEDUCED
 (in *Regency Christmas Proposals*)

And in Mills & Boon® Historical *Undone!* eBooks:

SHIPWRECKED AND SEDUCED†
TO BED A LIBERTINE
THE MAID'S LOVER
TO COURT, CAPTURE AND CONQUER
GIRL IN THE BEADED MASK
UNLACING THE LADY IN WAITING
ONE WICKED CHRISTMAS

The Chase Muses trilogy
†linked by character

THE TAMING OF THE ROGUE
features characters you will have met in
TO COURT, CAPTURE AND CONQUER
a Mills & Boon® Historical *Undone!* eBook

**Did you know that some of these novels
are also available as eBooks?
Visit www.millsandboon.co.uk**

Chapter One

London, 1589

God's wounds, but it was another fight. And Anna was sure she could guess what the cause was, too.

She put down the costume she was mending, and peered over the railing of the upper gallery to the stage below. Morning rehearsal had not yet begun for Lord Henshaw's Men, and only a few of the players sat there, desultorily running their lines as Old Madge swept up the used rushes of yesterday's performance. It seemed an ordinary start to a day at the White Heron Theatre—perhaps she had imagined that shout.

Nay, for there it was again, moving closer from the lane outside. A man's hoarse yell, a woman's scream. A mocking laugh.

The men on the stage heard it, too, breaking

off mid-sentence to turn curiously towards the bolted doors.

'It seems Master Alden has returned,' Anna called down to them, her voice calm and steady. Unlike the rest of her. Her hands trembled as she longed to grab Robert Alden and give him a violent shake! And then to drag him close and kiss him…

'Fool,' she whispered, not knowing if she meant him—or herself. She had fought hard to impose control on her life, and she wasn't going to let a ridiculously handsome, troublemaking actor wreak havoc on that.

'Shall we bring him in?' asked Ethan Camp, the company's comedian. He relished a good brawl.

'I suppose we must,' Anna said. 'He owes us a new play, and we'll never have it if his arms are broken.'

She spun round and hurried towards the narrow staircase, lifting her grey wool skirts as she dashed down the winding wooden steps past the lower galleries, empty and echoing so early in the day, and into the yard which was open to the sky above. The quarrel was louder there, as if the participants played to the groundlings.

But Anna knew too well that if any blood was

shed it would not be from a burst pig's bladder hidden under a costume.

Ancient Elias, the porter, was already unlocking the doors, the players drawing their daggers. Even Madge leaned on her broom, looking on with keen interest.

As if theatre life was not already unpredictable enough, Anna thought wryly. Robert Alden could always be relied upon to liven things up.

And that was why she was such a fool. She finally had her life orderly again, after the end of a most ill-advised marriage and a blessed widowhood. She helped her father with his many businesses, especially the White Heron, and she loved the challenge of it all. The fact that she was good at the work, and was needed, was something new and welcome. She could do her work and hide backstage. She had no more use for the perils of romance. Especially with an *actor*.

But when she looked at Rob Alden she felt like a silly girl again. A blushing, giggling clot-pole of a girl, just like all the legions of ladies who only came to the theatre to watch him on stage. To toss flowers at his feet and swoon. To lift their skirts for him in one of the boxes when they thought no one was looking.

He was a handsome, tempting devil, indeed. One with the magical gift of poetry in addition to his azure eyes and tight backside. Anna refused to be tempted. Refused to be another of his easy conquests. Her task was only to lure plays from him, those wondrous tales that drew vast crowds and great profits. A play by Robert Alden was always a great success, and ran for days and days to sold-out crowds.

But there would be no beautiful words if he killed himself in a brawl, which Anna feared he might. He had a reputation even in tumultuous Southwark for his temper.

As soon as the doors swung open she dashed through them, clutching the fearsome weapon of her sewing scissors even as she wished she had the short sword she carried when she collected her father's rents. The actors were right behind her.

Southwark was fairly quiet in the morning hours. A district that made a living in dubious pleasures like bear pits, brothels and taverns—all the things that were banished from within the city walls and into the suburbs—could never easily rouse itself after a long night's revelry. The thick pearl-grey mist drifting off the river hung over the shuttered, close-packed buildings and the muddy, mucky lanes.

But a few shutters were thrown open, sleepy faces peering down to see what the trouble was. *Trouble* always attracted attention in Southwark, no matter what the hour. But everyone soon melted away once it was over.

Anna first saw the woman—a buxom female clad in once-bright, now-dingy yellow satin, her matching yellow hair straggling over her shoulders. She was crying, the tears carving streaks in her thick face paint.

Anna's gaze darted to the man who stood in front of the whore, waving a sword around wildly. A great, portly bear of a man, with a reddened face and thick black beard. He looked quite unhappy, ready to explode, and Anna felt a cold touch of disquiet in her belly. The man was obviously drunk, and that made him even more unpredictable.

Unlike a play, where the script made it clear how all would end. Had Rob gone too far this time?

She turned to face Rob, who seemed most unconcerned by the whole scene. Probably he, too, was ale-shot, but he gave no indication of it. His blue eyes shone like a summer sky, his grin was

merry and mocking, as if imminent disembowel-
ment was greatly amusing.

Unlike his opponent, Rob was lean and lithe,
with an actor's powerful grace. His unlaced white
shirt revealed a smooth, muscled expanse of bare
chest—and a wide smear of blood. He held a rapier, lightly twirling the hilt in his hands as the
weak sunlight flashed on its blade and on the gold
rings adorning his ink-stained fingers.

Anna knew that he was a skilled fighter. Everyone knew that in Southwark. She had seen it too
many times, both on stage and in the streets. The
man's mocking tongue and quick temper were ir-
resistible temptations to brawlers. But somehow
this time felt different. There was a tense charge
to the air, a feeling of time standing still before
crashing down on them.

'Mistress Barrett!' Rob said, giving her an elaborate bow. 'I see you have come to witness our
revels.'

'What seems to be the trouble this time?' she
asked, glancing carefully between Rob and the
enraged bear-man.

'He's a boar-pig of a cheat!' the bear-man roared.
'He owes me money for the lightskirt.'

The woman's sobs grew louder. ''Tweren't like

that. I told you! *Some* men aren't brutes like you. I weren't working then…'

'Aye,' Rob said cheerfully. 'Some of us know how to be a gentleman and woo a lady properly.'

Gentleman? Anna pursed her lips to keep from laughing. Robert Alden was many things—witty, clever, and damnably handsome. Gentlemanly wasn't one of them.

This was just another quarrel—over payment to a Winchester goose. Yet somehow she still sensed there was more to it. Something else was happening underneath this common, everyday disagreement.

She opened her mouth to argue, turning back to Rob, but just then that strange tension snapped and chaos broke free in the quiet morning. With an echoing shout, the bear-man lunged at Rob, all flailing arms and flashing blades, faster than she could have imagined possible.

His men, half-hidden in the shadows, tumbled after him, shouting, and everything threatened to hurtle over into a full-blown battle. Anna pressed herself back against the wall.

But she had underestimated Rob. Debauched he might look, yet the long night had lost him none of his actor's grace. Swift as the tiger in the Queen's menagerie, he sidestepped his attacker, reaching out to grab his arm. Using the man's bulk against him, Rob flipped him to the ground. A brittle snap rang through the air, causing the bear-man's minions to freeze in place as he howled in agony.

Rob gestured to them with his blade. 'Who is next, then?' he called.

Predictably, no one took that offer. They scooped up their fallen leader and ran away, the sobbing whore reluctantly following them. The sudden explosion of violence receded as fast as it had come.

'I hope you are content now,' Anna murmured.

Rob leaned his palm against the wall near her head, laughing. 'I am, rather. They ran like the gutter rats they are. Didn't you find it amusing, Mistress Barrett?'

'No, I did not. I think…' Then she saw it. The smear of blood on his bared chest was a thicker, brighter red, staining his rumpled shirt. 'You're hurt!'

She reached out to touch him, but he drew away with a hiss. ''Tis a scratch,' he said.

'A scratch can lead to the churchyard if it's not seen to,' she protested. 'I am the daughter of Tom Alwick, remember? I'm certainly no stranger to wounds. Please, let me see.'

He glanced past her at the gawping actors, reluctant to lose their excitement so fast. 'Not here,' he muttered.

'What? Do you fear having your modesty offended? Fine, we can go to the tiring-house.'

'I will happily shed my garments for you, Mistress Barrett. You need only ask...' Suddenly Rob swayed, his bronzed face ashen.

Anna caught him against her, her arm around his lean waist, as alarm shot through her. Robert Alden was never pale. Something troubling indeed must have happened in the night.

'Rob, what is it?' she gasped.

'No one must know,' he said roughly, his breath stirring the curls at her temple as he leaned against her.

Know what? 'I will not let them,' she whispered. 'Come inside with me now, and all will be well.'

If only she could believe that herself.

Chapter Two

Anna led Rob through the twisting maze of corridors behind the stage of the White Heron. It was eerily silent there, with Rob's breath echoing off the rough wooden walls. The smell of dust, face paint and blood was thick in her throat, and Rob's body was too warm as he leaned on her shoulder—as if he had a fever.

Despite her efforts not to worry, Anna couldn't help it. All her life, with her father and her husband, and now with her father again, she had lived among men of hot and unpredictable tempers. Fights and feuds, duels, even sudden and violent death, were things all too commonplace in the streets of Southwark and Bankside. She had learned the hard lessons of dealing with such men.

But Rob Alden—despite his own quick temper, he had always seemed above such things, able to win a brawl with a quick flick of his sword and a careless laugh. He was known and feared in this world. Men said his smile hid a lethal heart, and they avoided him when they could. Anna had seen this time and again, and puzzled over it. Rob walked through life as if enchanted. Unlike her own existence.

Had the enchantment worn away?

She pushed away that cold, clammy fear and led him into the deserted tiring-house behind the stage. Chests full of costumes and properties were stacked along the walls, and a false cannon gleamed in a dark corner. Anna pushed aside a pile of blunted rapiers and made Rob sit down on a scarred old clothes chest.

He slowly lowered himself to the makeshift seat, watching her warily. There was no hint of his carefree laughter, his constant sunny flirtation. He looked older, harder, the sharp, sculpted angles of his handsome face cast in shadows. How had she never noticed that coldness before?

It made her even more cautious of him—of the threat his good looks posed to her and her hard-won peace.

'What happened?' she said. She turned away from the steady, piercing glow of his eyes and dug out her basket from a cupboard. She always kept bandages and salves nearby for these all-too-frequent moments. There were always injuries in the theatre.

'You saw for yourself,' Rob said. His voice was as hard as his expression, with no hint of the light humour he usually used to cloak his true self.

Whatever Rob Alden's true self might be. Anna wasn't sure she wanted to know.

'A quarrel over a whore?' Anna said.

'Aye. It happens all the time, alas.'

'Indeed, it does.' Her father was the landlord of brothels. She knew what went on behind those doors, and actors were the worst sort of trouble there. Yet she couldn't shake away the sense that something more was happening here.

She watched Rob as he pulled his shirt off over his head. He winced as the cloth brushed over his shoulder, and Anna could see why. A long gash arced over his upper ribs into the angle of his shoulder—a jagged red line that barely missed his heart. It was crusted over with dried blood, but some fresh, redder liquid still seeped out onto his smooth burnished skin.

There were older scars, as well—stark white re-minders of other fights and wounds that marred his perfect beauty, making Anna remember the daily danger of this life.

She dampened a clean cloth and carefully dabbed at the new wound. She breathed shallowly, slowly, and kept her expression bland and calm. She had learned a thing or two about artifice from working around actors. Nothing should ever be what it seemed.

'A quarrel over payment?' she asked as she lightly sponged away the dried blood to examine the depth of the wound.

His breath roughened but he didn't move away from her. He just watched her with that steady, unreadable look on his face, with those blue eyes that seemed to see so much yet give nothing away.

Anna slowly raised her gaze to meet his. She saw why the bawds fought over him as they did. He was the last sort of man she needed in her life, but he was a rare specimen of manhood with that face, and that lean, strong body displayed before her now. He was a danger just by simply being himself, and whatever it was he kept so well hidden only made him more so.

She dropped her attention back to the work of cleaning the wound. The coppery tang of blood was a timely reminder.

'Aye,' he answered after a long, heavy pause. 'Her keeper tried to charge me more than agreed on after we were done. Something I'm sure your esteemed father would never do in one of *his* houses.'

Was that sarcasm in his voice? Anna nearly laughed. She wouldn't put anything past her father and his business practices. He was such an old rogue. But not even he would cheat Robert Alden.

And neither would anyone else in Southwark. Too many had felt the chill of Rob's dagger, and ever since he'd been tossed into Bridewell Prison for a short spell after a fatal duel he had grown even colder. That had been before he'd become a sharer in Lord Henshaw's Men, and one of their most popular actors and playwrights, so Anna didn't know the details of the crime. But she had heard all the gossip.

'And he did this to you? The bawd's pimp?' she said, as she dabbed some of the sticky salve onto the clean wound. 'For I would wager it was not the girl herself who took a blade to you.'

A hint of his usual careless grin whispered over his lips. 'Nay, she couldn't bear to ruin my handsome looks. But it wasn't that boar-pig of a pimp who did this.'

'It wasn't? Two brawls in one night? That's a great deal even for you, Rob.'

'It was an old quarrel. Nothing to worry about at all, fair Anna.'

'Then I hope it was resolved at last. Or someday someone *will* ruin your looks, I fear.'

'I'm touched that you worry about me.'

Anna laughed. She reached for a roll of bandages and wrapped the linen tightly over Rob's shoulder. The white cloth was stark against his bare skin. 'I worry about my family's business. With no more Robert Alden plays the White Heron would surely suffer a loss of receipts, and my father has many expenses.'

Rob suddenly caught her wrist in his grasp, his fingers wrapping round it in a tight, warm caress. For all his wounded state, he was still very strong. He drew her closer—so close she could feel his breath on her throat, the alluring heat of his body against hers.

'You wound me, Anna,' he said, and for once there was no laughter in his deep, velvet-smooth voice. 'Is that truly what you think of me?'

She wasn't sure what she thought of him. He had confused her ever since she'd met him, when she'd come back to her father's house after the blessed end of her wretched marriage. He was unpredictable, attractive, changeable...

Dangerous.

She tried to pull her hand away from him, to create a safer distance between them. For an instant his hand tightened and she thought he wasn't going to let her go. She swayed towards him, not even realising what she was doing.

He pressed a quick, hard kiss to the inside of her wrist. 'Of course you do,' he muttered, and let her go.

Anna stumbled back a step. She still felt dizzy, baffled, and she didn't like that feeling at all. In her marriage she'd had no power, no control, and she had worked hard since to make her life her own. She didn't want Robert Alden, with his handsome face and wild ways, tossing her back into turmoil again.

She wouldn't allow it.

She scooped up his rumpled shirt from where he had dropped it on the clothes chest and tossed it to him. Despite his wound, he caught it neatly with one hand.

'We all need you here, Robert,' she said. 'Your careless behaviour endangers us all.'

He laughed, and Anna thought she heard a bitter

note to it, underneath the dismissive carelessness. Did he see what he did to them? Did he care at all?

He pulled the shirt over his head, covering the bandage, and said, 'I have disappointed you again, fairest Anna. But don't despair—I will have the new play to you within a fortnight. I'm sure even I can stay healthy and whole for that long.'

Anna wasn't so sure. Temptations lurked around every corner in Southwark, and Rob wasn't one to deny them. Her doubt must have shown on her face, for Rob laughed again.

'Perhaps you would want to lock me up in your garret?' he said. 'I could slip you the pages under the door as I write them, and with every scene you could reward me with bread and ale—and whatever else you might care to bestow.'

With kisses, maybe, like his bawds? Exasperated, Anna threw the rest of the bandages at his head. 'Don't tempt me, Robert Alden—I may do just that!' She whirled round and dashed from the room, his laughter following her as she went.

'I look forward to being your captive, Anna,' he called. 'I can think of so many ways we could pass the time…'

She slammed the door behind her, cutting off his infuriating laughter, and made her way back to the open air and light of the theatre. The actors were all gathered there, milling around on stage as if waiting to see what would happen next.

'What are you all loitering about for?' Anna shouted. She was thoroughly fed up with actors and their wild doings. 'We have a performance this very afternoon and there is no time to waste.'

They quickly went back to their rehearsal, and Anna returned to her sewing in the gallery, trying to get back to the day's many tasks. But her hands were trembling so much she could scarcely wield the needle.

Chapter Three

As soon as Anna was gone from the tiring-house, the door safely shut between them, Rob slumped back down onto the chest. His shoulder felt as if it was on fire, the salve burning as it knitted the flesh back together, and his mind was heavy with weariness after the long night he had just passed.

He rubbed his hands hard over his face and pushed back the rumpled waves of his hair. It had been meant to be a simple task—a quick one. Go to a party, wait until everyone was ale-shot, and find the documents. Compared to what he usually did for Queen and country, it was simpler than crossing the lane.

Only it had not worked out quite that way. He had the papers—but he had also got a dagger to the shoulder.

'Surely it is time for me to retire,' he said, and

then gave a wry laugh. No one retired from the service of Secretary Walsingham—unless it was in a wooden box to the churchyard. But, God's teeth, he was growing weary of it all.

He prodded at his shoulder and felt the ridge of the neat bandage there against his skin, which made him think of Anna Barrett. He remembered the cool softness of her hands on his bare skin as she nursed him, the cautious light in her jewel-green eyes as she examined the wound. She smelled of roses and fresh sunlight, and her body was so slender and supple, had felt so warm against his as she'd leaned close. So close he could almost have slipped his arm around her waist and pulled her to him for a kiss…

She was beautiful, with her glossy red-brown hair and pale skin, the lush, full pink lips that seemed to contradict her prickly distance. Rob had long been a great appreciator of female beauty and softness, and the moment he'd met her all those months ago he'd been drawn to her. There was passion under her coolness, a flash of raw fire that beckoned to him.

But she was untouchable. Everyone in Southwark said she had no desire for men, or for women, either. She was above all of them, chilly and glittering, like the North Star. All the men who tried their luck with her were laughingly turned away.

So Rob did not try. There were too many willing women for him to waste his time on other than Anna Barrett. But he did like to tease her, flirt with her, just to see that rose-pink glow rise in her cheeks, feel the spark of her temper. He liked even more to touch her whenever he could, in those rare moments she let him close enough, and feel the heat of her body.

He dared do no more. Anna Barrett was above him, just as that star was, in this sordid world of Southwark, but not of it, and he wouldn't drag her down into his work. He was not that heartless, surely, not quite that far gone. Not yet.

Yet there were moments, flashes of something he usually kept hidden even from himself, when he wondered what it would be like to have her admiration. To kiss those soft lips and feel her respond to him, open to him.

Given the way she'd run from the tiring-house, today was not that day. And he had to keep it that way. She had to go on thinking he had been wounded in a tawdry quarrel over some Doll Tearsheet—just as she had thought so many times before. She had to see him as the face he presented to the world: a careless brawler.

'Your careless behaviour endangers us all,' she had said, and she was more right than she knew. The White Heron was the closest thing to a real home Rob had known for a long time, the Lord Henshaw's Men his only family now. He had to protect them.

He laced up his shirt, pushing away the lingering pain in his shoulder. He could smell Anna's rose-water perfume on the linen folds, and he dragged in a deep breath to hold it with him for one more fleeting instant. That bitter weariness was pressing down on him, but he couldn't rest now, couldn't take refuge in the softness of Anna Barrett. He had to deliver those papers.

There was a quick knock at the door, and Rob shook away the last of the pain to gather the concealing cloak of a careless player around him again. The two sides were so much a part of him now it was as easy as changing papier-mâché masks on stage. But could it all become *too* easy? Did he lose his real self in the switch?

'Rob, are you there?' a man called. 'They told me you were hiding in the tiring-house.'

It was his friend and sometimes co-conspirator Lord Edward Hartley. 'Come in, Edward,' Rob said. 'Obviously I am not hiding so very well.'

Edward pushed open the door and slipped inside, closing it behind him. As usual he was dressed in the very height of Court fashion—black velvet doublet slashed with crimson satin, a short cloak embroidered with gold thread, and a plumed cap. He looked like a bright peacock dropped into the drab, dusty backstage area of the theatre.

But Robert knew the steel that lurked behind that jewelled velvet. Edward had saved his life many times, as Rob had saved his in turn. They both served the same cause. With him, Rob could relax his ever-constant vigilance just a bit—just for a moment.

Edward held out a rough pottery jar. 'I heard tell there was a brawl of some sort this morning. I thought perhaps you could use this.'

'Word does travel fast,' Rob said as he reached for the jar and uncorked it. The heady smell of home-made mead rose up in a thick, alcoholic cloud, and he tipped his head back for a long drink. It burned going down, doing its task most effectively. 'I thought you had gone off to the country with your beauteous Lady Elizabeth.'

At the mention of his lady-love, Edward grinned like a passion-struck fool. 'Not as of yet. Our departure was delayed for a few days, which is a good thing if you need stitching up after a fight.'

Rob wiped the back of his hand across his mouth. 'No stitching up required this time. Mistress Barrett mended me well enough.'

'Did she, now?' Edward's brow arched as he reached for the jar to take a drink of his own. 'And does the fair Mistress Barrett know the true nature of this quarrel?'

Rob remembered the look on Anna's face as she told him how his behaviour affected them all. He took another drink of the mead, but even that couldn't quite erase the memory of her frown. 'She knows I quarrelled over a whore's payment. Like everyone else.'

Edward nodded. 'And the papers?'

'I have them.'

'Shall I go with you to deliver them to Seething Lane, then? Maybe with two of us there will be no more trouble on the way.'

'Perhaps tomorrow.' Rob corked the jar again, and resisted the strong urge to dash it to pieces on the flagstone floor. It was his damnable quick temper that had got him here in the first place. He had vowed never to let it get the better of him again, yet it had led to the bloody fight—and almost revealing himself to Anna. 'There is something I must do first.'

Chapter Four

Anna bent her head over the ledger books spread across her desk, trying to concentrate on the neat rows of numbers tabulating that day's receipts from the theatre. She usually loved keeping the accounts—in the end, figures always added up to the correct answer. Unlike human life, they were regular and predictable. She understood them.

Tonight, though, the black ink numbers kept blurring before her eyes. Images kept flashing through her mind, bright and vivid, of Robert Alden and that blood on his shoulder. The solemn look in his eyes as he looked up at her, as if he hid ancient and terrible secrets deep inside—secrets he had only allowed her to glimpse for that one moment before he concealed them again.

'Fie on it all,' she cursed, and threw down her quill in frustration. Tiny droplets of ink scattered across the page. Of course Robert had secrets. Everyone in their world did. It was a dirty, crowded life, and everyone had to survive any way they could. She saw it every day. No one emerged with clean hands or hearts, least of all those who relied on the theatre for their living. She held enough secrets and regrets of her own—she didn't need anyone else's.

Yet something in his eyes had moved her today, quite against her will. Rob Alden was a handsome, merry devil, known to be as quick with a mocking laugh as with his rapier. Today he had looked old and sad, as if he had seen far too much. As if one too many friends had suddenly turned enemy.

Then that glimpse had been gone, and he was hidden again behind his handsome face. But she couldn't forget that one flashing, sad look.

'Don't be such a gaping fool,' Anna said out loud. She was as bad as that sobbing bawd in her cheap yellow dress, weeping over Rob in the street. There was no time for such nonsense, no time for soft emotions—especially over a rogue who did not deserve them and would only laugh at them. Actors were good at counterfeiting love onstage, and rotten at living it.

She carefully scraped the spilled ink off the vellum and tried to return to the neat columns of figures. Shillings and pounds—that was what she needed to ponder now, what she could understand.

Suddenly the house's front door, just beyond her sitting room, flew open, and her father stumbled in. Through the door she caught a glimpse of the White Heron across their small garden, the theatre dark and quiet now in the gathering twilight. The afternoon's revels were long ended by this hour, the crowds gone back to their homes across the river or to more dubious pleasures in the nearby taverns and bawdy houses.

It seemed that was where her father had been, as well. Tom Alwick's russet wool doublet was buttoned crookedly, his hat set askew on his rumpled grey hair. Even from across the room she could smell the cheap wine.

Anna carefully set aside her pen and closed the account book. Her precious quiet hour was done. There would be no time for reading poetry now, as their usual evening routine began. At least her father, unlike her late husband, was an affable drunk. Tom was more likely to regale her with wild tales before he fell to snoring in front of the fire. Sometimes he would cry for her mother—

dead since Anna was a toddler of three, but never forgotten by her father.

Her late husband, Charles Barrett, had used to slap her and break their plate before insisting on his marital rights. So, aye, she much preferred this life here with her father.

'Anna, my darling one!' Tom cried, stumbling on the raised threshold of the sitting room. He reached out with one flailing hand to catch his balance, nearly tearing down an expensive painted cloth from the panelled wall.

Anna leaped up from her chair and caught him by the shoulders before he could ruin their furnishings. She knew too well where every farthing came from to pay for their comfortable house. He leaned against her as she led him to the chair by the fire.

'Are you working again?' he asked, as he fell back onto the embroidered cushions.

Anna moved her sewing basket away and gently lifted his feet onto a stool as she said, 'I was going over the receipts for today's performance. The takings were down a bit, though Lord Edward Hartley took his usual box for the performance.'

'*The Maid's Dilemma* is an old play,' Tom said.

'We'll have rich takings indeed once we open Rob's new play, I swear it.'

'*If* we open it,' Anna murmured as she tugged off her father's boots. They were damp and muddy from his lurch through the Southwark streets, and she set them by the fire to dry.

'What do you mean, my dearest? Rob has never been late delivering a play! And they are always great earners. Audiences love them.'

Of course they were great earners, Anna thought. Women came flocking to see them, hoping for a glimpse of the writer acting onstage himself, and they always paid extra to sit in the upper galleries, rent cushions and buy refreshments.

Anna couldn't really blame them. His plays *were* extraordinary, no matter how maddening the man was. They were wondrous tales of the powers and dangers of kingship, of betrayal and love and revenge, and deep, stirring emotions. They were written with beautiful, poetic words rarely heard on the stage, and the audience was always in floods of tears by the end.

Even Anna, who saw plays every week, was always moved by Robert Alden's words, and the new, wondrous worlds they created. They were worth the trouble he caused.

Usually.

She sat down in the chair across from her father's. 'His last play had delays being passed by the Master of the Revels. It was weeks before we had a licence to stage it. He grows careless with his plots.'

Tom waved this away with an airy gesture, and almost toppled out of his chair. 'Audiences love a bit of controversy. Making them wait only makes them even more excited to see it.'

'Not if you've already paid good coin for a play we can't use!'

'All will be well, Anna, I am sure. You're working too hard of late. It makes you worry too much.'

'I like the work.' It kept her busy—and kept her hidden at the same time.

Tom narrowed his eyes as he gave her a sharp look, the wine haze lifted for an instant. 'You are too young and comely to bury yourself in account books all the time. You should think about suitors again.'

Anna laughed bitterly. 'One husband was enough, Father.'

'Charles Barrett was a stupid brute, and I was a fool to let you marry him,' Thomas said. 'But not all men are like him.'

Nay—some were like Robert Alden. Too handsome and witty for their own good, or for any woman's good at all. 'I am content as I am. Don't we have a comfortable life here?'

'*My* life has certainly been more comfortable since you came back. This house is wonderfully kept, and my profits from the businesses have doubled.'

'Because I make you invest them instead of spending them all on wine and ale.'

'Exactly so, my dearest. But I should not be selfish and keep you here.'

'I told you, I am quite well where I am, Father. I promise. Now, what about some supper? I can send Madge to the tavern for some venison stew, and there is fresh bread…'

'Oh, I almost forgot!' Tom cried. 'I did invite some people to dine with us. They will surely be here at any moment.'

Anna sighed. Of course they would. Her father was always inviting guests for a meal, or a game of cards which usually went on until morning. It was seldom they had a quiet evening alone.

'Then I will have Madge fetch some extra stew, and perhaps a few pies,' she said, and went to ring the bell for the maid. At least her father's guests seldom expected grand fare. 'Who is coming this evening?'

'Some of the actors, of course. Spencer and Cartley and Camp, and perhaps one or two of their friends. We need to discuss the new play and the casting.' Tom paused, never a good sign. 'And Robert. I may have asked him, as well, when I saw him at the Three Bells earlier.'

'Robert was at the Three Bells?' Anna asked in surprise. She would have thought after his adventures of last night he would have eschewed taverns and gone back to his lodgings to collapse.

She should know better. No matter what occurred, he always kept moving. It was almost as if he was one of his own heroic creations.

But she had touched him today, been near to him—looked into his eyes for that one fleeting, vulnerable instant. She knew how warmly human he truly was.

'I heard there was a bit of a disturbance this morning,' her father said. 'But he was writing in his usual corner of the tavern, so all must be well. We can press him about the new play when he arrives.'

Anna braced her palm on the carved fireplace mantel, staring down into the crackling flames.

Robert Alden was coming here tonight. She didn't want to see him again so soon after mending his wound. How could she look at him across her table and keep that secret?

How could she stop herself from reaching out to touch him?

'Father—' she began, only to be interrupted by a pounding at the door.

'I will go,' Tom said as he tried to push himself out of his chair.

Anna shook her head. 'Nay, I will go. It seems Madge is otherwise occupied.'

She took a deep breath as she made her way slowly to the door, steeling herself to see Rob again and to remain expressionless. Yet it was not Rob who waited there on the threshold, it was Henry Ennis, another of the actors in Lord Henshaw's Men.

As he smiled at her and bowed, Anna pushed away that unwanted and unaccountable pang of disappointment and said, 'Master Ennis. We haven't seen you at the White Heron in a few days.'

Henry's smile widened and he reached for her hand to bestow upon her fingers an elaborate salute that made her laugh. Next to Robert, Henry Ennis was the most handsome of the company, slim and angelically blond where Rob was dark as the devil. Henry always seemed to be laughing and cheerful, as open and easy as a fine summer's day, with no hidden depths or concealed secrets.

Anna always enjoyed being around him. He made her laugh along with him, and forget her duties and worries. He never made her feel flustered or confused, as Rob always did.

Against her own will, she glanced past Henry's shoulder to the shadowed garden behind him. But no one was there.

'My beauteous Anna,' Henry said as she took his arm to lead him into the corridor. 'It has pained me greatly to be away from you, but as I had no role in the last production I thought it best I travel to the country to visit my family. They have been neglected of late.'

'Family?' Anna said in surprise. In their strange, vagabond London life she often forgot the actors might have *real* families tucked away somewhere. They formed their own bonds among others of their kind, with her father's house as their temporary hearth.

Did Rob have a family, too? A wife and blue-eyed children, in a cosy village somewhere?

'My mother and sister in Kent,' Henry said. 'I have not seen them in many months.'

'Then I hope you found them well?'

'Very well. A bit bored, mayhap—they always long for tales of London.'

Anna gave him a teasing smile. 'I'm sure they especially long for tales of your London courtships. Does your mother not wish for handsome grandchildren to dandle on her knee?'

Henry laughed ruefully, his handsome face turning faintly pink. 'Perhaps she does. I should so like…' His words trailed away and he shook his head, turning away from her.

'Should so like what, Henry? Come, we are friends! Surely you can talk to me?'

'I should so like for her to meet *you*, Anna. She would like you very much, I think,' he said shyly.

Anna was so shocked by his quiet, serious words that she stopped abruptly in the dining-chamber doorway. Henry wished for her to meet his *mother*? But surely their friendship was only that—a friendship? Though he was kind and sweet-natured, and so handsome…

She studied him in speculation in the flickering half-light of the smoky candles. Aye, he *was* handsome, and so earnest as he watched her. Perhaps friends was a fine place to start. Friends was safe and pleasant—not a threat to her calm serenity, the quiet life she had worked so hard to earn and build.

But as she looked at Henry Ennis she saw not his pale grey eyes, glowing with wary hope as he watched her, waiting for—something. She didn't feel his arm under her hand. She saw Robert's bright blue eyes mocking her as she bandaged his shoulder, staring deep, deep into her hidden soul and letting her glimpse his for one moment. It was his bare, warm skin she felt.

Anna made herself laugh, and tugged Henry towards the dining chamber. 'I am not the sort of lady mothers like very much, Henry. And I fear I shall never leave the city now. The country air is far too clean and sweet for me after so long in London.'

Henry seemed to take her hint, and he laughed merrily, as if that instant of seriousness had never been. Perhaps she had merely imagined it. It had been a long, strange day, after all.

'And my mother will never come to London,' Henry said. 'She is quite certain villains lurk on every street corner, ready to cut an unwary throat. So perhaps you will never meet, after all.'

'Perhaps your mother is right to keep her distance,' Anna murmured. And far wiser than she was herself, living in the very centre of such a perilous world. But she had no desire to leave; this was her home, the only place she could belong. A quiet country hearth was not for her.

There was another knock at the door, and Anna left Henry at the table with her father so she could hurry and answer it. More of the actors waited for her there, far more than her father claimed to have invited. They greeted her exuberantly, kissing her cheek and lifting her from her feet in fierce hugs, before they dashed into the house looking for food and drink. It seemed her father's 'some people' invited to dine included the whole company, along with their always voracious appetites and endless need for wine.

Anna was accustomed to such evenings. Her father's hospitality was boundless, and his memory for such practical matters as how much food to serve was non-existent. Anna sent the servants for more dishes and jugs of wine from the tavern, and the evening passed in a swift, happy blur as she made sure everyone was served and there was enough bread and stew.

Finally she was able to collapse by the sitting-room fire with her own goblet of wine. She tucked up her feet on her father's footstool, listening to the shouts and laughter from supper. Her father would be busy until dawn, and then some of the actors could carry him up to his bed.

Anna reached into her sewing basket for the new volume of poetry she had bought at one of the stalls at St Paul's churchyard just that day. It was an anonymous sonnet cycle about the deep love of a shepherd for an unreachable goddess he'd once glimpsed at her bath, called *Demetrius and Diana.* Everyone was reading and talking of it, and she could see why. The words and emotions were beautiful, so filled with raw longing and the sad realisation that such a love was impossible. Life was only what it was—lonely and cold—and there was no escape from that, even through passion.

She lost herself in that world of sun-dappled sylvan glades and passionate desire, that need for another person. The noise from the company, which grew ever louder as the night wore on, vanished, and she knew only the poor shepherd and his impossible love.

'Why, Mistress Barrett, I see you are a secret romantic,' a deep, velvet-rough voice suddenly said, dragging her out of her dream world.

The book fell from her hands to clatter onto the stone hearth and she twisted round in her chair. It was Robert who stood there in the sitting room doorway, watching her as she read. He leaned his shoulder on the doorframe, his arms lazily crossed over his chest. A half smile lingered at the corners of his lips, but his eyes were dark and solemn as they studied her.

How long had he been standing there?

'You startled me,' she said, hating the way her voice trembled.

'I'm sorry. I didn't mean to frighten you,' he said.

'I didn't even know you were here. I heard no knock at the door.'

'I have only just arrived. Madge let me in.' Rob pushed away from the door and moved slowly to her side, loose-limbed and as deceptively lazy as a cat. As Anna watched, tense, he knelt by her chair and picked up the dropped book.

He took her hand in his, very gently, his fingers light on hers, and carefully laid the book on her palm. But he didn't let go of her. He curled her hand around the leather binding and held his over it.

It was a light caress, cool and gentle, and Anna knew she could draw away whenever she chose. Yet somehow she just—couldn't. She stared down at their joined hands as if mesmerised.

He stared down at them, too, almost as if he could also feel that shimmering, heated, invisible bond tightening around them, closer and closer. The crackle of the fire, the laughter of the company—it all seemed so far away. There was only Robert and herself here now.

'Are you enjoying the travails of poor Demetrius the shepherd?' he asked.

'Very much,' she whispered. She stared hard at the book, its brown cover held by their joined hands. She feared what might happen if she looked into his eyes. Would she crack and crumble away, vanishing into him forever?

What spell did he cast over her?

'The poetry is beautiful,' she went on. 'I can see every ray of sunlight, every summer leaf in those woods—I can feel Demetrius's grief. What a terrible thing it must be to feel like that about another.'

'How terrible *not* to feel that way,' he said. 'Life is an empty, cold shell without passion.'

Anna laughed. It seemed she was not the only 'secret romantic.' 'Is it better to burn than to freeze? Passion consumes until there is nothing left but ash. Demetrius is miserable because of his desire for Diana.'

'True. Diana can't love him back. It isn't in her nature. But if she could, it would be glorious beyond imagining. It is glorious even without her return, because at least Demetrius *knows* he can love. He can feel truly alive because of it.'

She smiled and gently laid her free hand against his cheek. The prickle of a day's growth of beard tickled at her palm. Beneath it his skin was warm and satin-taut. A muscle flexed under her touch. 'I believe *you* are the secret romantic, Robert. Do you envy the shepherd, then?'

He grinned up at her, and turned his head to press a quick kiss to the hollow of her palm. 'In a way I do. He gets to be alive—truly alive—even if it's only for a moment.'

'Until that love kills him.'

'Until then. I see you have peeked ahead at the ending.'

Anna sat back in her chair, finally breaking their hold on each other. But though not touching him, not physically close, she felt bound to him.

'Are you not alive, then, Robert?' she asked.

He sat back on the hearth, resting lazily on his elbows as he stretched his legs out before him and crossed his booted feet at the ankles. He had charged that morning's rumpled, stained shirt for one of his dandyish and expensive doublets of burgundy-red velvet, slashed at the sleeves with black satin and trimmed with shining rows of gold buttons. His boots were fine, soft Spanish leather, polished to a glowing sheen, his breeches of thin, fine-spun wool. A teardrop pearl hung at his ear.

He was dressed to impress someone tonight, and Anna suspected it was not meant to be her.

'Sometimes I feel I'm already cold in the grave, fair Anna,' he answered. His tone was light, teasing, but she thought she heard a hard ring beneath it—the tinge of truth. 'The true, deep feelings of Demetrius are lost to me now. I just counterfeit them onstage.'

'Aye,' she murmured. 'I think I know what you mean.'

His head tilted to the side as he studied her. 'Do you?'

'Aye. My life is not one of deep emotions, as the poor shepherd has. It is quiet and calm—cold, some might say. But I prefer its chill to the pain of burning.'

'Your husband?' Robert asked, his voice low and steady, as if he didn't want to frighten her away.

As if Charles Barrett could frighten her now. His black soul was dead and buried. But before that, before they'd made the mistake of marrying and it had all gone so horribly wrong, she had once longed for him. Those feelings had clouded her judgement and led her far astray.

'I never want that again,' she said firmly.

'So you are like Diana now?' he said. 'Above the maelstrom of human emotion and desire?'

Anna laughed. 'I am no virgin goddess.'

Suddenly there was a crashing sound in the corridor, a burst of drunken laughter. Someone bumped into the wall outside, making the painted cloths sway.

Robert held his finger lightly to his lips and rose to his feet.

'Shh,' he whispered. 'Let's walk in the garden for a time, where they can't find us.'

'The garden?' Anna asked, confused. To be alone with him, in the dark of night, with no one lurking outside the door? It was—tempting.

Too tempting. Who knew what she might do

there? She didn't even seem to know herself when she was with him.

But as he held his hand out to her, she found herself reaching for it.

'There is a beautiful moon tonight, my Diana,' he said. 'And I find I am in no fit mood for company.'

She nodded, and together they tiptoed down the corridor and out of the front door into the night. Once they were outside, the raucous roar of the gathering faded away to a mere distant hum.

The garden that lay between the house and the darkened theatre was quiet and full of shadows from the shifting of the moon's glow between drifting clouds. A tall stone wall held back the flow of Southwark life beyond—the taverns and bustling brothels, the shouts and shrieks and the clash of steel and fists. It all seemed very far away in that moment.

Anna sat down on a stone bench and tipped her head back to stare at the silvery-pale moon in the blue-black velvet sky. It was nearly full, staring down impassively at the wild human world below.

'It *is* lovely,' she said softly. 'I don't look at the sky enough.'

'Our lives are too frantic to remember such simple joys,' he answered. He rested his foot on the bench beside her and braced his forearm on his knee—so, so close, but not yet touching.

'Your life is terribly busy, yes?' she asked. She held tighter to the cold, solid stone beneath her, to keep away the temptation to lean against him. 'Writing, acting, dodging demanding theatre owners, assignations with admiring ladies—fights with their husbands...'

Rob laughed. 'Such a great opinion you have of me, Anna. I would have you know I work hard for my coin every day. And if I choose to enjoy myself when the work is done—well, life is too short *not* to seek out pleasure.'

Anna smiled up at him. He was so good at seeking out pleasure, it seemed, at drawing out every hidden morsel of joy in their striving, heaving existence. What was that like? What would it feel like to let go of control and duty for one mere moment and just—*be?*

She feared the cost of that one moment would be too high. But it was tempting, nonetheless, especially when he looked at her like that under the shimmering moonglow.

'Perhaps we do need to stop and glance at the

stars once in a while,' she said. 'Lest we forget they are even there at all.'

'It's difficult to see them in the city,' Rob said. He sat down beside her, his shoulder pressed very lightly against hers. He did only that—sat beside her—and yet she was so very aware of the hard, lean line of his body, the heat of his skin on hers through the layers of their clothes, the raw strength of him.

'I've never lived anywhere but London. Not for long anyway,' Anna said. 'This is the only sky I know.'

'When I was a lad I lived in the countryside,' he said. His voice was quiet in the darkness, as if suddenly he was far away from the garden. Somewhere she couldn't quite see or follow.

'Did you?'

'Aye, and often on summer nights I would slip out of my bed and go running down to the river, where there was only the water and the sky, perfect silence. I would lie down in the tall grass at the riverbank and stare up at the stars, making up tales for myself of other worlds we could not see. Wondrous places beyond the stars.'

Anna was fascinated by this small glimpse of Rob's past, his hidden self. She had never thought of him as a boy before; he seemed to have just sprung up fully formed onstage, sword in his hand, poetry on his lips.

'You must have been the despair of your mother, running away like that,' she said.

He smiled at her, a flash of his usual careless grin, but it swiftly faded. 'Not at all. My mother died when I was very young. Our aunt then stayed with us for a time, but she cared not what we did as long as we didn't dirty her nicely scrubbed floors.'

'Oh,' Anna said sadly. 'I am sorry.'

'For what, fair Anna?'

'For your losing your mother so young. My own mother died when I was three.'

Rob studied her so carefully she felt a warm blush creeping stealthily into her cheeks. She was very glad of the cover of darkness—the moon was behind the clouds. 'Do you remember her?' he asked.

She shook her head. 'Not very much at all. She would sing to me as I fell asleep at night, and sometimes I think I remember the way her touch felt on my cheek, or the smell of her perfume. My father says she was very beautiful and very gentle, that there could be no lady to compare to her and that is why he never married again.' Anna laughed. 'So it seems I inherited little from her, having neither beauty nor gentleness!'

'I would disagree—about the beauty part, anyway,' Rob said, his old light flirtatiousness coming back, encroaching on their fleeting moment of intimacy.

'I am not gentle?'

'Gentleness is quite overrated. Spirit—that is what a man should always look for in a female.'

Anna thought of the weeping whore in her tattered yellow dress. She had not seemed especially spirited, but then Anna hadn't seen what had come before the morning quarrel. Maybe the night had been spirited, indeed.

Had it all only been that morning? It seemed like days ago, so very distant from this quiet moment.

And she felt a most unwanted twinge of pleasure that he might think she was spirited—and beautiful. Even though she knew very well it was only a mere flirtatious comment—a toss-away he no doubt said often to many women. But she had long ago lost her youthful spirit. It was buried in the real world.

'Surely *spirit* can cause more trouble than it is worth?' she said sternly. 'For instance—how is your shoulder tonight?'

He flexed his shoulders as if to test them before answering her. His muscles rippled against the fine fabric of his doublet.

'Better, I thank you,' he said. 'I had a very fine nurse.'

Anna waited to see if he would say more, tell her how he had come to be wounded in the first place, but he did not. A silence fell around them, heavy and soft as the night itself. She let herself lean closer against him, and didn't even move away when his arm came lightly around her shoulders.

'Tell me about those worlds you saw beyond the stars,' she said. 'Tell me what it felt like to escape there.'

'Escape?' he said. She could feel the way he watched her in the night, so steady, so intense, as if he wanted to see all her secrets. 'What do you want to escape from, Anna?'

Everything, she wanted to say. At least for that one moment she wanted not to be herself, here in her workaday life, her workaday self. She wanted him to be not himself, either. If only they were two strangers, who knew nothing of each other or of what the world held beyond this garden.

'It's more what I want to escape *to,* I think,'

she said. 'Something beautiful, clean and good. Something peaceful.'

'Something beautiful?' he said. 'Yes. I think I've been looking for that all my life.'

Anna felt the sudden gentle brush of his hand against her cheek. His touch was light, and yet it seemed to leave shimmering sparks in its wake across her skin. She reared back, startled, but he didn't leave her. His palm cupped her cheek, holding her as if she was made of the most fragile porcelain, and she swayed towards him.

Slowly, enticingly, his hand slid down her throat to the ribbon trim of her neckline. He toyed with it lightly between his fingers, his dark gaze following his touch. He didn't even brush the bare, soft swell of her breast above the unfashionably modest bodice, yet she trembled as if he did. She felt unbearably tense and brittle, as if she would snap if he did not touch her.

'Why do you always wear grey?' he asked, twining the bit of ribbon between his fingers.

'I—I like grey,' she whispered. ''Tis easy to keep clean.' And easy to fade into the background. It was a suitable colour for a woman who spent her time hovering behind the scenes.

'In my star kingdom you would wear white satin

and blue velvet, sewn with pearls and embroidered with shining silver thread.'

He stroked one long strand of her hair that had escaped its pins and trailed over her shoulder, tracing the curve of the curl. She felt the heat of his touch against her skin.

'And you would have ribbons and strands of jewels in your hair.'

Anna laughed unsteadily. 'That would not be very practical as I went about my tasks. I would be always tripping over the satins and pearls and getting them dirty.'

'Ah, but in that kingdom you would have no such tasks. You would be queen of all you surveyed, seated on your golden throne as everyone hurried to serve your every whim.'

'Gold and silver and pearls?' she said, mesmerised by his touch, his words. 'La, but I do like the sound of this kingdom of yours.'

He twisted his fingers into her hair and drew her close, so close she could feel his warm breath whisper over her skin. He cradled the back of her head on his palm, holding her to him.

'You deserve all of that, Anna,' he said. All hint of his usual teasing manner was gone, and there was only dark seriousness in his words and in the way he watched her. 'That should be your life, not—this. Not Southwark.'

Anna felt a sharp prickle behind her eyes and was afraid she would cry. She could *not* do that—not here, not with him! She already felt too open and vulnerable. She tried to turn away but he held on to her, his hand in her hair. His touch didn't hurt, but he wouldn't let her go.

'You know naught of my life,' she said.

'I'm a poet, Anna,' he answered. 'It is my lot in life to see everything—even that which I would rather not. And I see your sadness.'

'I am not sad!' Not if she could help it. Emotions, like sadness and anger and love, only brought trouble. She preferred serenity now.

'You are, fair Anna.' He pulled her even closer, until his forehead rested lightly against hers. She closed her eyes, but he was still there—very close. 'I see that because it calls out to the sadness in me. We both see too much, feel too much. We just don't want to admit it.'

Nay, she did not! She didn't want to hear this, know this. She tried to twist away, but Rob suddenly bent his head and kissed the soft, sensitive spot just below her ear. She felt him touch her there with the tip of his tongue.

She gasped at the rush of hot, sizzling sensation. Her hands clutched at the front of his doublet, crushing the fine velvet as she tried to hold on and keep from falling. Her eyes closed and her head fell back as she gave in to the whirling tidepool of her desire. His mouth, open and hot, slid slowly along her neck to bite lightly at the curve of her shoulder.

'Robert!' she cried, and his arms closed around her waist to lift her onto his lap as his lips met hers, rough and urgent.

Anna had never felt so weak and strange. Something deep and instinctive, primal, rose up deep inside her, blotting out the world around her so that she knew only him and this moment with him. Only his kiss.

She felt the press of his tongue against her lips and she opened for him. He tasted of wine and mint, of something dark and deep that she craved far too much. She wrapped her hands around the back of his neck, as if she could hold him to her if he tried to leave, and felt the rough silk of his wavy dark hair on her skin.

She heard him moan deep inside his throat as her tongue met his, and the sound made her want him even more—madly so. He was so *alive,* the most wondrously alive person she had ever known, and she craved the heat and pulse of him. For that one instant he made her feel alive, too—free of her calm, cool, still existence.

He made her feel too much—he frightened her, her feelings frightened her. She was drowning in him.

She tensed, and Rob seemed to sense her sudden flash of fear. He tore his lips from hers, and the clouds suddenly skittered away from the moon. Its silvery light streamed down onto his face, casting it into angular shadows. For a second he was starkly exposed to her, and she saw the horror in his eyes, as if he realised just what he was doing. Whom he was kissing.

Anna felt as if a freezing winter wind washed over her, her passion turned to cold, bitter ashes around her. What was she doing? How could Rob say he saw her, knew her, when in that moment she didn't even know herself?

She pushed him away, and as his arms slid from her body she forced herself up from his lap. Without him holding her she felt shaky and cold, but she knew she had to get away from him.

If only she could run away from herself, as well. As she dashed towards the house she heard him call her name, yet she couldn't stop. She just kept running—past the dining room where her father and his friends still roared with laughter, and up the narrow stairs to her bedchamber. She slammed and bolted the door behind her, as if that could keep out what had happened.

She stumbled past the curtained bed, already turned back for the night by their maid, and went to the window. It was open to let in the night's breeze, and she could see that garden below, full of shadows and secrets.

Rob wasn't there any longer. The stone bench was empty. Had he also fled from what had exploded between them?

Somehow she couldn't imagine Rob Alden fleeing from anything. She didn't know anyone who ran into danger as he did.

Anna shut the window and sank slowly to the floor, her skirts pooling around her. She pressed her hands to her eyes, blotting out the night. Soon it would be dawn, and a new day's tasks would be before her. Soon she could lose herself in the busy noise of her life, and this would all be as a dream. A foolish dream.

It had to be.

Chapter Five

'And this fair place, this Eden, is as nothing compared to your—your...'

Rob stared down at the words on the page, and an intense, fiery wave of anger washed over him. They weren't right—the right words simply wouldn't come that morning. They were imprisoned behind an impenetrable wall, locked away. There were no tender love words to be conjured that day. Not by him.

There was only that anger, burning away everything else. Anger and something he had never known before, something he despised—guilt. The conscience he'd thought he didn't have, couldn't afford, pricked at him like sharpened poniards.

'Z'wounds,' he cursed, and threw down his pen. Ink splashed over the papers scattered across his table, blotting out the words he had just written. Work was the last thing he could think of today.

Anna Barrett filled his thoughts—and created that anger.

Rob sat back in his chair and flexed his hand, the ink-stained fingers stiff from trying to write tenderness and love where there was none. He thought of how that hand had touched Anna last night, how he hadn't been able to stop himself from giving in to the luscious temptation of her rose-scented skin, the softness of her hair.

The way her mouth had tasted against his— like ripe, sweet summer fruit to a starving man. Everything else had vanished when they were alone like that, just the two of them in the night, and he had lost himself in her. The control that was so vital to his life had disappeared as if in a puff of mist, and he'd been desperate for her.

He'd wanted, *needed,* the softness of her, and if they had been in a private chamber with none passing by he would surely have lifted her skirts and taken her in that rush of sudden, desperate lust.

Thank the stars they had been outside, with a houseful of people mere feet away. That Anna had come to her senses when it had seemed he had none and pushed him away.

That look of blank surprise on her face as she'd run from him had awoken him from his sensual dream as nothing else could have. The memory of it now made him even angrier—though whether at Anna or himself, or at the whole world, he couldn't say. If only there was a brawl to be had, here and now! A fight would erase all else, burn away the emotion that ran too fast, and he could forget. For a moment.

Rob pushed back from the table so swiftly his chair clattered to the rough wooden floor. He kicked it out of the way and went to thrust open the window and let in some of the early morning light.

His rented room at the top of the Three Bells tavern looked down on one of the back alleys of the Southwark neighbourhood, so high he was above the overhanging eaves of the buildings that nearly touched above the road. It meant he had more light and air than the dank lower chambers—better for his long hours of solitary writing. The fetid smells of the dirt lane were more distant, as well, and he could think and work here. It was his sanctuary, rough and small as it was.

Today it didn't feel like a sanctuary. It felt like a prison, binding him up alone with unwelcome feelings and desires.

Desires for Anna Barrett, of all women. Rob leaned his palms on the scarred wooden ledge and stared down at the alley below. He didn't see the passing water-girls or the drunks straggling home from the night's revels. He saw Anna, her full, soft lips pink and damp from his kisses, her bright green eyes wide and startled. Her body so soft and pliant against his.

Anna Barrett—the prickliest, most distant female he knew—*soft* in his embrace. Anna Barrett oversetting his emotions, which he had long thought mastered. Who could have thought it? Someone who shaped human ends had a sense of humour.

It was surprising, and he had thought he could never be surprised again. That alone was enticing.

But he could not afford to be *enticed* by Anna, or to have anything to do with her at all. If she knew the truth about him—about what he was doing at the White Heron—she would castrate him herself with a rusty stage rapier and toss his severed member into the Thames.

Rob turned away from the window and the

piercing daylight that rose above the jagged roof-tops, pulling his rumpled, ink-stained shirt over his head. The morning moved apace, and he had work to do.

If only today's task was half as pleasant as being in the garden with Anna Barrett. He could easily face every danger if such a reward waited at the end.

But it was thinking like that—careless and impulsive, seeking pleasure at all costs—that had brought him to this place. It was the Alden family's downfall, always.

As Rob splashed cold water from the basin over his face and bare chest, he thought of his family. He usually refused to think of them at all. Memories of his time before London, before Southwark, were futile and foolish. They were gone and he had made his choices. The past was no more. His parents would have disowned him for all he did now. His short stint in prison after a brawl had shown him what his life had become—how far he was from his old life. His parents would have been disappointed, indeed.

But his sister—pretty Mary, gone from him now for so long—she still lingered with him. Sometimes he seemed to sense her sad spirit at his shoulder, and it was that memory that drove him forward, that kept him alive amidst all the danger and his own careless ways. He had to do right by her, to fulfil his goal before he could let go and be at peace.

That had long been the implacable force driving him onward. He wouldn't let Anna Barrett be an obstacle, no matter how well she kissed. No matter how much he wanted her.

Rob scrubbed hard at his face with a rough cloth, as if he could wash away last night and the emotions it had aroused in his long-cold heart. Wash away all the past. That was impossible, but he could at least make himself look a bit more respectable. Like a man with important business to conduct.

He pulled on a clean shirt and reached for his best doublet—the crimson velvet sewn with gold buttons he'd worn last night and which lay discarded on his rumpled bed. But it still smelled of roses and night air, of Anna and their closeness in the garden.

'God's teeth,' he muttered, and tossed it aside. His next-best doublet, a dark purple velvet and black leather, would have to do, and was more sombre, anyway. Better for where he was going.

He donned it quickly and smoothed the tangled waves of his hair before he reached for his short black cloak—and the packet of papers.

He had to journey to Seething Lane before the day was too far gone.

'Anna, dearest? Are you well this morning?'

'Hmm? What did you say, Father?' Anna asked as she stared out of the window of the dining room. The garden in the morning light, with the slow traffic of Southwark waking up just beyond, seemed so—ordinary. The same trees and over-grown shrubs she saw every day. How had she ever been so carried away by dreams and fantasies in such a place? Even under night's cover?

It was a terrible, twisting puzzle that had kept her awake until dawn.

'It's just that you seem distracted, daughter,' her father said. 'You're about to spill that beer.'

Anna looked down, startled, to see that the pitcher of small beer she was pouring into pottery goblets was indeed about to spill. She quickly put it down on the table, and reached for a cloth to wipe up the last drops.

'Fie on it all,' she murmured. 'I'm sorry, Father. I suppose I'm just a bit tired today.'

'Sit down and have some bread,' Tom said, pushing a platter of bread and cheese across the table to her. 'I shouldn't have asked so many people to supper yesterday. We talked too late into the night.'

No, he shouldn't have asked them, Anna thought as she listlessly poked at a piece of bread. Maybe then she would have spent the evening quietly with her book, not wandering off in dark gardens with Robert Alden, forgetting herself and acting like a fool.

She felt her cheeks turn hot at the memory of their kiss, of the way she'd flung herself onto his lap and held him so tightly, as if she was drowning and only he could save her. But there had been such a feeling of inevitability about it all—like the fate that led characters in a play to their inescapable ends. Something dark and needful had been growing between them for a long time. Something she didn't understand and didn't want.

Anna took a long sip of the beer. Perhaps it was best something *had* happened. Now it was done and past, and they could forget it.

But what if it was not so past? What if it happened again and she found she truly was a strumpet with no control?

She almost laughed at the thought. Strumpet

or not, she knew Rob was pursued by so many ladies—Winchester geese and fine Court women alike. She saw them all the time at the White Heron, his admirers clustered around the stage with shining eyes and low-cut bodices. He certainly didn't need a grey-clad widow like her.

She just had to forget him—put last night's folly down to a wild dream and move forward. It was as simple as that.

Only *that* didn't seem so very simple, even in the hard light of day.

'We will have a few quiet evenings for a time,' her father said. 'No more late dinners. I can meet with the actors at the tavern to read the new plays.'

'Invite them here whenever you like, Father,' Anna said. She refilled his goblet, careful not to spill any beer this time. 'I do not mind.'

'I don't want to make more work for you, dearest, not when you do so much already. Perhaps you would like a holiday in the country?'

'A holiday?' Anna said, startled. Her father was a London man, born and bred; the dirty water of the Thames was in his blood. He *never* thought they should go to the country.

'Aye. You seem to need a rest, and soon the hot

weather will be upon us. What if the plague comes again?'

'It won't.' But the country—fresh air and quiet, long walks, space to think, to *be*. A place away from the theatre and Rob Alden. It sounded quite enticing. But… 'And I have too much work just now to go away.'

Thomas shrugged. 'If you say so. But think about it, my dear. We could both use a change of scene—especially right now.'

Anna laughed. 'You would die of boredom away from London, Father! Why this sudden urge to go to the country?' A suspicion struck her. 'Are you in some sort of trouble?'

'Trouble? Certainly not!' he blustered. But he wouldn't meet her gaze, and his rough, lined cheeks looked red. 'Whatever would make you say such a thing? When am I ever in trouble?'

All the time, Anna thought. Southwark was ripe with trouble around every corner—especially for men like her father, who had business concerns in every narrow street and dark corner. Yet he'd never wanted to run away from it before. He seemed to enjoy trouble.

Just as Robert did.

'I will think about going to the country for a

time,' she said. 'When business grows slow in the hotter weather. But for now I have things I must do.'

Her father nodded, somewhat mollified. But his face still bore that guilty flush. 'What are you doing today, my dear?'

'It's rent day, and a few tenants are still behind in their payments. I'm going to visit them myself and have a word with them. You must keep a watch on the rehearsal at the White Heron, Father, or they will waste away the whole morning.'

He nodded, but Anna feared he was inclined to laze away the morning with them. She rose from her chair and kissed the top of his balding head. *The old rogue*—how she loved him, despite everything. He was all she had, her only family, and she was all *he* had, as well. She had to look out for him.

'I will be back by afternoon, Father,' she said. 'Don't worry about a thing.'

He reached up to pat her hand. 'I don't worry, Anna. Not while you are here.'

Anna left the dining chamber and went up to her room to fetch her hat and shawl. As she pinned the high-crowned grey hat to her neatly coiled hair, she caught a glimpse of her pale face in the small looking glass. Usually she only took a quick look, to be sure she was tidy, but today she looked longer, studied herself.

Her father had always claimed she was pretty because she looked like her mother, but Anna had never thought herself so. She saw the finely arrayed Court ladies, with their golden curls and rouge-pink cheeks, their white bosoms displayed above jewelled bodices. She saw the admiration they gathered from men, and knew she did not resemble them. Her hair, though thick and long, was brown and straight, her eyes too tilted and her chin too pointed. She was pale and thin, her gowns plain grey, as Rob had pointed out. Her lips were fine enough, but were too often pressed thin with worry.

She was not a vivid beauty, likely to catch and hold the eye of a handsome devil like Robert.

'He must have been very ale-shot last night,' she said, and jabbed the pin harder into her hat. Perhaps she had been, as well—or at least drunk on the moonlight and on his words, the rare glimpse he'd given her of his past.

But that had been last night. This was today, and she had work to do.

Anna looped her wool shawl over her shoulders and reached for her market basket. Her father was still at the table with his beer when she went downstairs, looking uncharacteristically sad and reflective. Something was happening with him, she was sure of it. But she had no time to puzzle it out now; the mysteries of men would have to wait. She had business of pence and pounds today, and *that* she could decipher and understand.

Men, she vowed, she would never fathom.

Anna was nearly to Mother Nan's bawdy house, her first rent-collecting stop of the day, when she caught a sudden glimpse of Rob through the crowd. He was taller than most of the people passing around him, the plumes on his cap waving like a beacon, and her heart suddenly beat faster at the sight of him.

There was no time to prepare herself for seeing him again after last night, and she felt very flustered and uncertain. She hated that feeling. How dared he make her feel so discomposed?

And—and how dared he not even notice her?

As Anna watched him, pressing herself against the whitewashed wall in case he glanced her way, he kept walking quickly on his path, looking neither to the right nor the left but just straight ahead. The people around him, the crowded, quarrelling knots and tangles of humanity, made way for him as naturally as if he was a prince. They didn't jostle him or grab his arm to entreat him to buy their wares, and no one dared try and rob him. It was extraordinary.

Yet Rob appeared to be lost in his own thoughts. Under the narrow brim of his fine cap his brow was furrowed, his expression dark as a storm cloud. There was not even a hint of reckless laughter about him, only some intense purpose that drove him onward.

Where on earth was he going? Anna was intrigued in spite of herself. In her world it never paid to be curious. Only minding one's own tasks kept trouble away in this neighbourhood, and not even always then. And Rob always seemed to bring trouble with him.

'Oh, what am I doing?' she whispered, but she followed him anyway, as if her feet could no longer obey her. She hurried after him, keeping those plumes in sight as her guide. She had to be very careful not to let him see her.

She had never known Rob to be like this before, so solemn and purposeful, so lost in his own thoughts. Was he in some sort of debt or planning a crime? Or perhaps he was planning to sell his new play right out from under her father's nose.

They left the most crowded streets behind, leaving the thick knots of people and the busy shops for the pathway that ran alongside the river itself. Luckily there were still enough people gathered there for her to stay out of sight, using them for shields. Boatmen plied their trade, looking for passengers to ferry to the opposite bank, and fishmongers announced their fresh catch.

Robert kept walking, and Anna had to quicken her steps to keep up with him. They passed warehouses, close-packed merchants' houses, and London Bridge came into view, with the boiled heads of the executed staring down sightlessly at the crush of humanity. Rob started to cross the huge edifice and Anna realised with a sudden cold shock where he was heading—towards the silent stone hulk of the Tower.

Anna shrank back from its tall, thick walls and gates, its waving banners and the guards who patrolled the ramparts. She had never been there herself, but she had heard such terrible tales of what happened behind those blank walls. Pain and blood and fear as could only be faintly imagined in revenge plays were a reality there, and most who were swallowed up by it never returned. Even from where she stood, at a safe distance along the river, she could feel the cold, clammy reach of it.

What business could Rob have there? She could well imagine he would do something to cause his arrest. Actors were always getting into fights and being thrown into gaol, and there had been rumours he had once fetched up in Bridewell. Yet surely no one, not even a bold player like Rob, would voluntarily go near the Tower?

She hurried across the bridge herself and stood up on tiptoe, straining to catch a glimpse of him. She finally saw his plumes again, and to her relief he was not entering the dark environs of the Tower but continuing along the river on the other side. She ran after him, dodging around pedestrians to keep him in her sight as he made his way into the tangle of streets just beyond the Tower's walls.

He went past more shops and houses, not even glancing at them. Gradually the buildings grew farther apart, with large gardens and empty spaces between them and the road, until he came to what had once been the entrance to an old Carthusian monastery. A vast complex had once lain here, covering many acres and containing churches, dining halls, scriptoriums and butteries and barns.

Now there were large homes, quiet and watchful behind their new gates.

At one of them, a tall half-timbered place of solemn, tidy silence and glinting windows, Rob stopped at last. He glanced over his shoulder, and Anna dived into the nearest doorway to stay out of sight. As she peeked out cautiously, he sounded the brass knocker on the heavy iron-bound door. A black-clad manservant, as solemn as the house, answered.

'He has been expecting you, Master Alden,' the man said as he ushered Robert inside. The door swung shut, and it was as if the house closed in on itself and Rob was swallowed up by it as assuredly as if it was the Tower itself.

Anna stared at the closed-up structure in growing concern. What was that place? And what business did he have there? She did not have a good feeling about it.

A pale heart-shaped face suddenly appeared at one of the upstairs windows, easing it open to peer down at the street. It was a woman, thin and snow-white, but pretty, her light brown hair covered by a lacy cap and a fine starched ruff trimming her silk gown. The watery-grey daylight sparkled on her jewelled rings.

Anna realized that she recognised the woman. She sometimes visited the White Heron to sit in the upper galleries with her fine Court friends. It was Frances, Countess of Essex—wife of one of the Queen's great favourites and daughter of the fearsome Secretary Walsingham, whose very name struck terror in everyone in Southwark.

'Oh, Robert,' Anna whispered. 'What trouble are you in now?'

Chapter Six

'Wait here, if you please, Master Alden,' the dour manservant said to Rob. He gestured to a bench set against the wall in a long, bare corridor. 'The Secretary will receive you shortly.'

'I thought he had long been expecting me,' Rob said, but the man just sniffed and hurried on his way. Rob sat down on the bench to wait; it was a move no doubt calculated to increase the disquiet any visit to this house in Seething Lane would cause.

He had been here too many times, heard and seen too many things in its rooms and corridors to be too concerned. Still, it was always best to be gone from here quickly.

The house was dark and cool, smelling of fine wax candles, ink, and lemon wood polish. The smooth wooden floors under his feet were immaculately clean, the walls so white they almost gleamed. Lady Walsingham was a careful house-keeper.

Yet underneath there was a smell of something bitter and sharp, like herbal medicines—and blood. They did say Secretary Walsingham was ill—more so after the stresses of the threatened Spanish invasion the year before. But not even the great defeat of the Armada, or this rumoured ill-ness, seemed to have slowed the man at all.

He was as terribly vigilant as ever. No corner of England escaped his net.

And no filament of that net, even one as obscure as Rob, ever escaped, either.

He swept off his cap and raked his hand through his hair. This was the only way he could protect the ones he cared about—the only way he could see them safe. He had always known that. But lately it had become harder and harder.

Especially when he thought of Anna Barrett, and the way she looked at him from her jewel-bright eyes…

'Master Alden. My father will see you now,' a woman's soft voice said.

Rob forced away the vision of Anna and looked up to find Secretary Walsingham's daughter watching him from an open doorway. Her fine gown and jewels glistened in the shadows.

'Lady Essex,' Rob said, rising to his feet to give her a bow. 'I did not realise you were visiting your family today.'

'I come as often as I can. My father needs me now.' She led him down the corridor and up a winding staircase, past the watchful eyes of the many portraits hung along its length. 'Don't let him keep you too long. He should rest, no matter how much he protests.'

'I will certainly be as quick as I can, my lady,' Rob said. He had no desire to stay in this house any longer than necessary.

She gave him a quick smile over her shoulder. 'My friends and I did so enjoy *The Duchess's Revenge*. We thought it your best work yet.'

'Thank you, Lady Essex. I'm glad it pleased you.'

'Your plays always do—especially in these days when distraction is most welcome, indeed. When can we expect a new work?'

'Very soon, God willing.' When his work here in Seething Lane had come to an end.

'Don't let my father keep you away from it. We're most eager to see a new play. Always remember that.' Lady Essex opened a door on the landing and left him there with a swish of her skirts. Rob slowly entered the chamber and shut the door behind him.

It was surprisingly small, this room where so much of England's business was conducted. A small, stuffy office, plainly furnished, with stacks of papers and ledgers on every surface and even piled on the floor.

Walsingham's assistant, Master Phellipes—a small, yellow-faced, bespectacled man—sat by the window, with his head bent over his code work. The Secretary himself was at his desk in the corner, a letter spread open before him.

'Master Alden,' he said quietly. Walsingham always spoke quietly, calmly, whether he remarked on the weather or sent a traitor to the Tower. 'Have you any news for us today?'

'Nothing that can yet be proved,' Rob answered. 'But work progresses.'

Walsingham tapped his fingers against the letter, regarding Rob with his red-rimmed, murky eyes. 'Were you working when you took part in that little disturbance outside the White Heron? A quarrel over a bawd, I hear.'

'It may have seemed so. I had to come up with

a quick excuse to cover my stealing of this.' Rob took out a small, folded packet of papers and passed it across the desk.

Walsingham glanced at it. 'A step in the right direction. Yet we still do not have the names of the traitors in Lord Henshaw's Men. We know only that they pass coded information to Spain's contacts via plays and such. Surely you are well placed to discover them?'

Rob watched Walsingham steadily. He had no fear of the Queen's Secretary, for he had never done him double-dealing in his secret work here. But Walsingham held so many lives in his hands, and one slip could mean doom for more than himself. This was Robert's first task of such magnitude—tracking down a traitor in Tom Alwick's theatre. It was a change from coding, courier work and fighting. It was a dangerous task on all sides.

He could not fail at it. No matter who was caught in Walsingham's wide net.

He pushed away the image of Anna's smile and said, 'I am close.'

'I'm glad to hear it,' Walsingham answered. 'Phellipes is busily decoding a letter another agent intercepted, which should be of more help to us in this matter. Once we have that information I will send you word. But for now, tell me all your impressions of Lord Henshaw's Men and their home at the White Heron...'

It was a half hour more before Rob left Walsingham's house, ushered out through the door by Lady Walsingham herself, whose pale, worried face spoke of her concerns for her husband, working so hard through his illness. Once outside in the lane, he drew in a deep breath. Even the thick, fetid city air of the Tower Ward was better than the dark closeness of the house.

Rob frowned as he thought of Walsingham and Phellipes, bent over endless letters, tracking down traitors among the theatre people he spent his own days with. One of them used his art for a darker purpose, but which one and why? He could not be wrong in this. So very much was at stake.

He put on his cap and turned back towards the river. His thoughts were still in that dark house, and for a moment he didn't notice the lady lurking across the street. But then a flash of grey, a surreptitious movement, caught his eyes and he swung round with his hand on the hilt of his sword.

To his shock, he saw it was Anna Barrett who tried to duck down a side street out of sight. What was *she* doing so far from home, so near the lion's den? What was she looking for—and what did she know?

Rob strode after her, determined to find out.

Chapter Seven

'What are you doing so far from home, Mistress Barrett?'

Anna whirled round, her heart pounding at the sudden sound of Rob's voice. When he had emerged from that house, alone and with a distracted cast to his face, Anna had been so startled she'd stumbled back against the wall behind her hiding place. He had not been in there very long.

As he started towards her, she spun and hurried down the alleyway—only to find her path blocked by a blank stone wall. She ran back the way she'd come and tried to retrace her steps to the river. Rob was no longer in sight, and she thought she could breathe again.

But she was quite wrong. She ran down to the riverbank—only to be brought up short by the sight of Rob standing there, negotiating with a boatman. He glanced back over his shoulder, as if he could sense her standing there, and she whirled around to feign interest in a tray of flower posies.

What a terrible intelligencer I would be, she thought, holding her breath as she prayed he would leave now, that he hadn't seen her.

Her prayers were in vain.

At his words, she turned to him and tried to give him a smile. If only she could hear above the pounding of her heart in her ears!

'Why, Robert Alden,' she said. 'I could ask the same of you. Do you have business at the Tower, mayhap? It does seem strangely appropriate...'

He suddenly reached out and caught her arm in a hard clasp. It wasn't painful, but it was as implacable as a chain, and Anna found she couldn't break away. He leaned close to her, his face hard and blank as he studied her.

He seemed like a complete stranger, not at all the tender, passionate lover who had kissed her in the garden. It made her feel cold, despite the warm breeze that swept down the river.

'You saw where I went,' he said. His voice was as fearsomely blank as his face.

Anna tried to tug her arm free, but he wouldn't let go. He held her so easily, so effortlessly. She swallowed past the sudden dry knot in her throat and said, 'I don't know what you mean, Robert. I care not where you go.'

'I tell lies for my profession, Mistress Barrett,' he said. 'You can't out-deceive an actor—especially with eyes like yours.'

'Eyes like mine?'

'So green and pretty—so transparent, like a clear country pool. You can't hide from me.'

'I have naught to hide.' Anna stiffened her shoulders and threw her head back to look at him directly. She wouldn't cower, no matter how frightened she might feel. 'Not like you, it seems.'

'Come with me.' Still holding on to her arm, Rob steered her back to the walkway. Once again the crowd seemed to make way for him, and he moved quickly, so easily, though Anna had to almost run to keep up with him.

She wanted to break away, to run—not to know whatever secrets he held. But something deep in her heart, the spark of some long-lost sense of adventure she had worked so hard to erase after her marriage, *did* want to know. She had long thought there were many things Rob hid—angles and shadows he dwelt behind, where no one could follow.

Was she about to discover what they were? She felt as if she stood on a stony windswept ledge, peering down into a roiling sea. One small shove and she would topple over and be lost.

Rob looked down at her, his eyes very dark, like the bottom of that sea. She had the feeling he was already lost in those depths.

'Where are we going?' she asked.

He turned down one of the narrow, twisting lanes that led endlessly into other streets and squares, to a press of houses and people that formed an inescapable maze of their world. The light of the sky above was blotted out by the eaves of the roofs, and the flow of the river was lost behind them. All was stillness and darkness.

'Look out below!' someone shouted, and Rob pulled her under the shelter of a wall until the stream of waste water from the window above flowed into the latrine ditch in the middle of the road. He kept walking, not answering her.

At last they came to a tavern at the turning of the lane, not far from the White Heron. A sign painted with three golden bells swung over the half-open door. The place seemed quiet so early in the day. Only a few ragged men sat drinking in darkened corners, and a maidservant scrubbed at the floor.

Rob led Anna up the rickety wooden stairs, all the way to the top floor under the eaves. All the doors were closed along the narrow corridor, the rooms behind them silent, and the heavy smell of cabbage and boiled beef and tallow candles hung in the air.

He opened a door at the end of the corridor and pulled her inside. Only then did he let go of her arm.

As he turned away to bolt the door, Anna rubbed at her arm, where she could still feel the heat of his touch, and went to stand as far from him as she could. It was a small, spare room, with a sloping beamed ceiling and one window that looked out on the street far below. There was a bed with rumpled blankets and bolsters tossed about, a table under the window scattered with ink-blotted pages, and two straight-backed chairs. His fine red doublet from last night was tossed over a clothes chest.

Rob threw his cap down next to it and ran his hand through his hair, throwing the glossy dark waves into disarray. He looked somehow older today, his face drawn, his eyes shadowed and wary.

'Please, Anna, sit,' he said as he offered her one of the chairs. 'I'm sorry I have no refreshments to offer you. The Three Bells is a fine, private place to lodge, but I fear it lacks some of the more gracious amenities.' As Anna hesitated, he laughed. 'I promise you, fairest Anna, I will not hurt you. You wanted to know where I went. Well, now I shall tell you, even though I'm quite sure to regret it in the end.'

She slowly sat down, not taking her gaze away from him. She placed her basket on the floor, along with her shawl, and carefully unpinned her hat. 'I am not so sure I do want to know.'

'Ah, but I have the feeling you already know. Or at least you have your suspicions.' Rob took the other chair and swung it round to sit down on it backwards, facing her over its chipped wooden slats.

They watched each other, as if they could not turn away even if they tried. Anna felt those same invisible bonds she'd felt in the garden tighten around her again, binding them together in some mysterious way she could not escape. They were all alone here in this room, so high above the world.

'Was that Secretary Walsingham's house?' she asked. She clasped her hands in her lap, twisting her fingers together to hold herself still.

'You know about Walsingham?'

'Everyone in Southwark knows about Walsingham. We can scarcely escape him,' she said. 'They say he has long known everything that happens in England, and beyond. That he has superhuman powers and uses them to protect Queen Elizabeth from plots of all sorts.'

Rob gave a bitter laugh. 'He has no superhuman powers, Anna, but he *is* like a great, strong spider, looking over all of us. He thinks he sees terrible papist plots around every corner, and he will do what he must to crush them. He and his circle thrive in these days of suspicion and fear.'

Suspicion and fear—had there ever been days *not* filled with those? Anna could remember none such. 'And are you one of his circle?'

Many people worked for Walsingham, or for his political rivals the Cecils, or for Lord Leicester before he'd died last year. Everyone knew that. Each person had to survive as best they could, and life was nothing but a succession of masks in the end. They were changed as needed, and no one knew the truth about anyone else.

But somehow to be faced with real evidence that Robert was one of those secret men, that he too wore masks upon masks, made her head spin. It felt as if her world was tipping, everything falling top to bottom in chaos—and the blinds crumbled from her eyes.

'Writers and actors are among his favourite recruits,' Rob said. 'We have some education, we must be observant to ply our trade. We move about the country on tours, we know people of all sorts and ranks—and we always need money. I work for him sometimes, aye, when there is a task he thinks I can perform.'

'And you have a task now?'

For the first time his steady, watchful gaze flickered away from her and he shrugged. 'I keep in touch at Seething Lane. These are uncertain days, with the Spanish still hovering in every corner and the succession not certain.'

Anna slumped back in her chair. So *this* was his secret—or one of them anyway—he was an intelligencer. Recruited for his skills of observation, his deceptive acting abilities.

What had he observed of her?

'How did you come to this work?' she asked.

He shrugged again. 'Because it is a way forward in the world, I suppose, and writers who live by their pens and their wits have few of those. It puts coins in my purse and I meet influential people.'

'Such as Lady Essex?'

'They do say her husband has taken his late step-father Leicester's place in the Queen's favour. It can't hurt to know them.'

Anna studied his face carefully, wishing she too had a writer's power of observation, of knowing the secrets of the human heart. She had a disquieting sense that he was not telling her all his secrets. That there was more to his work than money and connections.

But she could only bear one secret at a time.

Rob suddenly knelt beside her chair and took her hands in his. Unlike the hard grasp he'd used to lead her here, his touch was gentle. He twined his fingers with hers and raised them to his lips for a swift kiss.

'I have given my secret into these hands alone, fairest Anna,' he said. 'You now have the power of life and death over me. I may be only a lowly courier for Walsingham, but if others came to know…'

Anna was sure Rob could never be a *lowly* anything. There was more to this twisted tale of his, but she was content for the moment. 'I will not say a word to anyone. If you will assure me of something.'

'What is that?'

'Are you in danger—*great* danger, I mean? More than usual? Or is anyone near us in danger?'

'I promise you, Anna, I will protect you whatever happens. You are in no danger from me.' He kissed her hands again, soft kisses to each fingertip and the hollow of her palm. He turned them over and touched the pulse pounding at her wrist with the tip of his tongue.

Anna caught her breath at the flood of sensation that washed through her at his touch. It was as if that invisible bond had become all too physical. They clung to each other as if that was all they had left in the world.

'I know I ask the impossible of you, Anna,' he said, cradling her palm against his cheek. 'But believe me when I beg you to trust me. You don't like me, I know—and with good reason—yet I will make sure nothing touches you in these matters.'

Anna laughed. She bent her head to softly kiss the top of his head, his hair tickling gently at her lips. 'Don't like you? Oh, Robert. It's true that you drive me mad sometimes. Yet I fear I like you all too well—even when I know I should not.'

'Then we share that. For I like you more than I should.' Rob rose up on his knees in front of her and gently cradled her face in his hands. He studied her closely, as if he sought to memorise what she looked like, to imprint her features on his memory.

Anna wrapped her fingers around his wrists and studied him in turn. All traces of his laughter, his recklessness had gone now, and in his eyes she saw the stark seriousness of his true heart. Rob was involved in matters she could scarcely fathom, despite her life lived on the fringes of London's underworld. She thought she knew greed and desperation, the turning of those masks from one false face to another, but she didn't know everything. She didn't know the truest depths.

She stared into them now, with Rob. And she had to admit it was frightening, but also so very enlivening. For once he did not hide from her. He trusted her.

Could she trust him? Did she dare to come out of hiding at last?

Then Rob's own mask slid neatly back into place, and he smiled at her. 'Always beware, fairest Anna, of all men,' he said. 'For we are the basest deceivers.'

His hands slid into her hair, loosening its pins until it fell free over her shoulders. He wrapped long strands of it around his fists, using them to tie her to him, and drew her slowly towards him. He stared at her mouth as if fascinated by it, drawn to it.

She closed her eyes just as his lips brushed hers softly, lightly, once and then again. She felt the echo of his moan against her, the tightening of his touch in her hair, and the kiss deepened. His tongue swept past her parted lips to taste her fully, and she opened to him in welcome. She couldn't hide from him as she could from everyone else.

She remembered his taste, the way he felt, from the garden, and she had thought she remembered how his kiss made her feel and thus could be prepared for it. But that drowning, flying, exultant sensation swept over her all over again, and she was lost in it.

For so long she had been alone in life cold and afraid of feeling again, afraid of the terrible danger of vulnerable emotions. In his arms she didn't feel alone any longer. She wasn't even afraid, even as she knew he was probably the most dangerous man in her world. She just felt alive and warm—and free. The cold fell away at last.

She wanted to be alive, even if it was only for a moment. A moment couldn't hurt her. A moment was nothing.

She wrapped her arms around his shoulders to bring him closer to her. She slid off the chair and knelt before him, until their bodies were pressed together and nothing could come between them at all. His hands fell free from her hair to unfasten the front of her jacket and push it away from her shoulders.

There was no smooth deftness to his movements, as Anna would have expected from a man so experienced at removing women's garments. He was rough and quick, as if desperate to remove that one barrier—as desperate as Anna was to have it gone.

He tossed it away and his mouth slid from hers to kiss her neck, the soft curve where it met her shoulder just above her gathered chemise. His teeth nipped at her skin lightly, making her gasp, and then he traced the spot with his tongue. Anna's head fell back to give his kisses greater access, and she closed her eyes to let the feelings wash over her.

For once she revelled in them, and did not push them away. After all, this was a fleeting moment in the sea of her life and she had to hold on to it before it ebbed away.

Blindly, she reached out to unfasten his doublet. The buttons stuck in the stiff velvet, making her groan with frustration, but at last they gave way and she peeled the cloth away from his body. She pulled off his shirt, as well, and tossed the garments away.

She ran her palms over his bare chest, the skin smooth and warm, slightly damp under her touch. She felt the roughness of the bandage on his shoulder—a stark reminder of just how dangerous his secrets were. How dangerous it was to be here with him. She bent her head and pressed an open-mouthed kiss below the bandage, near where his heart beat so strongly.

'Anna,' he growled, and he lifted her up in his arms as he rose to his feet. He spun round to the bed and laid her down amid the rumpled blankets that still smelled of him.

She opened her eyes to stare up at him as he stood before her, his magnificent body, honed by swordcraft and stage acrobatics, bare to her. He studied her, as well, his blue eyes almost a burning black.

She held out her arms to him and he fell to the bed beside her, kissing her again. There was no artful seduction to their embrace, no fine poetry or pastoral gentleness. There was only a fire, a raw longing that burned away all else.

He caught the hem of her skirt in his fist and dragged it up until she felt the cool air of the room rush over the bare flesh above her stocking. It was quickly turned to warmth as he touched her through the thin knit silk of the stocking, his finger dipping behind the velvet ribbon of her garter.

'Such fine underthings you hide from the world, Mistress Barrett,' he whispered teasingly. 'So shocking.'

And he was the first to see them in a very long time—definitely the first to appreciate them. Anna tugged his lips back down to hers for another kiss, their tongues touching and tangling. He parted her legs and fell between them as she tilted her hips to cradle him against her. She felt the heavy, rigid press of his erection through his breeches, and it sent a tingling thrill through her.

He wanted her, too—just as she wanted him.

She wrapped her legs around his waist and held on to him as their kiss slid deeper and deeper. Through that blurry, hot mist of desire she felt him tug the loose edge of her chemise lower to reveal her pale breast. He slid down her body to kiss the soft swell of it.

The tip of his tongue circled her aching nipple, only lightly caressing and teasing. Anna arched her back, trying to bring him closer, but he laughed and kissed the other breast, the soft, vulnerable curve of it just above the angle of her ribs.

'Such pretty bosoms you have, Anna,' he said, blowing ever so gently on a nipple as she trembled. 'It's a shame you hide them away as you do, for they are rare beauties.'

'Teasing wretch,' she moaned.

'Oh? Is this what you want, then?' He kissed her again, just at the hollow between her 'pretty bosoms.' 'Or—this?'

At last he drew her pouting nipple deep into his mouth to suckle it, wet and hot and hungry.

Anna wound her fingers into his hair, holding him against her. He was so *good* at that— too good, for she couldn't see straight when he touched her like that.

Rob slid even lower down her arched body, his mouth open against her skin. He kissed every freckle, every soft, sensitive spot, until he knelt between her legs. As Anna watched, breathless, he rose up on his knees before her and reached for her leg.

Through the thin silk of her stocking he kissed the curve of her foot, nipped lightly at her ankle, the vulnerable spot just behind it. His lips traced a warm path up the back of her calf, the turn of her knee—the angle of her thigh. His tongue dipped behind her garter, as his finger had earlier, and touched her naked, hot skin.

'What are you doing?' she gasped as he knelt lower on the bed, looping her legs over his shoulders. She was open to him, completely bare—not even her husband had ever seen her thus.

She wasn't sure how she felt about that, about such vulnerability, but Rob held on to her when she tried to close her legs.

'Let me, Anna, please,' he said hoarsely. 'You are so beautiful. I have to taste you, feel you...'

And then he did just that. His fingers spread her hidden folds open to him and his tongue delved into her in the most intimate of kisses.

Anna's head fell back to the pillow and her eyes fluttered closed. Slowly she let her whole body relax into the bed, let her thoughts and fears float away, and just—*felt*. Felt every touch, every sensation. Once she did it was as if she flew free into the sunlit sky.

A burning pleasure built up deep inside her, expanding and growing until it exploded and covered her in its sparkling light.

She had heard women at the bawdy houses and

taverns laugh about such things, but she had never felt it before. It was wondrous. Dizzying.

Rob lowered her legs back to the bed and drew her skirts over her bare skin. He pulled himself up to lie beside her on the pillows and took her gently into his arms.

Anna felt him kiss her closed eyelids, her forehead, the pulse that beat in her temples. He smelled of mint and the clean salt of sweat—and of her own body.

'Did I please you, fairest Anna?' he whispered.

Anna opened her eyes and turned her head on the pillow to study him. His hair fell in tangled waves over his brow and his eyes were shadowed with—could it be worry? Concern? Did he actually think of her feelings now? A tiny fragment of worry and hope touched her deep inside, but she dared not explore that further.

She reached up and traced his cheek with the tips of her fingers. 'I am overwhelmed,' she said truthfully. He had swept over her careful life like a summer rain, exposing hopes she had thought long buried.

Rob laughed, and turned his head to kiss her palm. 'Then I'm honoured to have overwhelmed you.'

She raised herself up on her elbow to study him.

His face against the white pillow seemed dark and drawn, the elegant angles of his features tight, as if he was in some sort of pain.

'You have not taken your pleasure,' she said. She laid her hand flat on his naked chest and felt the erratic pounding of his heart, the thrum of his need. His penis was a hard ridge under his breeches.

'I'm fine,' he said brusquely.

'And I know you are not,' she argued. 'I am no fine miss in an ivory castle. I know what happens to a man when he is unsatisfied.' She slid her hand lower, over his lean waist, the hard plain of his hip. 'Let me…'

Rob caught her wrist in a hard grasp before she could brush against his erection.

'I'm quite well,' he said. His voice sounded rough, and his hold on her was tight. Something about him told Anna she shouldn't argue, even as she longed to with every fibre of her being.

He had just given her such pleasure—had given her the most intimate moment she had ever known with another person. Why would he not let her do the same for him?

Why would he not be with her in every way?

But he was surely right to cut this—whatever it was—now.

Anna nodded and he slowly let go of her hand. 'I should go,' she said. 'You seem to want to be solitary.'

'Nay, Anna, don't go yet,' he said, his voice growing gentler. 'I don't want to be alone. Not right now. I just…'

She nodded. Sometimes she also had no words when unexpected emotions overwhelmed all her senses and she couldn't explain them even to herself. Moments just like this one. Lovemaking would only make that confusion a thousand times worse.

And what if there was a child? She had lost the one baby she'd conceived with her husband before it could even quicken, and had never had another, but with Rob who knew what could happen? She couldn't have a babe now. She had to hide even as she longed for him to draw her out.

Still—her body did not know how to be sensible. It still wanted him, ached for him. She had to be stronger than her rebellious body.

Rob urged her to lie down on the pillows, and he eased her chemise back into place over her shoulders, re-tied the ribbons. As she closed her eyes, she felt him lie down beside her and take her into the circle of his arms. He smoothed her hair back from her brow and kissed her cheek in a soft, lingering touch.

'Just sleep now, Anna,' he whispered. 'Stay with me. I'll keep you safe here.'

Despite everything she had discovered today, against all odds, she *did* feel safe. Held there in his arms, she slowly drifted into dreams. Even if they were dreams that could never come true.

Rob gently smoothed the tangled waves of Anna's hair as she slept in his arms, draping it like a silken cloak over his chest and shoulders as if he could use it to bind her to him. To make her his forever—even if she discovered the whole, terrible truth.

She slept peacefully, curled on her side against his chest, perfectly matched with him there as if they were made to be just so. Her breath was soft over his skin, and a tiny smile curled the corners of her dark pink lips in some secret dream.

She looked so young and soft in her sleep, her face free of the caution she usually carried with her, the hardness that reflected her life and the suspicion she bore so rightly for the people around her. As he lightly traced her cheekbone with the back of his hand, and watched as a pale pink blush suffused her skin, he had a sudden vision, as if in the pastoral romance of a poem.

He saw Anna sitting beneath a tree at the edge of a green meadow, the shade of its spreading leaves dappling her face and hair and casting patterns over her white dress. Her hair was loose, red-brown waves over her shoulders, and the silken strands were strewn with summer flowers. As she leaned back he could see the swell of her belly under the soft folds of her skirt—she was with child.

A brilliant smile lit up her whole face. A smile filled with such peace and joy. And she held out her hand to him in welcome…

Z'wounds, he thought. Such peace would never be his, or hers, either. They had their lot in life, their place in the world, and he had learned long ago it wasn't beneath some pretty country tree. Anna would never welcome him thus—and certainly would never grow round and glowing with his child—once she knew what he had to do.

He had certainly tried his damnedest to stay away from Anna Barrett, ever since he'd joined Lord Henshaw's Men. He'd never thought to have a moment like this one, and he wanted to hold on to it—hold on to *her*—as long as he could. As long as he dared.

At least he had shown a trace of self-restraint, though his body certainly didn't thank him for it. It ached and throbbed with sheer lust, with the strong urge to drive itself into her and lose itself in her softness and heat.

He gently brushed aside a lock of her hair and kissed the curve of her neck. She smelled of roses still, a sweet antidote to the stinking world outside. She murmured in her sleep and burrowed under the blankets.

Rob drew them up over her shoulders and eased himself away from her to let her sleep in peace—and remove himself from temptation. Their clothes lay scattered on the floor, and he scooped them up to drape them over the chair.

'Grey again,' he muttered as he rubbed at the plain-cut sleeve of her jacket. Why did she hide herself behind its drabness like that? She should be arrayed in purples, blues and greens, satins and brocades that showed off her beauty.

Or perhaps that was the whole point—to disguise and conceal. Just as he did. Only he hid behind attention-getting antics that disguised his real purpose, and she shrank back behind a thick grey cloud. She deserved so much more than to hide herself that way. She deserved all the finest life could offer.

He glanced at her where she slept so sweetly in his bed and wondered what secrets she sought to hide.

She stretched against the pillows, and her breasts were outlined by the thin blankets. Rob remembered how they'd felt under his hands, the sweet taste of her pebbled nipples on his tongue. The way she'd moaned with pleasure as he suckled her.

His body hardened all over again—painfully. It was a blasted terrible thing to decide to be *honourable* so suddenly. He spun away from the alluring sight of her slumbering in his bed and braced his palms on the edge of the desk. He tried to study the ink-scratched papers, but all he could see was Anna. All he could hear was her breath, the brush of her beautiful body against his blankets as she turned.

He impatiently tugged free the knotted lacings of his breeches and curled his fingers hard over the painful erection. Closing his eyes to picture Anna again in his arms, her legs spread to welcome him, her bare skin, he rubbed brusquely once, twice, again, until a modicum of relief came over him.

He had not done such since he was a callow boy, as there was never a lack of willing women in Southwark. It was nothing to what he really wanted—to have Anna Barrett fully, to possess her—but it would have to suffice.

Feeling wretched, Rob quickly cleaned himself with the cold water left in the basin and reached for a fresh shirt. Suddenly a knock sounded at the door—a too-loud rapping that tore into the quiet afternoon. Rob looked quickly to Anna. A frown drifted over her brow and she slid lower beneath the blankets, but she did not wake.

As he hurried to the door, he swiped a dagger from the table and carried it low at his side. No one should be disturbing him at such an hour. It was too early for most of the citizens of Southwark to be about, and he had paid his rent on time. He opened the door a mere inch and peered out.

It was a servant clad in Walsingham's sombre black-and-gold livery. His glance flickered past Rob's shoulder, as if he would try to peer into the room—even Walsingham's footmen, pages and maids were trained to be ever-observant, and to report back what they observed.

But Rob blocked the small opening with his body, and he was much taller than the servant.

The boy smirked and gave a little bow as he held out a neatly folded and sealed note. 'A message from the Secretary, Master Alden.'

'Did he fail to inform me of something earlier?' Rob asked, snatching the paper from his hand. 'I find that hard to believe.'

'Mr Secretary never forgets anything. Nothing escapes his notice.'

Rob shut the door and listened carefully until he heard footsteps move away down the stairs. Only then did he turn back to his room.

Anna was awake on the bed, watching him. That taut wariness was back on her face, the soft peace of slumber gone.

Rob leaned back against the door and watched as she sat up amid the piles of bedclothes. She shrugged her hair from her shoulders and tugged the folds of her chemise closer around her.

'Have you an errand to perform?' she enquired.

'Only one—to see you safely home,' he answered.

'There is no need. I know the way well enough, and I still have errands of my own before I return.' She slid to the edge of the bed and flicked her skirts out of her way, baring her legs. As Rob watched, fascinated, she smoothed her stockings and carefully tightened the ties of her garter. She scooped up her shoes and looked about for her lost jacket.

Rob caught it from the chair and held it out for her to slip in to. After an instant's hesitation, as if she was worried he planned some trick, she slid her arms into the sleeves. She stood very still as he skimmed her hair free of the collar and smoothed the strands down her back.

So, she was suspicious again. It stung, even as he knew she was quite right to be wary of him. She *should* suspect him.

She gently shrugged him away and went in search of her hairpins, scattered across the floor. 'I must make it to Mother Nan's before she grows too busy. She is behind on her rent, though she seems as thick with customers as ever.'

Rob reached for his doublet. 'Then let me help you. I can be persuasive when I wish to.'

She glanced at him over her shoulder. 'Aye, that you can. And I'm sure Mother Nan knows you well enough. Very well—come with me, then. But you shouldn't feel obligated to me.'

'Obligated?' That was surely the very last thing he felt towards Anna Barrett.

She came to him and pressed her palms against

his chest, where his doublet fell open. She went up on tiptoe and kissed him lightly, fleetingly. 'It was a most pleasant afternoon, Robert. Thank you.'

Pleasant? Was that what she really thought? Rob caught her hand and reeled her back into his arms. He kissed her, hard and hot, with every rough bit of his longing and lust in it. His tongue pressed deep into her mouth, tasting her until she went limp against him. She held tightly to his shoulders.

He wanted to sweep her up, toss her onto his bed and make love to her as he had longed to do. Their capers earlier had only honed that desire to a feverish pitch, higher and higher, until it almost burned them both to ash.

But he was able to pull back from that fire at the last possible instant. He held Anna away from him as she stared up at him, her eyes wide and startled, her lips parted, glistening bright pink from his kiss.

'We should go now,' he said hoarsely.

'Oh, aye,' she whispered. 'We most definitely should.'

Chapter Eight

'Anna? Is that you?'

Anna paused with her foot on the lowest step and silently cursed. She had taken great care to be quiet, gently opening the garden gate and creeping into the house with her shoes in her hand. It was an hour when her father was usually gone from home, seeking out a tavern or some other diversion, but she didn't want to chance being caught. Not when she was so discomposed.

The house had seemed so quiet, so deserted and dark, but it seemed her father was home, after all. His voice floated out from the half-open door of the sitting room.

'Anna?' he called again.

'Yes, Father,' she answered. 'It is me. My errands took longer than I planned, I fear.'

'Come in. Sit by the fire. We have a guest.'

A guest? That was the last thing she wanted—to sit and chat with one of her father's friends, calm and serene, as if nothing had happened at all. As if nothing had changed.

'In a moment, Father. I need to refresh myself after walking all day.'

'I'm sure you look quite well enough, Anna!' Her father appeared in the doorway and held out his hand to her. 'We have wine and a nice fire in here, and no grand company that expects fine satins and elaborate coiffures.'

Anna sighed in resignation and tucked a stray lock of hair back under her hat. 'Very well. Just for a moment.'

She stepped into the sitting room and saw that her father's guest was Henry Ennis. She wasn't very surprised to find him at their hearth. He and her father had seemed to become good friends, despite the difference in their ages, and he was almost always at the theatre when she went there.

She remembered his declaration last night, the way he had taken her hand and said he wanted her to meet his family. She was used to drunken actors declaring passion for her, and had learned to easily fend them off. They seldom remembered when they were sober anyway, and if they did they laughed about it and it was gone.

But Henry looked at her now with such hurt in his eyes, as if he remembered every second and rued it. As if—as if he had been serious. He rose from his chair and gave her a low bow.

'Mistress Barrett,' he said. 'You are looking quite lovely this evening. Most beautiful.'

She looked rumpled and dusty, and she knew it, but his words made her feel oddly uncomfortable—as did the way he looked at her. As if he *expected* something from her. Flustered, she turned away to put her basket down on the table beside the ledger books. The coins inside clinked—the rent paid at last from Mother Nan, thanks to Rob's blandishments.

'Thank you, Master Ennis,' she said. 'I hope you and my father have had a good conversation this evening.'

Her father sat down in his chair by the fire and propped his feet up by the grate. 'Henry here says he has been working on a play.'

'Have you really?' Anna said. She sat down as far from the light of the fire as she could, sure that her afternoon of lust with Rob Alden showed on her face. Her cheeks felt warm, and her lips still tingled. 'So you want to do more than act on the stage?'

'I can't be a player forever,' he said. 'But I want to stay in the theatre. Surely I have appeared in enough plays to know what the audience wants?'

'Blood—that's what they want,' her father said. 'And plenty of it. A funny bit for the clown can't hurt, either.'

'Surely they also want romance?' Anna protested. 'A grand passion they can cry over? At least the ladies do, and they are a large part of our daily receipts.'

'The ladies want to look at a handsome lad, like Henry here, no matter what the plot might be,' her father said with a laugh. 'Eh, Henry?'

Henry laughed, too, and in the firelight Anna saw that he *was* very handsome—surely as much a draw to the White Heron as Rob was. His golden cap of hair gleamed above a face as perfectly sculpted as an ancient statue, and his lean-hipped body was as elegantly clothed as any courtier's. He was the perfect romantic lead for any play, a vision of manly beauty.

And yet she was strangely unmoved when she looked at him, as if she were admiring a tapestry or carved chair, instead. He didn't make her feel as if she would burst out, as Rob did, as if she had to cry out from looking at him.

If she was to be prudent again, surely she should spend more time with Henry and less—much less—with Rob. Rob made her feel alive again, which was the most dangerous thing she could think of.

'There is blood aplenty in my tale, Master Alwick,' Henry said. 'But I will be sure there is romance, as well, to please Mistress Barrett.'

'Then I'll be happy to take a look at it when you have finished,' her father said. 'The White Heron always needs new plays. There's never enough supply for the demand. The public is greedy for them.'

'I hope it will be up to the standards of your usual writers,' Henry said quietly. 'Such as Master Alden. He is very popular.'

'Robert is a great writer, and the audience does flock to his plays,' said her father. 'But he's not nearly fast enough with his pen for their taste.'

Because he was so busy with Walsingham? Anna remembered that look on his face when he stepped out of Walsingham's vast spider lair of a house, so inward and serious. And the note that had arrived when he thought she slept…

He said he was a mere messenger for Walsingham—a code-breaker and cipher-writer. But what if there was more to it? What was he not telling her?

Yet another reason to be prudent and stay away from him. Yet she seemed to have used up all her prudence long ago.

'I must go now, I fear,' Henry said as he pushed himself up from his chair.

'Stay and dine with us,' her father urged. 'Tell us more about this play of yours.'

'Thank you for the invitation, Master Alwick, but I have an appointment I must keep.'

Anna was glad he was going and leaving the house quiet again. She had so much confusion swirling in her mind, so much she had to think about.

On the other hand—perhaps it was better not to think. Perhaps what she needed was action and activity.

'I will see you to the gate, Master Ennis,' she said. She wrapped her shawl tighter around her shoulders and led him out of the door and into the garden as her father lit his pipe and settled in for an evening next to the fire.

It was almost nightfall now, the sky a deep

purple-indigo tinged pale grey at the edges. The world seemed suspended in silence for just a moment, before darkness descended completely and Southwark came to noisy life.

'Thank you for coming to visit my father,' she said. 'He seems to need company more than ever of late, and it's good for him to think on business.'

'I am happy to spend time with him,' Henry answered. 'Especially if it pleases *you,* Anna. I would do anything at all for you—you know that now, I hope.'

Anna shook her head and started to turn away. 'I do know, Henry, and I am flattered by your kind attentions. But I…'

Henry caught her arm and swung her back towards him. His eyes gleamed in the twilight and his grasp was tight. She couldn't leave him now. He wouldn't let her go.

'I'm sorry if I spoke too soon,' he said. 'I should have waited, bided my time. But I could not. Not any longer.'

'Henry, please,' Anna said desperately. 'Can we not be friends, as we were? I do like you, but after my marriage I don't—I can't be married again. You have so many admirers—beautiful women far more worthy than me.'

His grasp tightened on her arm, crumpling the sleeve, and he dragged her closer. 'Their beauty is false! I want something real and true for once in my life. Something truly my own.'

Anna felt tears prickle at her eyes. She felt for Henry so much; she too longed for something true—something she feared did not really exist at all. Sometimes she ached with that longing.

But she was not that something. Not for anyone. Not any longer.

'Henry, nay, I beg you—'

Her words were cut off by his sudden kiss, his mouth hard and hungry on hers. His kiss wasn't terrible, not smothering and fearful as her husband's had been when he was drunk and lustful. She might even have enjoyed it another time—enjoyed being admired by a handsome young man who thought her something true and good.

But it did not make her feel as if she was falling, tumbling free into another world, as Rob's did. It awakened a flicker in her, but no flame.

She pushed as hard as she could against his chest, until his hold on her broke at last and he stumbled back from her.

'Anna,' he gasped, looking shocked by his own actions. His face flushed a deep red. 'I am sorry...'

She shook her head as she rubbed her fingers across her damp lips. 'I must go inside now, Henry. I know this will not happen again when next we meet.'

She spun round and ran back up the garden path before he could say anything else or kiss her again. As she turned to shut the door she glimpsed him still standing there by the gate, watching her. Waiting for—something. Something from her. Something she almost wished she could give.

But she felt hollow and tired. There had been entirely too much passion for one day.

Her father still sat by the fire, staring into its flickering glow as he puffed on his pipe. Anna dropped down onto the chair across from his and rubbed at her throbbing temples.

'Henry Ennis seems a fine young man,' her father said, not looking away from the fire. 'Ambitious and hard-working. He tells me he has a house in the country he intends to retire to one day.'

'Aye. Where his mother and sister live now,' Anna said.

'It sounds as if he is looking for a wife to add to the household.'

She laughed. 'Players should never marry.'

'Some should not, of a certes. As a lot they tend to be hot-tempered and impulsive, and they lose their coin as soon as they earn it. But Henry seems a different sort. A lady might do well to consider him.'

Did her father know about Henry's attentions to her? Anna studied him carefully, but he gave not a hint of what he was thinking, what he really wanted for her. He just chewed on that pipe.

'The right lady, perhaps,' she said. 'Are you going out tonight, Father, or should I send Madge to the tavern for some supper? I bought some apples at the market for our pudding. They're small and rather hard, but might make a fine pie.'

'Aye, my dear, if you are hungry. I will just take a little wine now, and sit by the fire awhile longer.'

'Not too much wine, Father. Not on an empty stomach. Or I shall be calling for a physick.' Anna went to kiss his cheek before she left the room. 'I must go tidy myself now. It has been a very long day.'

He caught her hand in his as she turned to go. 'You work too hard, dearest daughter. I tell you, you should consider Master Ennis. He could take care of you as you deserve.'

'Never fear. I can take care of myself quite well

enough—and you, too.' Anna gave her father a confident smile and another kiss, but inside she was just not so very sure any longer.

Rob tossed the tiny scraps of parchment into the fire, watching intently as they turned to black flakes of ash and melted away. If only the words could be so easily erased from his mind, so easily cast out of the world.

Behind him, the main room of the Three Bells was crowded with its usual denizens, getting drunk either loudly or morosely, losing money at cards, grabbing the serving maids who slapped them down. The smells of fried onions and cheap beef, spilled ale and damp wool blended thickly with the acrid smoke of the fire.

But Rob didn't see any of it. It was as distant as birdsong in the sky and as removed from him. He braced his fists on the arms of his chair and stared at the charred bits of Walsingham's note.

The Secretary had new information on the traitor among Lord Henshaw's Men—the one who hoped to profit from Spanish information passed under the disguise of the theatre. It was Tom Alwick.

Anna's own father. And Rob was assigned to

find the evidence that would bring him down forever, ruin him and bring him a traitor's death.

Rob sat back in the chair and stretched his long, booted legs towards the fire, as if its heat could melt the ice forming around his heart. He thought of Tom, always so affable, yet so shrewd about the plays he could sell and what the audience wanted. Tom, who almost always seemed at best half-drunk, and lately more apt to leave business affairs to Anna. Could he really be such a good actor himself as to hide treason behind such a façade of jokes and drink?

Rob rubbed his hand hard over his jaw. Of course, Tom could be acting—anyone caught in Walsingham's web had to be a good liar or he would be dead in an instant. Yet Rob had learned hard lessons ever since he was a child—lessons on seeing beyond what people presented to the world and into the very heart of the matter. He had to be observant to write his characters, and to do his job for Walsingham. It was how he stayed alive in the face of daily danger.

Tom seemed to be no actor, no deceiver. A ruthless businessman, aye, but one who was fair to his tenants and employees. A man getting on in years and seeking solace in wine and ale for a too-long life.

Rob didn't believe he was the spy. Surely it had to be someone around him? Someone in his business…?

Someone like Anna?

'Nay,' he muttered. His remembered the sweetness of her kiss, the wonder in her eyes as she found pleasure in his arms. The softness she hid under her sharp tongue and stern grey garments. Anna wasn't a traitor.

Yet doubt, once planted, lingered. She was clever and she had access to all her father's business concerns. It was said around Southwark that her husband's death had left her penniless, forcing her to return to her father's house.

He had to consider all possibilities in this conundrum. It was often the least likely one that proved true. Even if it was not Anna, she could be helping the villain—whether wittingly or not. He had to discover the truth, and take care of the matter before Walsingham could.

He had become very good at taking care of matters over the years, ridding the Queen of her enemies any way he could. He couldn't let Anna

Barrett cloud his judgement or stand in his way. Too much depended on this one task.

He heard a footfall behind him—the tap of a boot's sole on the sticky floor more purposeful than the general cacophony of the room—and he reached for the hilt of his dagger.

'What visions do you see in those flames, Robert?' Edward Hartley asked.

Rob relaxed, no longer preparing to do battle, and looked back at his friend. Edward stood out from the usual Three Bells crowd in his bright green satin Court clothes, but as usual no one dared assault him—even to steal his finery.

'I was merely seeking a quiet moment to myself,' Rob said.

Edward arched his brow as he took the chair across from Rob. 'Here?'

'I do my best thinking in the midst of a crowd.'

'Then you must have something brilliant indeed in mind. It's even noisier than usual here tonight, not to mention noisome.'

'And you're far from home for such a late hour. Is the beauteous Lady Elizabeth gone from London now?'

'Not as yet. We're to meet later tonight.' Edward

took a long drink from the goblet in his hand. 'I heard you were at Seething Lane this morning.'

'So I was.'

'Any progress?'

Rob shrugged. 'Perhaps. None I care for, though.'

'Ah. Well, I may be able to help you in your task, my friend. I've had word that Sir Thomas Sheldon is back in London, penniless again and even more careless than usual.'

'Is that so?' Rob sat up in interest. Sir Thomas Sheldon had long been an enemy to Edward, as Edward blamed the man for his brother's untimely death. Edward had been seeking a way to ruin him, and lately Rob had learned Sheldon's loyalty could definitely be for sale to the highest bidder. He was possibly even involved in this threatened treason in Southwark, though likely not as the main mover. He seemed too clumsy for that.

'We may have him now,' Edward said. 'I have a plan to set a trap that could benefit us both, and I need your help.'

'Of course you have it. What are you thinking of?'

'Elizabeth and I are having a party at Hart Castle next week. We have invited Sheldon and some of his friends, as I have heard he looks to sell his estate next to mine and considers me a possible buyer. Once we have them trapped on our own ground, they won't be able to wriggle free so easily.' Sheldon was a rich, thieving, Court-toadying man, who had recently attempted to marry Edward's love Elizabeth's young niece. She ran away with Elizabeth's help—and inadvertently brought Edward and his Elizabeth together.

'And Sheldon has agreed to come?'

'Oh, aye. He is always seeking his own advancement—not to mention the sale of his estate. And I have also dangled the promise of some young heiresses before him. He has been seeking a wealthy wife ever since Elizabeth's niece got away from him. He took the bait quick enough.'

'And you want me to help reel him in?'

'No one is better at that than you, my friend. And you must invite anyone who can help us to this little gathering.' Edward grinned. 'It should be a most rewarding few days.'

'Anyone?' Rob stared back at the fire, as if there truly were visions to be found there. Could he lure Anna to Hart Castle? Perhaps once she was away from London, from her father and his friends, he could find out more from her. He could discover if she or her father were involved in this scheme.

Then he would know what to do.

'I will be there,' he promised. He had to be. The game was afoot and he had to see it to its end, even as his guilt over hurting Anna pricked at him in a most inconvenient and painful way. He had set his course long ago. He had to finish it.

Chapter Nine

The clash of steel blades rang out with a metallic clang in the morning air. Men shouted insults at each other, and laughed when their opponents responded with angry volleys of futile blows. It was the final, decisive battle between two warring clans.

Anna watched it all from her perch in the upper gallery, between stitches on a torn costume. She called out lines when an actor faltered, and noted repairs that needed to be made to the stage. The morning light, bright and golden for once, clear of the grey clouds, showed chips in the painted finish of the columns and faded spots on the mural of Zeus and the gods emblazoned below the musicians' balcony.

One of the fighters tumbled off the stage into the rush-strewn yard and rolled nimbly back to his feet. If only all battles were so easy as that, Anna thought. A whirl of colourful insults and blows that hurt no one, and then everyone went to the tavern for tankards of ale.

But Walsingham and men of his high ilk didn't work as simply as that. There were no shouts—just a dagger in a dark alley or a hidden room and it was as if nothing had happened at all.

She looked up from her needle to find Rob on the stage. He held no sword, only the pages of the play he had written, and he directed the men in their battle. The seemingly chaotic brawl was carefully choreographed for maximum effect as seen from the level of the audience, and Rob leaped nimbly among the action, shouting out encouragement. Sometimes he would clamber atop the base of one of the columns to direct the movement.

He waved up at Anna and gave her a merry grin, and despite everything she found herself smiling back. Rob was in his element on that stage, burning with raw, wondrous life. He was a different man from the passionate, intense lover, or the darkly brooding man who had left Walsingham's house. Which was the *real* Robert Alden? It was too enticing a riddle.

Anna laughed and waved back at him. He swung

lightly around the column and dropped back onto the stage.

'Nay, Ethan, hold the sword thus,' she heard him say. 'It's not a sow you're herding to market. Rapiers are delicate and changeable, perfect for both cutting and thrusting attacks, and they need a light touch—like a woman. You can't bash it around and expect it to go where you please.'

He took a stage blade from one of the apprentice actors and twirled the hilt in his palm. He swung it around, as if the heavy weapon weighed no more than a feather, and lunged forward with perfect control. 'In stage combat you must make it look real and fearsome, not comical. Take advantage of space, as you would in a true fight. Back your opponent into a pillar or a door. Use the element of surprise.'

Anna slowly lowered the costume she was mending to the bench and watched in fascination as Rob twisted and turned, as nimble as any Court acrobat, the blade singing through the air as he made its movements dance. Where had he learned such things? His movements were as graceful and beautiful as they were fatal. She couldn't turn her eyes from him.

One by one the other players stepped up to challenge him, and one by one he dispatched them. He laughed, as if having a merry time, as if fighting them off was no effort at all. His strongly muscled shoulders and back flexed beneath his thin shirt, the fabric growing damp with the exercise. He shook his hair back from his brow and with one flick of the sword sent another opponent tumbling from the stage.

No one else stepped forward. They all sat in collapsed heaps at the edge of the stage in their half costumes, defeated.

Rob laughed and tossed the gilded hilt from hand to hand. His own movements were slower now, yet still he leaped about the scenery as if defeating five men was as nothing. Only a fine morning's exercise.

'What? No one else?' he said. 'How will you endure a stage fight, my friends, let alone a street brawl?'

'We leave such things to you, Rob,' one of the others shouted. 'You are so good at it!'

'No thanks to my allies here at the White Heron,' Rob said. 'Come on—one more try.'

'I will take that challenge, Master Alden,' came a voice from the musicians' balcony at the back of the stage.

Rob's attention flew to the shadowed gallery. A man's bright hair emerged from the gloom, and he stepped to the carved railing.

It was Henry Ennis, and unlike the other laughing, teasing players he looked in solemn earnest. Anna slowly stood up and braced her palms on the gallery balustrade. Something new was suddenly in the cool morning air—something that seemed to crackle and snap like a whip. The other actors seemed to notice this, too, as they pulled themselves to their feet and reached for their discarded blades. Despite Rob's taunting words about his useless allies, Anna knew they were all well able to acquit themselves in a fight. They got into them often enough.

But she did not want to see one now, here at the White Heron. She thought of Rob's shoulder wound. It didn't seem to slow him at all, but surely he must feel it.

Yet he stood back, his arms held wide with the rapier dangling from one hand, and gave a low bow.

'The field is yours, Ennis,' he said.

As Anna watched in slowly dawning horror Rob raised his rapier, the greyish light from the sky beyond the open roof catching on the dull-coloured blade. She watched him assess his opponent with a strange half smile on his face. The two men circled each other warily, and then Henry let out a shout and lunged forward, with his blade arcing towards Rob's chest. Even from where she stood Anna could see the palpable, panicked fury in Henry's face and his movements. Why did he hate Robert so very much? This seemed no ordinary jealousy between players, but she could not fathom it.

Rob parried Henry's blade, his own sword arcing down to block the advance. The two blades clashed, scraping against each other in a harsh clatter as they tangled, parted, attacked again.

Henry's anger made him ruthless in his drive forward, and as an actor he was a practised swordsman. Rob managed to stay ahead of him, but Henry's fury only seemed to grow rather than burn out. The sharp side-tip of his blade caught Rob on the upper arm, drawing blood.

Anna pressed her hand to her mouth to hold back a scream. Even the gathered actors, who had at first shouted encouragement, grew terribly silent. No one intervened in the fight.

As she watched, Henry gave a strangled shout and raised his sword, as if to thrust at Rob's neck. Rob ducked nimbly under the attack and dropped down to deliver a counter-thrust. His blade cut Henry's thigh—a shallow wound that sent Henry crashing to the stage.

Henry tried to stab at him again, but Rob kicked him back down and pressed the tip of his blade to his opponent's chest.

'Enough of this,' Rob said roughly. 'What are you even fighting me for?'

'You care nothing for her,' Henry shouted. 'You are a hedge-pig, a heartless swine.'

'Mayhap I am,' Rob answered. 'But I won't fight a man so out of his wits.' He tossed down his blade and turned away, stumbling suddenly as he pressed his hand to his wounded side.

His fingers came away stained crimson.

Some of the other men fell on Henry to restrain him as Rob's friends caught him before he could fall. Anna ran down the narrow wooden stairwell and emerged into the pit as the scene broke into noise and confusion. 'Follow me,' she ordered them, and led the way backstage.

'Bring him in here,' Anna said, clearing piles of costumes from the crates and chests. 'I will see to him while you take Henry to the physick.'

Once they were all gone, and everything was quiet in the little room, Anna felt the tense fear of those few, flashing moments of violence drain away and found she was shaking. Even Rob was quiet. He had said nothing since his fall to the stage, with his head bleeding and Henry Ennis left to shout from the wound to his leg.

Anna took a deep breath to steady herself, and leaned over to study the trickle of blood on Rob's forehead. He watched her closely in that heavy silence.

'This seems to be becoming a terrible habit of yours,' she said. She carefully dabbed with a handkerchief at the gash, only to find it was luckily more blood than wound. 'You were fortunate again. I don't think this will need any stitches.'

'I'm better off than Ennis, then.'

'I should think so. That leg wound was beyond my meagre nursing skills.'

'The fool shouldn't have challenged me.'

'True. Though I don't think my father will see the distinction. He will only know you have robbed him for the time being of one of his chief players.' She wiped away the last of the blood. 'Why does Henry hate you so? I have never seen him like that.' Except for that one flash of fury when she had turned down his offer. But that had been quickly gone.

Rob gave a humourless laugh. 'Do you truly not know, fairest Anna?'

'I know you have enemies, but why another actor? You provide their livelihood with your plays.'

'I think Ennis prizes something more than a fine part in one of my plays. Ouch!' he growled. 'I think Ennis has seen how I look at you and he is jealous.'

Anna gave one last prod at the wound before she bound a strip of clean linen around his head as a bandage. She feared she *did* know what he meant—Henry had conceived some foolish passion for her, or rather for some imaginary lady he thought her to be. But she didn't want to think of Henry and where his feelings had led him. She had other things to worry about.

Such as her own feelings for the man who sat before her now. She felt even more foolish than Henry. If he had noticed, surely others would, as well. She had to be careful.

'Just keep your quarrels out of the playhouse,' she said sternly.

'I will do my best—for you, Anna. But I don't control what some other hothead might do.'

'Henry will have to learn to behave himself, as

well.' She sat down beside Robert on the chest and kissed him quickly. His lips parted in surprise beneath hers and he reached out for her, catching her around the waist to pull her closer to him.

'I won't always be there to mend your wounds, Robert,' she said. 'Promise me you will take care from now on. Try not to dash headlong into trouble.' She tried to keep her voice brisk and impersonal, concealing her concern even as she knew it was too late.

Rob gently kissed her temple, the wave of hair over her brow, and smoothed it back from her face. 'I fear trouble has a tendency to seek me out wherever I go.'

'And you never seek it out, I suppose?' she asked wryly.

'Perhaps when I was younger trouble had a certain appeal. But I find I grow older and wiser with each day that passes.'

If only that was true, Anna thought, for both of them. But wisdom felt so far, far away.

'You should leave London for a time,' she said. 'Go away to somewhere quiet where you can write.'

'I have recently been invited to a country house by Lord Edward Hartley.'

'Hartley?' Anna knew him—or at least knew *of* him. He was one of Queen Elizabeth's favourite courtiers, a man of good-looks and fashion, as well as a man of culture and sport. He sponsored poets and musicians, and often took the most expensive box at the White Heron for a play, bringing a party of friends with him. Surely at his house Rob could work and be safe from harm—at least for a time.

But while he was gone she would not see him. How grey would the days be then? How would she go back to her old ways once he was gone?

'You should go there,' she said, pushing away that sad pang she did not want to feel. 'The country air will be good for you.'

'And mayhap for you, Anna?'

'Me?'

Rob tightened his caressing hold on her waist and gave her a cajoling smile. 'Come with me to the country. We'll stroll the green sylvan lanes, lie by the river, dance under the stars, be as the shepherd and his shepherdess…'

Anna laughed and tried to push him away, even as she was tempted. To be somewhere quiet and peaceful, with Robert, away from the troubles and stink of London—it sounded like a dream.

An impossible dream. A wild player like Robert

was not for the grey likes of her. She had always known that.

'I have work to do,' she said carefully.

'It can wait for a few days. Please, Anna, come with me to the country. You will give me inspiration for my work there, and meet my friends.'

'I have nothing to wear at a grand house,' she said, her protests growing weaker. 'I only have grey, remember?'

Rob reached for one of the costumes and held it up—a handful of purple velvet and glossy satin ribbons. 'We can borrow these. Stage costumes are as fine as anything seen in a palace.'

'Aye, and as expensive, too!' Costumes were the greatest expense of any company of players—the audience didn't want to see kings and queens on stage clad in trumpery rags. She knew their price because she mended and laundered them herself.

But if she was careful, and took only what was not needed for the current productions, it should be well enough. She gently touched the velvet skirt and imagined wearing it as she strolled by a bright country stream on Rob's arm. London, her father, Walsingham—all of it far away. Surely she could be someone else for just a few days? See what centre stage felt like, just once? If she could summon enough courage.

'Well,' she said. 'I suppose someone should keep a watch on you, Robert Alden, and make certain you do finish this play and stay away from fights.'

'Then you will come with me?'

'I will. But only for a few days.'

Rob laughed and kissed her again—a hard, hot kiss full of promise. 'You will not be sorry, Anna. I swear that to you.'

Anna wrapped her arms around his neck and held him close. Nay, she would *not* be sorry. Not this time.

Not yet.

Chapter Ten

Robert stared across the small garden at the country cottage, his gaze narrowed. It all looked so peaceful—half-closed shutters blocking out the bright day, flowers tangling over the gate. Calm and quiet and ordinary. Far from the bustle of London.

Why, then, couldn't he bring himself to go inside? Why did the sight of it fill him with the hollowness of guilt?

Because he *was* guilty, of course. He knew that all too well. It lived with him day and night, drove him onward.

As he stared at the whitewashed walls he felt almost as he had in those days when his brawling had landed him briefly in gaol. The sky lowering over him, dark and oppressive. The terrible, sick knowledge he had failed those he loved.

That was when Walsingham had found him, dragged him from the cell and offered him a task. Given him a purpose again—a way to atone at last. But the walls still pressed in on him. They were built around his own soul.

Rob pushed open the gate and stepped into the garden. It gave a low, rusty squeak and sent a flock of birds soaring from the tree by the door. They flew into the sky, but he was still bound to the earth.

He knocked on the door and it swung open, to reveal a small, plump older woman in a stained apron. The sight of her round, reddened face calmed him. She was always the same, never changing since she had been his nurse when he was an unruly child, and she could control him with a quick swat and a kiss on the cheek.

'Hello, Nelly,' he said.

A smile lit her weathered face and she clapped her hands together. 'Master Robert! We weren't expecting you until later this month. London is a fair journey.'

'Not so long when *you* are at the end of it.' And when he had something he had to do. Rob stepped into the dim coolness of the hall and swept off his cap before he leaned down to kiss Nelly's brow. 'How are you, Nelly?'

'Oh, I'm well enough, as always.' Nelly shut the door and glanced over his shoulder at the silent depths of the house. 'Is aught amiss with you?'

Everything was amiss, he thought wryly. Anna Barrett had thrown everything into tumult. That was why he was here today—because everything was changing. He had to protect everyone.

'Why do you ask?' he said.

'Because we usually don't see you here when the theatres are still open.' She reached up to pat his cheek with a plump, roughened hand. 'You work much too hard, Master Robert.'

'Only to keep you in luxury, Nelly dearest,' he teased.

'Such a rogue,' she said with a laugh. 'You always were, even as a small lad.'

'So I haven't changed?' He felt like an entirely different person now, no longer the careless youth who had rambled across the countryside.

'Oh, you've changed.' Nelly shook her head sadly. 'When you were a boy you were always so light-hearted, laughing and running off on a lark with Lord Edward. Now you're so…'

'So what?'

She gently patted his cheek again. 'There's such a hardness in your eyes now. You never laugh much any more.'

Rob crossed his arms over his chest. 'There is little enough to laugh about—am I not right, Nelly?' That was why he had come here today, why he did what he did every day. The careless boy who had worn his heart on his sleeve was long gone. He had to be cold now.

'How go things today?' he asked, gesturing towards the rooms at the back of the house.

A frown creased Nelly's ruddy cheeks. 'Quiet enough. But there've been some sleepless nights of late.'

'Nightmares?' He had so hoped those would vanish in the quiet of the country.

Nelly nodded. 'They went away for the longest time. Now they seem to have returned.'

What new fear could have brought them back, when there had been peace for so long? Rob's jaw tightened. 'Is it safe to go back there, then?'

'It might do some good. She almost seemed to know you last time.'

Almost.

Nelly turned and led him down a narrow corridor to a small sitting room at the back of the house that overlooked the last bit of garden and the lane beyond. A fire crackled in the grate and the windows were half-open, making the space cosy but open.

At first Rob didn't see her. A half-finished tapestry was stretched on a frame by the window, where she usually worked, and there was the usual clutter of workboxes and threads. But she wasn't sitting there.

He found her standing by the fire, staring down into the flames with a pensive half smile on her face. A bright wool shawl was wrapped around her shoulders and her dark hair fell down her back in loose waves. She looked so much like his sister of vanished years—the shy, sweet Mary who had followed along behind him, eager for the attention of her older brother.

The brother who was meant to be her protector and who had failed her.

Then she turned, and the smile vanished. Her blue eyes went blank as ice, and he saw the scars on her left cheek. The stark reminder of her ruined life, of how he had to help her now.

'Now, see, Mary love, your brother has come to see you,' Nelly said in her hearty, cheerful voice. She put her arm around Mary's thin shoulders and led her to the chair by the window. 'Isn't that lovely?'

Mary watched Rob carefully, warily, with no hint of recognition. She hadn't really known him in years. To her, he was only a man, and thus an enemy to be feared.

But the manners Nelly had instilled in them both as children were still strong. She gave him a little nod and said, 'How do you do?'

Rob stepped closer slowly, carefully, and took out a packet from inside his cloak. 'I brought you some thread from London, Mary. Nelly said you required some green silk for a forest scene you are creating.'

'For me?' Mary stared at the packet as if it would bite her. Nelly always opened the packets for her when he was safely gone. 'Why would you bring gifts for me?'

'Because…' Against his judgement, Rob took a step closer to her. He knew he had to keep his distance, to be very careful, but sometimes his love for his sister was too strong for his caution. Her fear was too painful. 'Because I want you to be happy, Mary. I care about you.'

Some of his pain must have shown, because Mary suddenly shrank back against Nelly with a hoarse sob. 'But I don't even know you! Who are you?'

'Mistress Mary—' Nelly began, but Mary cut her off with a cry, shaking her head wildly.

'Who is he?' Mary cried. 'Why is here? Has he come to take me away?'

'Never, Mary,' Rob said, his heart aching. She only cried louder.

Nelly caught his eye over Mary's head and gave him a little nod, gesturing toward the door. Even though it went against all his instincts to leave without comforting Mary, he knew Nelly was right. Only his absence would soothe her now.

He spun round and left the sitting room. Once out in the corridor, he slapped his hands against the wall and closed his eyes against the anger and the pain. The raw, burning fury at the men who had done this to Mary. And at himself.

But he could still hear her sobs.

He had not been able to take care of her then. He would now. No matter what he had to do.

Chapter Eleven

'You *do* have fine friends, Rob,' Anna said with a laugh as their carriage flew past the outskirts of London's looming buildings and burst out into the wide lanes of the countryside. It was a luxurious conveyance, painted red and black and upholstered in soft velvet cushions. Footmen and outriders in the Hartley livery guarded against highwaymen and vagabonds.

As Anna ran her palm over the lush fabric and rested her feet on the little gilded stool below, Rob sprawled out on the seat next to her. He seemed to match the rich carriage in his fine gold-button-trimmed velvet doublet with the pearl drop in his ear. Gold rings flashed as he reached for her hand.

'Nothing but the best for you, my lady,' he said, and kissed her wrist before twining his fingers with hers. 'You should be carried thus every day, your feet never touching the ground.'

Anna laughed and squeezed his hand. 'I would never get anywhere in London in such a carriage—it would be much too slow. But it is lovely. It's like flying out here.'

She peered out of the window to see the country flashing by, a blur of green and brown as they passed hedgerows and towering trees, grey stone walls, a few cottages glimpsed in the distance and then gone. The wheels bounced along the rutted road, dry and dusty from lack of rain, and she could hear the whistle of the wind past the doors.

'I can't believe I have run away like this,' she said, feeling her heart beat faster, her spirit rising at this change of scene—and at the man who sat beside her, holding her hand. It felt as if she hadn't just run away from London, from her everyday work and duties, but run *to* Robert. To something she didn't yet understand and couldn't put into words, not being a poet like he was—but she knew she needed whatever it was. A deep, secret longing to be free. And it was Rob who made her feel this way, made her feel able to face the world and be bold once again.

She spun towards him on the wide cushioned

seat and looped her arms around his neck. He gave her a wide, white grin and reached for her waist to draw her even closer.

He seemed free here, too, as if just leaving London's walls had lifted a heavy chain from his soul. They could leave all else behind, at least for the short time they were alone here in the carriage, and just be Rob and Anna.

'I wish I could keep you away for always,' he said, lowering the leather shade of the curtain to close them in darkness.

'Always?'

'Well, at least for a year or two. Or five.'

'And where would we stay for five years?' she said, revelling in his smile, his touch. She resolutely pushed away all traces of fear. Today she would be brave. She would enjoy life, enjoy the moment.

'In an enchanted castle, of course. An ancient stone fortress covered in flowering vines and hidden from the world.'

'It sounds chilly.'

'Ah, but you forget—it's an enchanted castle, with magical hearths that light into warm fires the instant a chill creeps in. Ghostly servants bring wine and delicacies for the table, and jewels and gossamer silks appear for you to wear. There is sweet, dulcet music and perfumed oils, and long marble halls for you to dance in.'

'Dance alone?'

'Never! I will always be there to partner you, whenever you have the whim to dance.'

'I'm glad to hear it.' Anna tangled her finger-tips in the waves of his hair that fell over the collar of his doublet. It was soft and rough all at the same time, twisting around her. 'We'll be alone in this castle?'

'Until you tire of it and flee from me.'

Anna feared she would never tire of him. There were always new facets of him to discover, new secrets to learn. Would she ever break free of this fascination with him?

One day she would have to. Soon she would have to go back to her quiet life again and forget what the centre stage of life was like. Had to forget Robert. But not yet.

'I couldn't tire of a place where my food is prepared and fresh clothes appear whenever I want them,' she said. 'No darning, no rent collecting...'

'Nothing but dancing with me.'

'I could bear that well enough. For a time.'

'Then I would have to see to it that you never

grow weary of our time together,' he said softly, and kissed the curve of her cheek, the side of her neck. 'I would make you my prisoner for all time.'

Anna laughed, and her eyes fluttered closed as the warmth of his kisses flooded into her. Her head fell back as he nudged aside the high edge of her jacket and pressed his mouth to the delicate hollow of her throat.

'I fear *you* would be the one bored by our little castle,' she whispered. 'No admiring audience for your plays, no applause…'

'You're the only admiring audience I need, fairest Anna. I would write my poetry only for you.'

His mouth met hers, rough and hungry, as if he was starved for the taste of her. Her lips parted to let him in, their tongues touching, claiming each other and the passion they had held back for too long. Her hands tightened in his hair, holding him with her.

Through the blurry haze of their kiss she felt his touch at the fastenings of her jacket. He tugged them free and she let him push the fabric away from her shoulders. The warm air swept over her through her thin chemise, the confines of her stays, and then his body was against hers.

He pressed her down to the seat, her back to the

soft velvet, and eased the chemise out of his way so he could press his hot, open-mouthed kiss to her shoulder, the soft curve of her breast. Her heart pounded and she could only hear the rush of its beating in her ears, the rough sound of his breath. They were all alone in their enchanted world, just as he had said. There was only him and her, their bodies coming together, the exquisite, forgetful pleasure.

'Rob,' she gasped as he tugged down the edge of her stays and freed her breast to his avid gaze. The tip of his tongue traced around the pink, puckered aureole and lower, to the soft, sensitive spot just beneath.

She closed her eyes tightly, and bit her lip to keep from shouting out as he drew her nipple deep into his mouth. His hand slid over her hip, the curve of her thigh, to grasp the edge of her skirt. He crumpled it in his fist and dragged it up, up, slowly tracing the wool fabric over her sensitive skin. He didn't stop until her legs were bare to him, the damp curls between her legs vulnerable.

Her thighs fell open in welcome and he knelt between them as he kissed her other breast. She felt the friction of his breeches against the soft silk of her stockings, the heat and iron strength of his erection.

As their mouths met again in desperate, art-less need, Anna slid her hands down Rob's back. Beneath the layers of his doublet and shirt she felt the ripple and shift of his lean muscles, the power of his shoulders as he braced himself above her. She traced the groove of his spine, the hollow of his back—his hard, taut buttocks.

'Anna,' he groaned as she explored the way he felt under her touch.

How strong he was, how beautiful. How she wanted him—more than she had ever wanted any-thing before. And he wanted her, too. She could feel that very well as she traced the length of his manhood under his velvet breeches. But the fear she had tried to banish rose up in her, cold, bring-ing her back to reality. They were in a jouncing carriage, nearing his friends' home—this was no time for passion! No time to let herself go.

She eased him away from her and slowly pushed herself to sit straight on the seat. He went readily enough, though he turned his face away from her and she could hear the harsh rasp of his breath. Her head was still spinning, and she felt so light and giddy she feared she might faint. She shook her head hard to clear it, and smoothed her skirts back over her legs.

She tried to laugh. 'I can't meet your grand friends looking like *this*.'

Rob turned back to her to take her face between his hands, holding her as delicately as if she was a pearl set in gold, and gently kissed her lips. 'You are beautiful, Anna. Never doubt that.'

Her heart ached at his words, and she feared she would start to cry. How overwhelming this day had been! How grand and strange, and most unsettling.

And it was not over yet.

'I am sure Lord Edward will not think so when he sees such a slattern enter his fine house,' she said. She reached for her discarded jacket and pulled it on over her wrinkled chemise. At least the fine grey wool was unmarred, and any creases could be blamed on travel. 'Could you hand me my comb from the basket?'

Rob retrieved her travelling basket from beneath the seat and gave it to her in silence. He seemed to sense she couldn't talk just yet—she had no words to express her feelings about what had just happened between them. She wasn't even sure what those feelings were.

But she did know that very soon she would be faced with Rob's grand friends and she would have to greet them properly.

As he sat down on the seat across from her, staring out of the window in silence, Anna tidied her hair and put on her hat. She smoothed the puffed sleeves of her jacket, the folds of her skirt and dabbed on some rosewater. Just as she finished her swift ablutions the carriage turned in to a pair of ornate iron gates, set in high brick walls and adorned with an elaborate crest. They had arrived.

The lane leading to the house was wide and neatly gravelled, meandering lazily past thick stands of trees and rolling meadows that offered enticing glimpses of distant ponds and columned temples. It was as vast and lovely as the park of any royal palace, and Anna couldn't help but feel nervous as she studied it all. She was accustomed to grand courtiers, their manners and styles and expectations, but that was in the theatre, in her own world, where she knew how to conduct dealings with them.

This was their world, and she feared she had much to learn about it.

Rob, however, didn't seem concerned at all. He buttoned his doublet and ran his hands through his hair to smooth back the tousled waves. And after such brief attentions, damn him, he looked more handsome than ever.

He glanced over at her, and some of her worries must have been written on her face for he gave her a reassuring smile.

'Edward Hartley and his friends aren't grand people, Anna,' he said. 'They just like to enjoy themselves and have a good time here in the country.'

'Enjoy themselves wandering their grounds for hours and hours?' she murmured. The lane turned, revealing the house just ahead. 'Or maybe counting their chimneys and windows? That would surely take several days, at least.'

Hart Castle was a huge place, and despite its old title, conjuring up images of turrets and bare walls, it was built of gleaming new red brick and golden stone. The windows sparkled like diamonds in the daylight, a hundred watchful glass eyes surveying their approach. The drive led up to the front doors, sweeping past formal knotwork gardens and a tall maze, around a stone statue of Artemis and her bow. A few guests already strolled the pathways between the bright flowerbeds, their rich silks and plumed hats rivaling the blossoms for colour and shine.

Anna was suddenly quite glad to have the rich stage costumes packed away in her trunk. They would be a useful disguise.

As the carriage lurched to a halt the front doors swung open and Lord Edward Hartley appeared there. Unlike the garden strollers, he was dressed for the country in a brown doublet and tall, scarred leather boots. He waved at them as Rob bounded down onto the drive.

'You're here at last,' Lord Edward said. 'Elizabeth was saying we would perish of boredom before you arrived. Come and amuse us.'

'Be quiet, Edward, or you'll frighten my lady away,' Rob said. 'It took all my powers of persuasion to lure her away from London. I had to promise her a quiet time here at Hart Castle.'

He held out his hand to Anna, and she took one more deep breath before she reached out to take it. He helped her to alight, but her legs were still shaking from the long journey so that she had to hold on to his arm as she curtsied.

'I can see very well why she was reluctant to leave London,' Lord Edward said. He snatched her hand from Rob and bowed over it. 'Her admirers must have been clinging to the back of the carriage as you left, I vow.'

Anna had to laugh at the silly, outrageous compliment, and the roguish grin on his handsome, aristocratic face. 'And I can see why you and Master Alden are such friends. You are both ridiculous flatterers.'

'You do wound me, Mistress Barrett,' Edward cried. 'I speak only the truth. And, as a teller of truth, I must say I don't know how such an old reprobate as my friend here has persuaded you to come with him. You must tell me his secrets.'

'Oh, my lord. I think both of you know far more about secrets than I ever could,' Anna said.

Edward laughed and led her up the wide stone steps and through the open doors into the house, Rob trailing behind them. The entrance hall was richly panelled in polished dark wood, hung with tapestries, the floor an intricate pattern of white and black tiles. An elaborately carved staircase twisted up to the floors above, lit by a window of old stained glass at its turning. A suit of armour lurked in the corner, as if watching over all the comings and goings of the house.

A lady appeared at the top of the stairs and waved down at them. She was not very tall, and she was attractive rather than fashionably beauti-ful, with a heart-shaped face and dark brown hair drawn back under a pearl-embroidered cap. She wore a simple gown of blue velvet with an em-broidered Spanish-style surcoat.

'I'm quite sure the lady must be too tired for your teasing, Edward,' she said, hurrying down the stairs. Her heeled shoes tapped against the gleaming wood. 'It's a long journey from London.'

Lord Edward's face seemed to glow from within at the sight of her, and a gentle smile touched his carved lips as he went to her and took her hands in his. Anna watched the two of them with a sharp pang that was terribly like envy. They seemed to belong together, so perfectly fitting as they moved across the hall hand in hand.

'Mistress Barrett, may I present Lady Elizabeth Gilbert?' Edward said.

As Anna curtsied and murmured, 'Lady Elizabeth,' the lady reached for her hand and laughed.

'I have been so eager to meet you, Mistress Barrett,' she said. 'I visit the playhouse as often as I can—as does Edward, as I'm sure you have seen. He makes a peacock parade wherever he goes.'

Edward clasped his hand over his heart. 'My love, you wound me. I am the soul of discretion.'

Elizabeth just shook her head. 'The Queen does not love you for your discretion, I fear.'

'Indeed we do know Lord Edward well at the White Heron,' Anna said, looking between the pair with wonder. She had seldom seen such a couple, so very comfortable with each other, teasing and joking, unable to look away from one another. How was such a match even possible? A vague wisp of hope floated through her at the sight of a couple so genuinely happy with each other.

She glanced back at Rob, who also watched Edward and Elizabeth with a little smile on his face. He leaned against the stone stand of the armour, all lazy elegance. He also seemed to belong here, in this beautiful house with these people, and Anna at last started to feel at ease herself. Rob had drawn her out into the wide world again.

'But now we can come to know you, as well, Mistress Barrett!' Elizabeth said. 'I want to hear the secrets of a playhouse, and the secrets of Robert, as well. For all his wit, he is a great cipher to us.'

'I fear I cannot help you with that, Lady Elizabeth,' Anna said ruefully. 'He is a cipher to me, as well.'

Rob's brow arched, and Elizabeth laughed. She took Anna's arm and whispered, 'Then we must speculate about him between us. Come, I will show you to your chamber and leave Edward and Robert the dull task of going to look at the new stable.'

'My love, I fear you only wish to be rid of us,' Edward said.

'Of course we do. Gentlemen are only in the way when ladies have confidences to share,' Elizabeth said. 'Now, run along. We will see you at dinner.'

As Edward and Rob turned back towards the doors Elizabeth led Anna up the staircase. Anna glanced down over the balustrade, but Rob had already vanished into the bright day outside.

'Now, Mistress Barrett,' Elizabeth said. 'Tell me all about you and Rob Alden. I am so longing to hear he is tamed at last…'

Chapter Twelve

Rob followed Edward out of the doors and back into the sunlit day, but his thoughts were with Anna as she went upstairs with Lady Elizabeth. Would she be all right on her own, in the midst of that vast house? Would she be nervous, or feel lost, or come to hate him for throwing her into the midst of these bright, brittle courtiers?

He had to laugh at himself for those worries—about Anna Barrett of all people. Surely she had never feared anything in her life? Especially not a pack of overdressed pleasure-seekers. He was turning soft-hearted towards her, and he couldn't do that. He couldn't afford to—not when he walked the tightrope of Walsingham's task, dragging Anna with him. Below them both lay the waiting abyss, lined with flashing blades and snapping teeth. He did what he must for the work, but the guilt of involving Anna in his own chosen danger lay heavy on him.

If he was to save them both he needed all his hard, cold wits about him. So did Anna. She couldn't gossip with Lady Elizabeth—who knew what she would hear?

Rob glanced at the upper windows of the house, sparkling like diamonds in the sun. He thought he glimpsed a pale face behind one of them, watching him, but then it vanished.

'Don't worry, Rob,' Edward said. 'Elizabeth will look after your lady.'

'She's not *my* lady,' Rob protested. He hated the sudden smug touch of satisfaction those words gave—*his* lady, his Anna. No matter how easily those thoughts came to him.

'Is she not?' Edward said with a grin. 'I'm sure Lord Maddingly will be glad of that. He arrives this evening, and Mistress Barrett seems just the sort of beauty he enjoys.'

Hot anger flooded through Rob, and he reached impulsively for the dagger at his belt. 'He'd best keep his distance from her if he doesn't want a blade at his poxy throat!'

Edward laughed. 'A mere joke, Robert, I swear.

But if she is *not* your lady you are doing a fair imitation of it. Are you up to some masquerade?'

'I hardly know any longer.' What was real and what was a counterfeit? He had lost his real self so long ago.

'That sounds intriguing. I hope there's a part for me in whatever you're planning.' Edward stopped to bow to one of the ladies in the garden who waved to him, a pretty blonde in yellow satin and gilded lace.

Rob recognised her—Lady Arabella Bowen, one of the Court ladies who lingered at the playhouse so often. She sent him secret notes and lacy garters, but that was as far as things had ever gone with that particular lady.

Thus far.

She waved to Rob, too, and covered her mouth as she giggled and blushed.

'I have the feeling Lady Bowen would be glad to hear that you and Mistress Barrett are only travel companions, as well,' Edward continued. 'Elizabeth says she asked about you as soon as she arrived.'

'There is no time for such things right now, I fear.' Rob studied Lady Bowen as she cavorted among the flowers with her friends. She was pretty indeed, a fluffy Court sweetmeat, with an obvious liking for actors. But he felt strangely unmoved as he looked at her. He could see only Anna's face now.

'My friend, there is *always* time for such things,' Edward said. 'Except for men like me, whose hearts have been entirely claimed. If you are not in the same situation…'

'I am not.' Not yet—and never, if he guarded himself as well as he had in the past. If he kept his armour in place. Even as he knew Anna would hate him after, and that knowledge pained him as nothing else could.

'Then Lady Bowen might be a fine distraction from your work.' Edward led Rob down a winding path that twisted around the house to the meadows and fields that rolled away into the distance. Once they were alone by the decorative lake, with no one to overhear, he said, 'Speaking of work, Rob, what progress have you made?'

'Walsingham believes he is closing in on the plotters,' Rob said. The plotters—including Anna's own father. He scooped up a flat stone from the ground and sent it skimming hard into the water. 'He still seeks their leader, and I think he does not yet know the essence of their plot. Only that they work for Spain.'

'Always Spain,' Edward said. 'Even when we defeat them we are not rid of them. But perhaps some of our guests will know information of help to us.'

'Which guests are you thinking of?'

'Ah, we shall have to discover that later, won't we?' Edward pointed to the crest of a distant hill, where a dark grey stone wall snaked its way through the lush green. 'Beyond that border lies Thomas Sheldon's new estate, which he bought after the downfall of the unfortunate Carringtons.'

'Sheldon lives there now?' Rob said in surprise. 'And you have not yet run him off?'

'It amuses me to watch him squirm so close by,' Edward said, his eyes narrowed as he studied that wall. 'And his days are numbered now. He has many interesting visitors—and I have many watchers along the road to make note of them. He grows careless. With these comings and goings, and the papers Elizabeth's enterprising niece snatched for us, he will soon be done.'

'And you think he has something to do with these new Spanish plotters?'

'The Spanish have gold, and lots of it. Of course Sheldon will deal with them. I will show you the papers later. I'm eager to see what you think of them.'

'Will we have to break into his house to search for more evidence?' Rob asked. House-breaking was not his favourite activity—it lacked the quick, sharp action of a fight, the satisfaction of meeting an enemy face to face. But sometimes it was the only way to accomplish a goal.

'No need,' Edward said. 'He will be at the ball here at Hart Castle a few nights hence. Perhaps the lady who is not *your* lady might care to dance with him? She seems very observant, even if she *is* here with you.'

Rob stared hard at the hillside, imagining Anna in Sheldon's fat arms, the villain braying down at her as he stared at her bodice. It made that hot fury return, stronger than ever.

He had never felt so possessive of a woman before—so protective. He could never do his task—clear her father, be rid of Walsingham—if he spent every moment waiting to skewer any man who looked at her, who wished to do her harm.

Especially when he feared he would be the first one to hurt her.

He shrugged, feigning indifference. 'You must ask her yourself, Edward. I told you—she is not my lady.'

'I do hope you will be comfortable here, Mistress Barrett,' Lady Elizabeth said as she bustled around the bedchamber. She fluffed a cushion on a chair and opened the window to let in the fresh country breeze.

Anna carefully laid her hat and gloves on a small carved table, staring around her at the room that was larger than the first floor of her father's house. An immense dark wood bed, etched with images of fruit, flowers and fantastical birds, was hung with deep green curtains and spread with an embroidered counterpane that matched the cushions of the cross-backed chairs by the fireplace. Large clothes chests lined the walls, which displayed a valuable oval looking glass and portraits of sumptuously garbed Hartleys. Her own luggage looked small and puny next to such furnishings.

'Oh, yes,' Anna murmured. 'I dare say I will be comfortable enough here.'

'If you have need of anything at all you need only ring for it, or ask me. My own apartment is across the corridor.' Lady Elizabeth suddenly hurried over to clasp Anna's hands in hers, a happy smile on her face. 'I am so very glad you've come here with Robert! He has never brought a lady to one of our parties before.'

Startled by such a fine lady's gesture of friendship, Anna managed to smile back. What a strange house this Hart Castle was! She was starting to feel as if she had tumbled down into a new, strange land, and Rob was her only anchor.

'Has he not?' Anna asked.

Lady Elizabeth shook her head. 'I do fear he is very lonely.'

Lonely? Robert? Anna almost laughed at the thought as she remembered the bawd in the dirty yellow gown, the ladies who crowded the galleries at the White Heron to toss flowers at his feet, and the woman in the garden below who stared at him.

But then she remembered something else—the shadow in his eyes sometimes when he looked at her in an unguarded instant. The tender way he held her in his arms once the storm of passion had passed. There *was* something raw and aching he hid deep inside, and it was that which called out to her so strongly, which drew her to him even as she knew she should run.

But he would never reveal that vulnerable heart to her—not fully and freely.

A burst of laughter rang through the open window, and Anna hurried to see what was happening, Elizabeth right behind her. The view was down to the driveway and statues below, the curve of the lane, the formal gardens and the trees beyond. A new carriage had just arrived, its glossy, crest-painted doors opening to disgorge its passengers.

They were two men and three women, all dressed in sumptuous satins and velvets, creamy pearls and plumed hats. The guests who had been strolling among the flowerbeds rushed to greet them amid more raucous laughter and shouts.

Lord Edward and Rob appeared from around the hidden side of the house, and one of the ladies broke away to hurry over to them. Blond curls and bright ribbons flying, she threw her arms around Rob's neck and squealed with joy.

Anna smiled wryly. 'Terribly lonely, I see.'

'Lady Arabella flirts with everyone,' Elizabeth said.

'And so does Robert.'

'Does he?' Elizabeth waved towards the scene below. Rob had unwound Lady Arabella's arms and held her away as she pouted up at him. Rob just laughed and strolled lazily to the house, disappearing up the front steps.

Lady Arabella then bounced over to another gentleman and took his arm. He seemed rather more receptive.

'Dinner tonight should be very interesting,' Elizabeth said. 'Now, Mistress Barrett, tell me all the news of London. I have not been back to town for many days, and I'm sure much has happened since then! Has the unhappy Moreton been released from the Tower yet? What of the French ambassador's quarrel with Lord Meyers?'

As they shared gossip of the city, and maids appeared to unpack Anna's borrowed trunks, Anna began to feel more at ease. Lady Elizabeth was not grand or snobbish, despite her title and the fact that she had been lady-in-waiting to the Queen, and they laughed and chattered as old friends. Anna could at last let go of her worry over her father, her confused thoughts of Rob and all that had happened between them, and just enjoy herself.

It was a strange and delicious feeling. It made her wonder what a life like this could be like—a life in the pretty countryside, with friends and a man to love, as Elizabeth obviously loved Lord Edward. It wouldn't be such a grand house as Hart

Castle, of course, but maybe a cottage with a little garden…

Anna almost laughed at herself. A country cottage was as beyond her reach as a palace would be, and a man like Robert would never share such a place. She just had to enjoy this fine holiday now. She was determined to find a way to enjoy life again at long last. Rob had given her that.

The light outside was turning a mellow golden-pink, the sun beginning to sink towards the horizon, when Elizabeth said, 'How is it grown so late? I must see to dinner and leave you to change your gown, Anna. You have let me chatter on too long!'

Suddenly there was the clatter of more carriage wheels down the drive.

'Who would be arriving so very late?' Elizabeth wondered, and Anna went with her to peer out of the window once more. The carriage was a sombre black one, and only one lady stepped out into the deserted garden.

As she looked up at the house the hood of her cloak fell back and Anna glimpsed a pale face and light brown hair—a face she had seen only recently.

'Lady Essex,' she whispered.

'So it is,' Elizabeth said with a frown. 'Whatever

is she doing here? Edward and her husband do not get along at all.'

'Mayhap she is on an errand for someone else?' Anna wondered out loud. Someone like her father, Secretary Walsingham? Was she sent here with some new, dangerous task for Robert?

'Whatever her purpose, I must go down and greet her,' said Elizabeth. 'I shall see you at dinner, Anna?'

'Of course.'

'I *am* glad you are here,' Elizabeth called back to her as she hurried from the room. 'I'm sure we shall be friends!'

Alone again, except for the maids setting up a bath by the fireplace and laying out her clothes, Anna turned back to the window. Lady Essex was gone now, and her empty carriage rolled towards the stables. Why *was* she here? And what was Robert really doing with someone as dangerous as Walsingham?

She had to find out if she was to help him and protect herself. And, just possibly, have a little fun while doing it.

Chapter Thirteen

Anna tiptoed down the staircase, past the glow of the stained-glass window and the silent hulk of the armour. She didn't feel quite like herself, dressed in the deep red velvet gown with gold brocade sleeves, trimmed with gold and cream ribbons and false rubies, a starched lace ruff fanning out around her head. Elizabeth's own maid had dressed her hair in a high swirl of waves and curls fastened with pearl pins, and she held a feathered fan clutched in her hand. Her grey gowns were packed away, along with her everyday life, and it felt strange and exhilarating not to be cloaked in their disguise.

Nay, she was *not* herself tonight. She was sure she was someone entirely different—someone flirtatious like the lady who had greeted Rob on the garden driveway, and assured like Lady Elizabeth. Someone who could coax secrets from a man.

She could hear the hum of voices from a half-open door at the end of the tapestry-lined corridor, a high-pitched burst of laughter. A servant hurried past, bearing a tray of silver goblets, and Anna followed him, slipping into the chamber behind him.

It was filled with the people she had glimpsed earlier in the garden, and even more she had never seen. They were all dressed fit for Court, in sumptuous, jewel-coloured velvets, flashing gold embroidery, and snow-white ruffs that all swirled together like the brilliant stained glass of the staircase window. One man was leaping about, seemingly to demonstrate new dance steps, and everyone laughed at his antics. Lady Essex, the surprise guest, was nowhere to be seen.

Rob stood by the fireplace at the far end of the room, with Lord Edward and a few other guests. He wore a black and purple doublet, and his hair was swept back from his face to reveal an onyx teardrop at his ear and the handsome, austere lines of his features. He didn't laugh with the others, but watched them with an almost brooding look in his eyes. Anna couldn't fathom what he was seeing and thinking as he observed all the merriment around him.

Then he glimpsed her there by the door. For an

instant his eyes widened and he went very still, as if stunned. They stared at each other for a long, frozen moment, and it was as if everyone else in the room vanished. The colour and noise became a mere blur, and all Anna could see was him. All she could remember was her new determination to enjoy herself for a while.

He suddenly smiled at her, a dazzling grin that banished every hint of the darkness that had hung around him only a moment before. He snatched two goblets from the servant's tray and made his way towards her. He came straight to her, ignoring any attempts to catch his attention, and bowed before her.

'Anna,' he said. 'You look most beautiful.'

'Beautiful? Nay, you're just startled to see me without my grey!' She felt unaccountably nervous with him. After the wild intimacies they had shared in the carriage, and in his bed at the Three Bells, she shouldn't feel shy with Rob at all. Yet she did—as if she would start giggling and blushing at any moment. She took the offered goblet and drank deeply of its fine Rhenish wine, hoping it would steady her and bring her back to herself.

All he did was shake his head, and stare as if he couldn't get enough of her.

The wine didn't steady her. It just made her feel giddier, and she laughed. 'Have you no poetic words for me, then?' she asked. But she wasn't sure she could take poetry just yet—the mere word 'beautiful' was sweet enough.

'I fear poetry fails me when it comes to you, Anna,' he said. He took her free hand in his and raised it to his lips. His kiss was warm and soft, lingering on her skin. He turned her palm over and pressed it to his cheek, the heat of him flowing into her and giving her strength.

'Come, let me introduce you to the other guests,' Rob said as he looped her arm through his.

'I would like to meet your friends,' she said. She wanted to be let into his world, his secrets. Would he let her in? Could she let herself in, and follow her resolve to enjoy herself? To enjoy her life, with Rob, for just a little longer…?

Rob watched Anna where she sat along the length of the banquet table. She was lit by the golden glow of the candles, the red lights in her dark hair like flames, her skin white as a pearl against the fine lace ruff she wore. She laughed at something the man beside her said, her cheeks flushing the palest of pinks.

The man leaned closer to her, as if to whisper in her ear, and Rob saw it was Lord Maddingly—one of the greatest libertines at Court. Women were said to follow him wherever he went, besotted, begging for his attention. And now that attention was entirely focused on Anna. He refilled her goblet from one of the silver ewers on the table and smiled at her.

Rob's fist closed hard on the hilt of his eating knife.

'Robert? Is something amiss?' asked Elizabeth, who sat beside him.

He forced his hand to open and dropped the knife to the table. It seemed he became a hot-tempered fool when it came to Anna. He had no right to feel jealous of anyone she spoke to, anyone she liked. Not when he would soon be forced to hurt her more than another man ever could.

He thought of poor Mary, and the memory of her scarred face. His promise to her held him back from Anna.

'Why do you ask that, Elizabeth?' he said. He reached for his own goblet and took a long drink of the strong spiced wine.

'Because you had that murderous look on your

face. I thought perhaps one of our cook's fine dishes had displeased you.'

'Your hospitality is the finest, as always.'

'Then what....' She looked along the table, and when her gaze alighted on Anna and Lord Maddingly, their heads bent together in close conversation, her eyes widened. 'I see.'

'What do you see?'

'Your fair young lady and Lord Maddingly. But you have nothing to fear from him.'

'Mistress Barrett can do as she likes,' Rob said. It took all his hard-won acting skills to make that sound convincing—even to himself.

'I have not known Mistress Barrett long, but she seems too sensible to believe Maddingly's nonsense.'

'Then why did you seat her next to him?'

'Why, Robert, is that *jealousy* in your tone? I thought she could do as she liked, with whomever she likes? I thought he might amuse her.'

Rob gave a snort. 'Amuse?'

'Aye, for his overblown compliments and attempts at poetry he can be most entertaining to those of us who don't take him seriously.' Elizabeth skewered a bit of chicken in cinnamon sauce from a nearby platter and slid it onto his trencher. 'Mistress Barrett's father owns the White Heron, does he not? I'm sure she knows just how to handle poetic blandishments from men who are too handsome for their own good. Even you.'

Rob looked again to Anna, who still whispered with Maddingly. She suddenly caught him watching her, and a soft smile touched her lips. She gave him a little nod before she turned away.

Perhaps she did know how to handle him, but he was beginning to suspect that all his long experience with women was no help at all when it came to Anna Barrett. She wasn't like anyone else he had ever known. She was so much better, so much more beautiful, so much—everything.

'Does she know about your work?' Elizabeth whispered.

Rob remembered how she had followed him to Walsingham's house, how she seemed determined to keep him from protecting her. But he was determined, as well. He had chosen his course. 'Not really.'

'You should tell her, then,' Elizabeth said, surprising him.

'Nay.' She would turn from him in an instant if she knew *all* the truth. He wasn't ready to lose her just yet. That would come all too soon. For now he wanted to revel in her smile, the touch of her hand, the very presence of her. He didn't deserve it, but he craved it so very much.

'She hardly seems the sort to swoon if faced with the realities of life. She does live in Southwark, after all.'

'I will not see her hurt,' Rob said hoarsely.

Elizabeth looked as if she wanted to say more, but she just shook her head. 'As you will. But, as my dear Edward had to learn, you men cannot protect us by keeping us in ignorance. We try to make Hart Castle an escape, a place apart from real life, but I fear the world will encroach even here.'

'And where is Lady Essex this evening?'

Elizabeth shrugged, a little frown creasing her brow. 'She said she was tired from her journey and wished to dine in her chamber. I think she will complete whatever brought her here and depart in the morning.'

'And have you discovered *why* she is here?' That was what he should do—concentrate on his work, on what he had to do. Not watch Anna laughing at the other end of the table. Not think of what he would do to her in her chamber later that night.

'She merely said she wished to escape the stench of London for a little while. Edward always invites her here—it's best to keep in Essex's favour right now, the Queen loves him so, and Edward has his own reasons for keeping well in with her father. But she has never actually come to Hart Castle before.'

'Then is she here on her husband's behalf or her father's?'

'Who knows? Perhaps she is here on her own errand.' Elizabeth leaned closer and whispered, 'Mistress Barrett and I might contrive to talk to her before she leaves. But Edward thinks perhaps Essex sent her here to steal his scientific manuscripts!'

'His manuscripts? Are they valuable to a man as averse to books as they say Essex is?' Rob asked, puzzled.

'Essex seeks to discredit all those the Queen favours besides himself. Edward has made certain interesting discoveries. Perhaps Mistress Barrett might like to see his laboratory after dinner? I know Edward won't mind at all if *you* see it.'

There was no time to share more secrets as a loud quarrel had erupted farther down the table and Elizabeth had to play soothing hostess and intervene.

Rob looked again to Anna, who was still laughing with Maddingly. She *did* look beautiful to-night, in her fine gown, her eyes glowing with enjoyment. Far from her home and duties she looked younger, freer, as if she had long missed fun and laughter. She shone in that bright gown, her drab grey left far behind.

He suddenly wished he could give her this all the time, make her life one of constant laughter and life. She deserved that—to be appreciated for her beauty, surrounded by merriment, working at nothing harder than embroidery and country rides.

Aye, she deserved all that and far, far more. She deserved far more than him, a player and intelligencer with a black past and a darker future. What had happened to Mary had changed him forever, just as it had her, and he could never go back to the way he was before. He could not afford tenderness.

But he could give her this time at Hart Castle and keep her safe in the days to come. If Maddingly could make her laugh, Rob shouldn't mind. Yet he found he *did* mind, violently so.

He rose from his seat and raised his goblet. 'A toast to our fine hosts!' he called. 'And to all the beauty they collect around them.'

'And the music,' Edward said with a laugh.

'Mayhap you will play a fine tune for us after our meal, Robert?'

'Oh, yes!' cried Lady Arabella, clapping her hands. 'A tender ballad full of love and longing.'

'A tale of ancient battles might be finer for *your* sensibilities, Lady Arabella,' Lord Maddingly answered.

'I believe our fair hostess should choose the song,' Rob said.

'Then I choose a song of love,' Elizabeth said, reaching for Edward's hand. 'Always.'

As Edward raised her jewelled fingers to his lips for a tender kiss, the company laughed and applauded. Rob looked to Anna, only to find that though she still smiled a cloud seemed to have passed over her face. She turned away from the sweet sight of Edward and Elizabeth's affection and reached for her wine.

Rob couldn't stay away from her. He hurried down the length of the table, past the laughing guests, to kneel down beside her. He took her hand in his amid the concealing folds of her skirt, and she gave him a startled smile.

'Are you having an enjoyable time, fairest Anna?' he asked quietly.

Anna smiled down at him, but he could still see

that lingering, hidden sadness behind her eyes. 'I don't see how anyone could fail to enjoy themselves here. It seems like an enchanted house.'

'A place of escape?'

'Yes. But not as glorious an escape as your plays.'

'Or as a song?' He kissed her wrist quickly, breathing deeply of the sweet rose scent of her skin, and drew her to her feet. 'Come, Anna—you shall name the song tonight...'

'Where are we going?' Anna asked, laughing as Rob led her up flight after flight of stairs. The reverberation of the company down in the great hall faded away below until there was only silence.

Rob held on to her with one hand and a lantern with the other, carrying it high to light their mysterious path. Up here there were no windows, no ray of light except the glowing circle of the candle behind glass. The dark panelled walls grew closer around them.

But Anna was not frightened. Rob held her by the hand, and she felt light and almost giddy from the evening they had passed. She couldn't remember the last time she had felt quite so carefree, able to laugh and eat fine food, drink good wine and listen to inconsequential talk of fashion and poetry that had nothing to do with ledger books and business. Surely she would soon tire of such frivolity, but for a night's change, an escape, it was quite nice.

Yet she would never choose to leave this strange dark stairwell with Robert to return to the brightest, merriest party. It seemed a fitting end to a dreamlike day.

'Rob! Where are we going?' she asked again.

He glanced back at her over his shoulder, his eyes shining darkly like night stars in the candlelight. 'You'll soon see.'

'Is it a chamber of horrible secrets, like in a play?' she queried. 'A dungeon where you keep all your enemies? Oh, nay, a dungeon could not be so high.'

'And it would be no place for you, would it, Anna?'

She laughed. 'Am I not your enemy, then?' Sometimes when he looked at her she could swear she was—not his enemy, but someone who stood in his way. And at other times he looked at her as if he was starved for the touch of her. Just as she was with him. She could never understand him, never keep up with his quicksilver changes.

Rob suddenly stopped on the stairs, so quickly she stumbled against him. In a flash he let go of her hand and caught her around the waist, pulling her up against his body. The light wavered around them.

'I hope you may never think of *me* that way,' he said.

Puzzled, Anna shook her head. As an enemy? Nay. He baffled and angered her, and left her confused, but she could never see him as her enemy. He was so, so much more to her. But she could never tell him that—never let him see how he was changing her very heart.

'Will I have to build a dungeon of my very own, then, just for you?' she teased.

'Or maybe I intend to lock you up here in the tower of Hart Castle,' he answered. He bent his head to kiss the side of her neck, the curve of her breast above her borrowed bodice. His mouth was hot, hungry, as he tasted her, awakening her own desire all over again. 'I could keep you all to myself here, away from the greedy eyes of rogues like Lord Maddingly.'

'Maddingly?' Anna said breathlessly. She wound her arms around his shoulders to keep from tumbling dizzily down the stairs. 'He seemed rather nice. I'm sure he can't be half as roguish as *you,* Robert Alden. You fly from lady to lady, leaving us all sighing sadly in your wake…'

He pressed her against the wall, holding her there with his body. Every curve and angle of them seemed to fit perfectly together, as if they were made to be just so. As Anna curled her hands into the soft fabric of his doublet, feeling the hard heat of his body underneath, he kissed her lips, open-mouthed, eager. Anna met him with equal passion and need.

'Oh, Anna,' he whispered as his kiss slid to her ear. 'I don't feel in the least roguish when I'm with you. I don't see any other woman. You've cast a terrible spell on me.'

'Terrible?' she breathed, feeling unsteady and unsure, as if she was just a dizzy young girl again.

She didn't like that feeling at all. She pushed Rob away and stiffened her shoulders. Too much had happened since she truly was an innocent girl—her bad marriage, her work, all she saw every day around her in Southwark that showed her how little men could be trusted.

Especially Robert, who looked at her now as if he was just as stunned and lost as she was by what was happening between them. She should mistrust him above the others, for he could make his way past her carefully built walls as no one else ever had. He was so stealthy she hardly noticed until there he was, in her heart.

'Show me your dungeon, then,' she said. 'We have come this far.'

Rob gave a brusque nod and spun away from her. She followed him up one more short flight of stairs to a landing at the very top of the house and a single door. He removed a key from inside his doublet and used it to open the door. It swung inward, perfectly silent on its heavy hinges, to reveal more darkness beyond.

He stepped aside with a low, courtly bow and said, 'If you care to enter, my lady?'

Anna peered past him doubtfully. Tall windows lined one wall of the space, letting in the faint glow of the moon which cast odd-shaped shadows on the floor and around incomprehensible objects. Perhaps it *was* a dungeon—a torture chamber such as the ones they said lurked beneath the Tower in London.

But she had come too far to turn back now. She swept inside and Rob followed, closing the door behind them. He set the lantern down and she could see the room better.

It was not a torture chamber, but something even more fantastical. The octagonal room was lined with shelves and shelves of books. Locked chests were stored beside them, and there were long tables and stools piled with more books. She saw globes in brass stands, and strange, shining metal instruments.

'What is this room?' she asked as she wandered inside, examining mysterious objects and enticing books. She paused at a long brass tube on a stand, fitted with mother-of-pearl decorations.

'It is Edward's room of wonders,' Rob answered. 'He and his guests come here for their studies.' He swung the tube round and showed her a small hole at the end. 'Look through here.'

Anna peered through the tiny lens of the contraption, and gasped at the sight that met her gaze. Rather than mere pinpoints of silvery light, the stars were great, glittering orbs that seemed to sparkle and burst against the velvet of the night sky.

''Tis glorious!' she whispered. 'What is this thing?'

'A telescope,' Rob said. He moved it slightly, giving her another marvellous view of distant, magical worlds. 'Edward had it made in Venice, by the master glassmakers there, and sent back here for his studies. He corresponds about optics with Master Kepler.'

'I could never have imagined such a thing.' Anna drew back from the telescope, half expecting the sky to have taken on a new cast. Yet it looked the same as ever. Even the sky here was terribly deceptive.

'Edward has set up a place here at Hart Castle where new discoveries can be made and the truth sought out in all its forms,' Rob said. 'Mathematics, astronomy, philosophy…'

'And you are a part of it all?'

He gave a wary smile. 'When I can be. My work is busy in London, and sometimes there are dangers in studying the ways of numbers and the stars. Some people do not understand it.'

Anna went to the open window and leaned against the ledge to study the faraway sky. It seemed so quiet, so placid, a sea of black velvet sewn with the tiniest of diamonds. Yet through that glass it was something else entirely.

'Once you told me there were other worlds beyond the stars, full of wonders and stories we have never heard,' she said.

'Did I?' Rob said. She heard him move close behind her, the rustle of velvet as he crossed his arms.

'When we sat together in my father's garden. I'm sure *you* know those stories, for I see them in your plays.'

He came to stand beside her at the window, his shoulder pressed to hers. He was with her now, yet still he felt as distant as those stars. 'I do know many a hidden tale.'

'I wish we could go there now, to that world beyond the stars,' she said.

'Perhaps we can,' Rob whispered in her ear. 'Just close your eyes, hold on to me—and let me take you there…'

Anna closed her eyes and felt his touch on her shoulders as he gently turned her in his arms. He softly kissed her temple, her cheek, each of her closed eyelids, and she couldn't breathe at his nearness. The world spun in sparkling darkness behind her eyes and she felt warm and shivering all at the same time.

She wrapped her arms around his shoulders and leaned into him, and his mouth claimed hers at last. Their kiss was hot and hungry, and she lost herself in it completely. The taste of him, the clean, spicy scent of him, the way his lips felt on hers and his fingers in her hair holding her with him—she *did* spin away into the stars, just with his touch.

And that was frightening, indeed.

Chapter Fourteen

'Fairest Anna, you do drive me mad,' Rob groaned as he carried her through the door of her chamber and kicked it shut behind them.

'I've often thought the same about you,' Anna whispered against his neck. She tasted the salt-sweetness of his skin with her tongue, a raw hunger for him sweeping over her like a hot summer wind.

Rob dropped her feet lightly to the floor, only to wrap one strong arm around her waist and tug her close to him. His mouth stopped her breath with a rough kiss, their tongues pressing deep to taste and possess. He lifted her up and carried her back against the door.

She wrapped her legs tight about his hips and moaned as she felt him grasp her heavy skirts and pull them up, tossing them out of his way.

His erection pressed against her belly, hard and insistent through the layers of fine wool and silk and linen.

His mouth traced a fiery ribbon of kisses along the side of her neck, her collarbone, where her fine gown fell away from her skin. She could feel his hunger, his need, as he kissed her—it echoed her own. Their careful masks fell away one by one, and there was only them—Anna and Robert—bound by their desire for each other. Tied together by whatever it was they hid from the rest of the world, whatever it was in them that called out to the other.

Rob unhooked her ruff and tossed it away, crushing the stiffly starched lace, and Anna's head fell back against the planks of the door. She closed her eyes and felt the searing heat of his kiss as he laid his open mouth against her breast. Her fashionable stays and velvet bodice pushed them into high, soft mounds, but it wasn't enough for him. He hooked his fingers into the jewelled edge of the gown and with one hard tug they spilled free into his hands.

He held them on his palms carefully, lightly, as if they were rare, beautiful jewels, and Anna felt his long poet's fingers reach for one of the aching, hardened nipples. He plucked at it, rolled it between his fingertips, until she cried out at the hot pleasure.

He bent his head and took it deep into his mouth, biting, suckling. She slid her hands into his hair, tangling her caress into the dark waves as her body arched and moved against his. He was hard between her legs, and she remembered what he had done to her in his room in London. Some mischevious spark flared into being inside her, and she let her legs fall away from his hips. Her feet touched the floor and she pushed him away from her.

'Anna, what are you doing?' he ground out roughly. 'Let me…'

She smiled up at him. His eyes were black with hunger, and his lips damp and seductive. His whole body seemed to vibrate with lust, and it gave her a wonderful new feeling of—power. He *did* want her. No matter what troubles lay beyond their door, he wanted her just as she wanted him.

'Nay,' she said. 'Let me.'

She reached down to slowly unfasten his breeches, letting her hands brush gently over his erection. His body stiffened and his eyes narrowed warily as he watched her, but he didn't move away.

He braced his palms flat against the door to either side of her head.

She eased aside the folds of cloth and ran her fingers over his naked penis. It was iron-hard and hot under her touch, velvet-soft, the veins throbbing. She rubbed harder, a smooth caress down its length and up again, and it jumped against her hand.

A tiny drop of moisture gleamed at its tip, and she caught it on her finger. As Rob watched her in close, avid interest, she raised it to her lips and tasted him.

He groaned and said, 'Anna, you will surely slay me.'

She laughed, feeling entirely unlike herself. She had never been seductive or bold—and it felt rather good. With him, anyway. 'I hope not. You would be no use to me that way, Robert, not tonight.'

She let go of his manhood and curled her hands into the front of his doublet to turn him, so their positions were reversed and *he* was the one against the door. Slowly she fell to her knees, her skirts billowing around her.

She held him again, the length of him balanced in her hands, and she leaned forward to run the tip of her tongue over him. His whole body shuddered and she felt his fingers plunge into her hair, dislodging her pins and sending the careful arrangement tumbling loose down her back. Feeling even bolder, she took him into her mouth.

She could smell the faint, salty musk of his male desire, his desire for *her,* and it fanned the flames of her own need higher, hotter. She curled her tongue around him and tasted him.

His hands wound the strands of her hair tighter around his wrists and he tugged her away from him. She looked up at him, puzzled, and he gave her a crooked, unsteady smile.

'Enough, fairest Anna,' he said, and his voice was deep, rough and shaking. He pulled her to her feet and reeled her body in close to his again, his arms wrapping hard around her waist. 'Or this night will be over before it even begins.'

Anna took his face between her hands and found that she was also shaking. They were both trembling from the terrible storm of their need for each other.

'I want to please you,' she whispered. Just as he had pleased her. She wanted no debt outstanding between them.

'You please me more than I could ever have

dreamed possible,' he said, and kissed the tip of her nose, the curve of her cheekbone. 'But I do want this night to last.'

He lifted her up in his arms and carried her to the waiting bed. He laid her down amid the soft, rose-scented bedclothes, and Anna reached out for him to pull him down with her. But he evaded her arms and slid his touch slowly down the length of her body. He touched the flare of her waist, the soft curve of her hip, her outstretched leg where her skirts fell back in a froth of lace and linen and velvet.

He kissed her ankle, his mouth hot through the fine silk stocking, and slid her velvet shoe from her foot. Anna raised herself on her elbows to watch him, breathless as she waited to see what he would do—what he would kiss next. He tossed the shoe away, like her ruff, and slowly kissed a path up her leg, biting at the soft spot behind her knee, the angle of her thigh, until he came to the bare skin above her garter.

He untied the scrap of satin and carefully unrolled the stocking until it drifted away from her foot.

She felt his hot, open-mouthed kiss on the slight indentation where her garter had been tied, so close to the curls between her thighs. He tasted it, soothed it with his tongue, and lightly blew on those wet curls.

Anna fell back to the bed, sinking deeper into the soft feather mattress, the decadent fine sheets. Rob dispensed with her other shoe and stocking and bit at the tender inside of her thigh. He pressed a kiss to her damp seam, but he didn't plunge deeper there, as she longed for him to do. Instead, he eased himself up along her body and nuzzled at the side of her neck as he untied her sleeves and undid her bodice.

He was most adept at divesting a woman of elaborate clothes, Anna thought hazily. Soon she wore only her thin linen chemise.

But he was much too overdressed. She sat up and pushed him back to the bed, straddling him as she unbuttoned his doublet and stripped it away from him. She tugged his shirt over his head and it drifted down to tangle with the blankets.

She studied his bare chest, the hard planes of fine, glistening bronzed skin over powerful muscles, the faint sprinkling of dark, curling hair that arrowed down to his loosened breeches. He was so wonderfully beautiful, with his broad shoulders and narrow hips, his skin glistening with the sweat of their active exertions. She could hardly believe that he was hers, even for this night.

She laid her hands lightly on his shoulders, feeling the heat and vitality of him against her, seeping into her, until it thawed that hard knot of ice she had carried with her ever since her marriage. She let her touch drift over him wonderingly, feeling every inch of him, the roughness of his hair, the hard, pebbled flat nipple that puckered under her hand, the flat hardness of his stomach.

His hands closed over her hips and he swung her down to the bed, his body covering hers as their mouths met hungrily.

He stripped away her chemise and left her completely bare to him. No one had ever seen her entire body naked before, and she suddenly felt ridiculously shy. She tore her lips from his and tried to turn away, but he wouldn't let her. His fingers were gentle, caressing, but inescapable as he held her still for his study.

'You are so beautiful, Anna,' he said, kissing the curve of her shoulder. 'Like a goddess of the night.'

And suddenly she felt beautiful. She felt free and light, totally wanton. She wrapped her legs around his waist and tugged him closer for another eager kiss. The hot brush of his roughened, ink-stained fingers on her sensitive flesh made her cry out at the flood of sensation.

Rob covered her mouth with his and caught her cry as he gave a deft twist of his hips and slid inside her, deep and slow. It had been a long while since she had coupled with a man, and at first the stretching, tight sensation of fullness felt very strange. As if he sensed this, he went very still for a moment. He braced himself above her and let her body adjust to his invasion, his breath harsh and alluring against her ear.

But once she was accustomed to the feeling it was far, far better than she remembered, and a deep, growing sensation of tingling delight grew where his body was joined to hers. She wrapped her legs around his waist and he drew back slowly, slowly, inch by inch, until she feared he would leave her. Then he thrust forward again, deeper and faster.

Anna rocked against him, drawing him even deeper, even closer. So close it seemed as if, for one vivid instant, their souls touched and she could *see* him. See his damaged, lonely, seeking self that was so much like her own secret self.

Then he drew back and thrust forward again,

and that glimpse was lost in a burning sun shower of light. Anna cried out and he moved faster, harder, thrusting against her as they both desperately sought the relief they craved so very much and that they knew could only be found together. She wrapped herself close around him, meeting his every movement, his every stroke, until that climax broke inside her and she almost screamed with the burning force of it.

Rob caught her scream with his mouth, taking it deep inside him and answering it with his own ecstatic shout. She felt the warmth of his release in her, and the way his back arched like a taut bowstring under her hands. His head fell back, his neck muscles corded with the force of his pleasure.

'Anna, Anna,' he groaned. Then he fell to the bed beside her, their arms and legs still tangled, their breath laboured in the humid, perfumed air around them.

He lay on his stomach, his face hidden from her along with his emotions. Anna struggled to catch her breath, to catch *herself* as she tumbled back down from the sun. Her whole body trembled and the force of her feelings almost frightened her. She wanted to laugh and weep all at the same time.

Beside her, Rob's breath slowly grew steadier,

his legs heavy on hers, and she thought he slept. She knew she should sleep, too—dawn would come soon enough, and the party would resume. Something had been said about riding out to go hawking, and she needed energy for such exercise. Yet even though she felt heavy with exhaustion, spent with passion, her mind soared and fizzed, and she knew she would not sleep yet.

She slowly sat up on the edge of the bed, careful not to wake Rob. If he woke, if he spoke to her, she would hardly know what to say to him. Her feelings were so tangled and knotted inside her that she didn't know what she felt. She no longer knew how to protect herself.

She caught up her chemise from the floor and took it with her to the half-open window. The night breeze felt wondrously cool on her bare, heated skin, and she let it wash over her like a cleansing tide. The moon glowed down on the slumbering garden, turning it into a shimmering, silent fairyland.

She liked the silence—the way it blanketed everything in a mysterious peace. It was never quiet in Southwark, and almost never peaceful. It slowly calmed her heart, and she breathed it all in deeply. She closed her eyes and let the peace inside.

She heard the rustle of bedclothes behind her, and the soft sound of Rob's bare feet as he crossed the floor, but she didn't open her eyes. She didn't dare, for fear the silent spell would shatter.

He gently swept her hair from her back and let it fall over her shoulder as he kissed the nape of her neck and wrapped his arms around her waist. He drew her back against his body, the two of them naked as the night curled around them.

'Can't you sleep?' he asked softly, as if he also feared to shatter the spell.

'Not yet. I wanted to look at the moon again. It always seems to hide behind the clouds and dirt in Southwark—unless you are with me to coax it to appear.'

'Hart Castle is a pretty place.'

'Very pretty, indeed. Edward and Elizabeth are fortunate.'

'Have you ever wanted a home like this?'

Anna laughed. 'Of course I have. But that would be like wishing to possess that moon. A house like this—it is not for a woman such as me: a poor widow, the daughter of a man whose coin comes from theatres and bawdy houses.'

'Nor for a poor, wandering actor like me,' Rob said ruefully. 'Yet surely it's good to have aspirations and dreams, no matter how moon-mad? To have something to desire? Don't you think?'

Anna shivered as she felt his warm mouth nibble at her neck and drift lower, over her shoulder and her naked back. His hands crept up to caress the soft underside of her breasts and her eyes drifted closed. Just as she started to fall back against him she felt his whole body stiffen and his head came up.

'Anna, what is this?' he said roughly.

And she remembered. The scars—the marks no one had ever seen. How could she have forgotten long enough for him to find them? It was as if a sudden cold rain doused the dreamlike night.

She drew away from him and tugged the chemise over her head, as if hiding them could make them vanish. ''Tis nothing.'

Rob took her arm and turned her to face him. He wouldn't let her turn away. 'They are whip marks.'

'Aye. A gift from my husband. But they are old.' And the memories felt more distant with every minute. Robert made her feel new, reborn.

'It does not matter how old they are,' he said, and she heard the hard, sharp edge of anger glinting through his words like a sword. 'He hurt you—he left scars on your skin.'

'It is a wife's lot,' Anna said bitterly, repeating what everyone had told her when Charles had got drunk and beat her—even her father. Despite the sadness in his eyes then, he had sent her back to her husband. He'd said he had no choice.

Rob was the first person ever to show such anger over how she had once been treated, and it made her feel sad all over again—and heartened.

'Nay, it is not,' he said, that fury even harder and brighter. 'How dare he do this to you? If I had been there…'

'If you had been there?'

'I would have killed him,' he said, and there was the solid ring of truth to those stark, simple words.

'I had no knight to ride to my rescue then,' she said, her throat dry with the tears she had held back for years. 'But I confess—I felt nothing but relief when he died.'

Rob drew her closer, slowly, gently, until she could rest her head against his chest and close her eyes. There in his arms, in his protective silence, she at last felt those bitter days of the past drop away and free her from their hard talons. They were gone, *really* gone, and she was here now with Robert.

Rob Alden was a dangerous man in many ways.

She knew that well. He served Walsingham, which meant great secrecy and peril, and he brawled and fought—she had seen the wounds of that. He also threatened to invade her guarded heart, to make her care about him, want him in ways beyond the bedchamber—ways he couldn't be hers. But he was not cruel in the way Charles Barrett had been. He took not the slightest pleasure from her pain, and in that she could be safe with him.

Rob softly kissed the top of her head and she felt him smooth her hair. Gentle, soothing movements, so at odds with that cold fury in his voice— *I would have killed him.*

'How could your father have married you to such a villain?' he demanded.

'My father could not have stopped such a head-strong, silly girl as I was,' Anna said with a laugh. 'Charles was handsome and charming—though not as charming as you, Rob Alden. And he prom-ised to take me away from Southwark, give me a new life. I was foolishly certain I knew what I was doing. But when we married and I left my fa-ther's house it all changed.'

Rob took her hand and led her to sit down on the edge of the bed. She shivered, though whether from the night breeze or the old memories she couldn't tell. He wrapped his doublet around her shoulders and she drew it close to her. Its soft, fine folds still smelled of him—clean mint and dark spice.

Strangely, even that made her feel safer. Wrapped around with a new armour that kept the past away.

He sat down beside her. 'He was not what you thought?'

Anna shook her head. 'In London he was charming and full of good humour. He flattered me and I was silly enough to let him. But once I was his wife he became so jealous and angry. He did not like me to leave the house, and when I had to go to market he made me bind my hair tight and leave off my London-style dresses.'

'And wear grey,' Rob said roughly.

'Aye. I could never be perfect enough, modest enough for him, though. And then he would hit me.' Anna pulled the doublet even closer over her shoulders. 'Fortunately we were not so long married. When he was buried, I sold what I could and used the coin to return to Southwark for good. I told my father we wouldn't speak of it, that our lives would go on as if I had never married. I've never talked about it—until now.'

'Then you honour me with your secrets, Anna.'

Rob slid behind her on the bed and wrapped his arms and legs around her to hold her close. He gently urged her to lean back against him, to let him hold her.

At first she leaned away, still caught by the old memories, the thin bonds that still held her to the past. But then she sighed and relaxed into his arms, and it was as if those last bonds snapped and she was really free.

Rob gently rocked her in his embrace, soothing her, and she closed her eyes. She hadn't felt so warm, so content, in a very long time—maybe never. She knew very well Rob could never be truly hers—not to keep. He was a vagabond actor and writer with troubles of his own, not likely to love a woman such as her. But he had given her the gift of listening to her, *really* listening, and had helped free her from those old ghosts.

He had shown her some men were not like Charles Barrett. For that she would always care for him.

And worry about him. As she ran her hand slowly up and down his muscled forearm she felt the rough, jagged line of a scar marring his skin. It reminded her of the perils of his life, and she shivered again to think of his constant danger. Of what a blank world it would be without him in it.

They both had scars to bear.

'I wonder you have never found yourself married, Rob,' she said. 'Many of the players have wives.'

Rob gave a humourless laugh. 'Because wedlock sounds such a fine state to you, Anna?'

'I made a foolish choice. I see that now. But my father often speaks of my mother tenderly.' She had to learn to make better choices now, to see things for what they were. Not always wrapped in warm, comforting night as she was now.

'My parents, too, had a harmonious union. But I didn't inherit their easy tempers. I'm too full of anger to make a good husband.'

Anna closed her hand over Rob's, holding him close. 'You use your anger to defend those weaker than yourself, never to bully them! I see that time after time.' He had changed *her* life entirely, all because of the wonderful life force of who he was. She would never be the same again.

'It is true that if your husband was alive now he would have to fear for his existence,' Rob said. That anger was still there in his voice, but banked and solid. 'Bullies should be thrashed in the streets and thrown into the Thames.'

'My bloodthirsty side agrees with you whole-heartedly,' Anna said with a laugh. 'Were *you* bullied as child, Rob? Is that what makes you so quick to fight now?' She found she wanted desperately to know this—to know more about him. To know everything, all he kept hidden in his heart.

'Nay, not I. Even as a child I was too eager with my fists, and the village lads avoided me. But there was someone I cared for who was hurt.'

'A sweetheart?' Anna asked, her heart aching at the deep, heavy sadness she sensed in his voice. It was as if for a single instant the dark core of his heart was opened to her and she glimpsed his hidden self. Just as she had dared show him hers.

Then the moment was over, as if a door had slammed shut, and Rob kissed her temple with a reckless laugh. 'Just someone who is long gone from my life, fairest Anna. But, as you urge me to marry, I say you should be the one to choose a spouse. Not all men are as your late husband, and you deserve a kind companion who will look after you.'

Anna smiled sadly, thinking of Henry Ennis and his attentions. He seemed good enough—if a bit too eager, and burningly jealous when she looked at Rob. But Henry could never be the man for her. That bittersweet feeling lingered like a faint, lost perfume that faded with every passing tick of the clock. 'Not I. I'm happy with my life as it is,' she said, staring out into the night beyond the window. It was deepest dark out there and perfectly quiet, without even a bird's song. 'It's a long while until morning.'

'What shall we do with so much time?' he asked teasingly. He bore her down to the bed and lay down on his side next to her, propped up on his elbow as he lazily studied the length of her body. His fingers deftly toyed with the ribbons of her chemise, his touch brushing her nipples through the thin linen.

A new sort of shiver took hold of Anna—a warm feeling deep in her belly of desire reborn. She had to hold on to Rob, on to her feelings for him, as long as she could. She had to relish the passion that sprang so easily between them, and remember it for the rest of her life.

'I can think of a few things…' he said deeply, seductively, and leaned over to kiss her mouth hungrily. It was a long time before she knew anything else but him.

Chapter Fifteen

Henry Ennis stopped at the end of Seething Lane, trying to catch his breath. He felt as if he had run all the way from Southwark, his chest tight and his throat aching. He loosened the high collar of his doublet with sweating hands, but still that heavy cloud pressed down on him.

He glanced back over his shoulder, but even as he thought to run away from his resolved task the door opened. One of Walsingham's men stood there, bearded and grey-faced in his black robe. He gave Henry a humourless twist of a smile.

'Master Ennis, at last,' he said. 'Secretary Walsingham has long been expecting you since he received your most intriguing message.'

Henry was forced to step into the dimly lit hall, and the door clanged shut behind him. He swept his cap from his head and twisted it between his hands as the man led him towards the stairs.

This had all seemed such a fine idea when his father's old friend Thomas Sheldon had approached him with his proposition: gather bits of information from his fellow actors and pass them on to Sheldon, and sometimes slide coded passages into pages of the play he was writing. It was so simple, and gained him a few extra coins.

It had seemed even better when he'd realised the Queen's Secretary would also pay for such nuggets of intelligence, and his coffers grew. Walsingham and Sheldon both paid for information that flowed both ways. He'd even dared to think that with the extra money he might marry Anna Barrett.

Until that hope had been shattered. He rubbed at the wound on his leg, and his hatred of Robert Alden, born when they were both newcomers to Lord Henshaw's Men, vying for the same roles, and nurtured over the years as Alden's star rose and Henry's stalled, flowed even hotter. When he'd seen Anna smile at Alden so tenderly, he'd snapped. It had been the final straw.

Why, then, was he so nervous? His hands were damp, his head pounding. He had to be strong now. Follow through on his plans. Soon his tormenter Alden would be gone from his life, and Anna would smile only at him.

He followed the man up the carved staircase and along a long, narrow corridor to a chamber at its end. Henry had never been so far before. Usually his messages were taken and his money handed over in the entrance hall. He didn't like this walk at all. But he had to carry on with his plan now.

He had no choice.

The door opened and he was ushered into a small chamber piled with papers and heavy with the smell of ink and herbs and close air. Walsingham's assistant, Master Phellipes, a sallow-faced, ferret-like man, was carefully steaming open wax seals by the window. It was said he could tamper with seals so well no one was ever the wiser that they had been read. Walsingham himself sat behind a desk with a ledger open before him.

'Ah, Master Ennis,' he said. 'I trust your leg is healing?'

'It is, Master Secretary,' Henry answered, swallowing past the nervous knot in his throat. Of course Walsingham would know about the fight at the White Heron.

'Excellent.' Walsingham sat back in his chair

and studied Henry over his steepled fingertips. 'Now, tell me how you know the traitor we seek within the White Heron...'

Chapter Sixteen

'Shall I race you across the park?' Rob challenged as he led Anna down the stairs of Hart Castle towards the open front doors.

Anna laughed, trailing behind him. 'You would win most handily, I fear. It's been a long while since I was on a horse, and then it was only a docile old mare that carried me to country markets.' She tugged on his hand, forcing him to stop and face her, and whispered, 'In truth, I'm a bit nervous about this excursion today. What if I fall off and make a fool of myself in front of everyone?'

Rob didn't laugh at her, as she'd half feared he might. He seemed to be afraid of nothing at all. He held her hands tightly in his and raised them to his lips for a gentle kiss.

'You needn't fear falling, Anna,' he said. ''Tis no wild hunt, racing through stream and bramble as the Queen enjoys. It's just a day of hawking in the sunshine, and a picnic. I'll be nearby, and so will Edward—we won't let anything happen to you.'

She smiled at him. 'You are quick in a fight, I know, Robert. Yet I doubt you are quite quick enough to fly to me in time to catch me, should my horse take a notion to throw me.'

Rob leaned closer and whispered in her ear, 'I have talents you have not even seen yet, fairest Anna. If we but had time, I would demonstrate...'

Anna watched, fascinated, as he tilted his head and skimmed his lips in a soft, tantalising kiss over her cheek. Lower and lower, close to her mouth, until her own lips parted on a sigh.

But he drew back in a flash and tugged again at her hand, leading her towards the door. 'I fear duty calls us, my dear,' he said.

'You are a wretch, Robert Alden,' she declared. 'I will have my revenge on you yet.'

He laughed. 'I look forward to it.'

The party was gathering on the gravelled driveway in front of the house, a milling crowd of people, dogs and horses in the pale, misty morning light. Pages circulated amongst them with trays of goblets filled with warming spiced wine against the chilly morning.

Anna carefully smoothed her skirt and straightened her hat. She wore her own grey skirt and doublet for riding, but she had a new tall-crowned red-velvet hat and red leather gloves much like the riding ensembles of the other ladies. At least she would look well enough when she went tumbling to the ground, she thought. It was strange how Robert made her feel so very confident and carefree when she was with him. So very unlike herself.

Elizabeth stood with Edward and a russet-clad man holding a hooded hawk at the edge of the crowd. She waved at Anna and broke away to hurry over to her, her green and gold riding clothes bright and summery in the grey mist.

'Good morning to you, Mistress Barrett! And to you, Robert,' Elizabeth said. 'Don't you look quite…well-rested today.'

'And you look most charming, as ever, Lady Elizabeth,' Rob said with a bow. 'The goddess of the sun, the herald of the day…'

'Pah, it is too early for your poetry! Go and talk to Edward. He is aching to show off his new hawk,' Elizabeth said with a shooing wave. 'I will introduce Mistress Barrett to her horse.'

She didn't wait for an answer, but looped her

arm with Anna's and led her towards a sleepy-looking grey mare. 'Robert said you haven't had the chance to ride very much of late, so I found the quietest mount in the stables for you,' Elizabeth said. 'She knows every inch of this park and will carry you most safely.'

'That was very kind of you, Lady Elizabeth.' Anna cautiously patted the horse's soft nose, and laughed when it whinnied and nudged at her. 'I'm sure we will do well enough together.'

'I'm sure you will.' Elizabeth laid her hand on the horse's bridle, watching Anna closely. 'Tell me, Mistress Barrett, are you enjoying yourself at Hart Castle?'

'Very much. I don't see how anyone could fail to enjoy being at such a fine house.'

'Yes. Though, I fear it was not always so happy a place.'

'How so, Lady Elizabeth?'

Elizabeth studied the gleaming windows of the house with a little frown. 'When I first met Edward—when he brought me here—it was a house of great sadness and seemed very lonely. Since Edward had lost his brother he seldom came here, because he could not face the old memories. His grief was too deep, and he and the house were both sunk in some terrible spell of sad lifelessness.'

'How awful,' Anna whispered. She looked across the drive to where Edward stood with Rob, both of them laughing at some jest. 'He doesn't seem so sad now.'

'Nay. Sometimes, my dear Mistress Barrett, a person merely needs a reason to truly live again. A purpose that banishes the past and awakens them to the wonders of the present moment. A true passion.'

'And he found that purpose with you?'

'Me—and other things. Life is too uncertain and precious to waste, and love too rare to lose,' Elizabeth said with a smile. 'He and I both had to learn that. Maybe what happened to us could be useful for others, as well—others who struggle.'

Anna stared at the horse's grey neck, unable to quite meet Elizabeth's gaze. 'You think I struggle?'

Elizabeth shrugged. 'I have not known you long, Mistress Barrett—Anna—but I see the light in your eyes when you look at Robert, the way the two of you smile at each other. It's as if there is no one else in the whole room—nothing else you see. That is also how I feel when I look at Edward.'

Somehow the understanding in Elizabeth's soft voice, the truth of her words, melted Anna's reserve. 'I do care about Rob. But there is so much I don't know about him, and what I do know tells me I must be cautious. My feelings frighten me a bit.'

Elizabeth nodded. 'We can't choose who we love, and I fear *our* hearts have not chosen easy men to care for. But my first marriage was not a happy one. My husband was much older than me, and not very kind. I thought I could never feel for a man as I do for Edward. I wasn't even sure I *wanted* to feel that way!'

'I am not sure, either,' Anna murmured. Could she put the past behind her forever, and move forward as she had these last few days?

'But I came to see it as a great gift, Anna, and you should, too!' Elizabeth declared. 'Just remember what I said—life is too fleeting for fear.'

'My friends, shall we ride out?' Edward called. 'The day grows apace!'

Elizabeth gave Anna one last smile and hurried over to her own horse as a groom came to help Anna into the saddle. As she settled her skirts around her Elizabeth's words echoed in her mind. *Too fleeting for fear.* Should she—could she—

reach out and seize this time with Rob, no matter how brief, as a gift?

Rob reined in his horse next to hers and gave her a wide, white grin of sheer pleasure in the day. 'Are you ready to run, Anna?' he asked.

She nodded and laughed. 'Aye, Rob. I am assuredly ready to run!'

'Where are we going?' Anna asked as Rob led her along the soft green banks of the river. He laughed that she whispered the words, as if they were sneaking away from the party in stealth, even though the chattering voices of the others were now a mere echo behind them.

Now the sumptuous picnic that had been laid out for the hunters in a shady grove had been consumed they were all falling into a happy lassitude, induced by fine wine and Elizabeth's soft song played on her lute. Rob had taken Anna's hand and lured her away from the group.

''Tis a secret,' he said, tossing her a roguish smile over his shoulder. 'Unless you don't trust where I might lead?'

Anna laughed. 'I don't trust you a whit, Robert Alden! Yet you always intrigue me so greatly I fear that I forget all prudence and follow you.'

'You are a secret adventurer, then, fairest Anna. I see it in your eyes. You try to hide it behind your sternness and your grey gowns, but you can't conceal it forever. We are both much too curious about the world around us for our own good.'

Anna smiled, but Rob could see a dark cloud pass fleetingly over her face. 'Perhaps I was curious once. Until I learned it is better not to be.'

He remembered her tale of her nasty husband, and the scars on her back from where the villain had tried to beat the curiosity, the bright spark out of her. Fury still burned within him that anyone would dare treat her so—would bully and oppress her, his beautiful Anna. Master Barrett was fortunate he was dead, or Rob would soon have tortured him most painfully into that state. He could never bear to see a woman scarred, like Anna and his sister.

Yet Barrett hadn't extinguished Anna's spark, her passion. He had merely forced it into hiding behind a brittle shell of caution. Rob intended to see it free once more. Surely he could give her that one small thing? A moment of freely won happiness, before he himself had to hurt her all over again?

Or maybe he was merely selfish and wanted

to taste her happiness for himself. He found he yearned for it as he never had anything else.

'Do you remember when I told you of my disobedient youth?' he asked. He wrapped his arm around her waist, holding her against his side as they strolled beside the water.

She wrapped her arm around him, too, leaning close. 'Aye, you said you would climb out of your window at night and run free to sit by the river and dream of your future plays and poems.'

'This was that very river.'

She looked down at the water, burbling gently past below the banks, her eyes wide with surprise. 'Is it truly?'

'I lived in Hartley Village, not so very far from this estate, and I often trespassed on this land to swim in the river or wander the woods. Edward's father was always at Court, waiting on the Queen in her younger days. There was no one to care what one small boy did here.'

'And you imagined tales of knights and kings and gods here? Just like in your plays?' she asked.

'Perhaps then they were more bloody and full of battles and revenge,' he said. 'The fashion now is for tales more romantical. I had no liking for such things then.'

Anna laughed. 'And now?'

'Now they are my favourite tales of all. What poet is not inspired by the beauty of his lady?' He caught her up in his arms and carried her over to a narrow wooden bridge as she laughed and held on to her hat. She was so very beautiful when she laughed, her face glowing in the bright day. 'Or by the music of her laughter?'

'Audiences do like tales of love,' she said. 'But they also love stories of bloody revenge just as much as ever.'

Rob didn't set her back on her feet, despite her wriggling in his arms, but carried her along the overgrown path that led away from the river. He couldn't let her go yet. 'Then I must strive to give them what they want. Love and passion, ending in a noisy, messy battle.'

'As it always does, I fear, in one way or another.' Anna laid her head on his shoulder with a sigh. 'I think you *do* give the people what they want in your plays. You see into their very hearts and your words speak to their deepest desires and fears. It is why they flock to the White Heron to see your work. You see the truth of people, deep down.'

He wished he could see the truth of her. All of her—not merely the tantalising glimpses she offered in the heat of their passion. But then he would have to show her the truth of himself in return, and he wasn't ready to lose her. Not yet. He hadn't realised how dry and barren his life had been before, how hungry he was for what Anna offered. Not just sex, but her laughter and secrets, too.

Had he found what he really needed now, all too late? Was this the true curse of his life? To see what he wrote of in his poetry but be unable ever to claim it? He would have laughed at the bitter irony if it did not make his heart ache.

'Then I must finish my new play quickly for your father,' he said. 'And hope you will approve of it.'

'I fear you won't finish by going to country parties and wandering the woods with me,' she said.

'On the contrary, fairest Anna—walking the woods with you is the finest inspiration.' Rob ducked beneath a low-hanging tangle of branches, Anna still held in his arms, and entered his old secret grove.

'Oh!' she gasped. 'What is this place?'

'It was my magical realm when I was a boy,' he said. 'I haven't been back for many years. I'm surprised it's still here at all.'

'Who could bear to destroy such a spot?' Anna asked. Rob gently set her on her feet and she drifted around the thick ring of trees, staring in wonder.

The trees were so closely grown that the circle was cast in deepest shade. The ground beneath was soft and emerald green, scattered with several large, flat rocks worn smooth by time. In the centre a blackened circle showed where there had once been an old fire-pit.

'When I was a boy I imagined it was the realm of Druids and the fairyfolk, from the old tales our kitchen maid would tell me when my mother wasn't listening,' Rob said. 'Or it could be the Dark Knight's fortress—or a place where spirits could be summoned.'

'It is an enchanted place. I'm sure of it,' Anna murmured. She removed her glove and ran her fingertips over the rough trunk of a tree. 'I've never been anywhere so quiet. So strange and haunted, yet so welcoming at the same time.'

Rob leaned against another tree, crossing his arms over his chest as he watched her. She tilted her face up to the faint rays of pale light that filtered through the trees, and spun around laughing.

He couldn't look away from her at all. Her beauty held him spellbound.

'This place likes you,' he said. 'It doesn't welcome everyone into its midst.'

She twirled to a stop, her skirts swaying, and smiled at him. 'Perhaps it welcomes you because you are the king of the enchanted grove and I am your guest.'

'I would that I were king of so much more, with lands and jewels to shower on you.' He wished he could give her everything, instead of the pain that was his only legacy to her. Wished he could be worthy of her.

'No gift could be finer than this moment, here in this place.' She slowly crossed the grove to stand before him, so very close, achingly close, but not touching. 'With you, Robert.'

He could bear it no longer. He grabbed her hands in his and drew her into his arms, their bodies pressed tight together as she went up on tiptoe. He kissed her with all the hunger in his heart.

She looped her arms about his neck, his hat falling to the ground as she laced her fingers through his hair and held on to him. His tongue traced the soft bow of her lips, urging her to open to him, welcome him, before he pressed inside to taste her.

She met him with a soft moan that drove his need to even hotter heights. They fell together to the ground, wrapped around each other, their kiss deepening.

Rob traced his mouth over her jaw, the softness of her ear, the curve of her throat, until he rested his head on her shoulder and just held on to her. Breathed in deeply of the warm, summer rose scent of her.

'I wish we could never leave this place,' she whispered. 'Do you think the fairies would carry us off to live in their realm forever?' She gently cradled his head against her and kissed his brow.

'They would make you their fairy queen.'

Anna laughed softly. 'And you their clown. But surely in fairy realms a queen and a clown could be happy together.'

'Happy forever, I'm sure.'

'Then while we are here we are in our very own realm,' she said. 'Nothing can touch us—not here.'

They held on to each other in silence as the light turned sparkling and golden around them and time itself seemed to stand still. It was only them, Robert and Anna, in the perfect silence of their own realm, watched by fairy eyes that kept away the wider world with the force of their spells—or by the force of Rob's own will, that wanted only one more moment with her.

But not even the most ferocious will, nor the spells of the fairies, could keep away the world forever.

Chapter Seventeen

Anna turned before the looking glass on her chamber wall, twisting her head one way then the other as she studied herself. She wasn't sure it was really her, Anna Barrett, who stood there, even as the reflected woman obeyed her movements.

Lady Elizabeth had loaned Anna her own maid again to help her dress and fix her hair for the ball, and the woman had worked wonders. She could almost be a fairy queen in truth, with her dark hair piled high in smooth, shining waves, pinned with pearl skewers and crowned with a delicate wire and pearl headdress.

She wore another gown borrowed from the White Heron's costume coffers—a bodice and overskirt of white and gold brocade, with a quilted petticoat of deep crimson velvet. Lady Elizabeth had also sent jewels—pearl earrings and a long, looping strand of more pearls—and a white feather fan and silver pomander hung from her waist.

Such a creature could surely sit upon a golden throne in Rob's enchanted grove, presiding over the fairy revels. But was it *her?*

'It is me tonight,' she said with a laugh, and reached for her bottle of scent.

Ever since the visit to Rob's fairy circle, ever since he had kissed her there and held her so close, she'd felt—different. Lighter. As if she drifted above the ground on a golden cloud, dancing with each step. She wished she knew the antidote to keep the spell from fading away. She wished that she could always feel just like this—always.

She turned away from the glass and the false image it held to tempt her. Soon this party would end. The days were flying past, faster with every moment, and soon she would go back to Southwark. Back to looking after her father, keeping his ledgers, badgering bawdy housekeepers for their rent. Wearing grey gowns and living backstage, behind the action and noise and colour.

'But in the meantime I will dance and dance,' she declared aloud. She whirled round and round in her fine skirts, whirling until she was dizzy and laughing.

Until she collided with a solid, strong male chest.

She heard the sound of Rob's laughter, and he reached out to catch her in his arms before she could topple to the ground.

'Have you begun the ball so early, my lady?' he asked. 'And without me?'

'I thought I should practise my steps,' she said, breathless from her spinning—and from his touch. 'I fear that particular dance might be rather unpolished for company.'

'Not once they've had their fill of Edward's fine Malmsey wine.' Rob nuzzled his lips just below her ear, his breath warm on her skin. 'You smell delicious, Anna.'

She wanted to melt deeper into his arms, seize him by the folds of his crimson velvet doublet and drag him closer and closer, but she could hear the faint strains of music from downstairs. She pushed him away.

'And you will muss Lady Elizabeth's maid's fine efforts,' she said. 'I fear one touch will bring this great edifice collapsing down.'

Rob kissed her hand in a most gallant, courtly manner, bowing low over it. 'You will be the most beautiful woman there. All the men will be brawling for the chance to dance with you.'

'I should hope not,' Anna said sternly. 'I should hate to see Lord Edward's grand hall wrecked for the sake of my clumsy pavane.'

'Nonetheless, you will have many partners tonight.' Rob suddenly looked serious. 'Edward has invited all the local gentry and some friends from London, as well as his house guests. The ball will be very crowded, and some of them are people you would not like to know.'

Anna laughed, but she was a bit discomfited by the sudden solemn look on his face. 'Rob, I collect my father's rent from Mother Nan and the proprietor of a bear pit. I work in a theatre. I am quite accustomed to the less genteel sort.'

'Some of these people make Mother Nan look the image of honesty,' he answered. 'Just try and stay close to me. And don't listen to anything they might tell you.'

'Oh, Robert. I can take care of myself—even amongst preening courtiers.'

'I know you can.' He kissed her hand again, a lingering caress, and held on to her as if he didn't want to let her go. 'But you should not have to.'

The music grew louder, and Anna feared if she stood there with him a moment longer she wouldn't want to leave. 'Shall we go down now?'

Rob held out his arm for her to take and gave her a bow. 'Your revels await, my lady.'

Anna laid her hand lightly on his arm, feeling his tight and corded muscles under her touch. He led her down the stairs to the foyer, where they joined a stream of guests pressing towards the great hall. It seemed as crowded as when the audience surged through the doors of the White Heron when a play was announced, with a jumble of laughter and shouted greetings, the hum of excitement, as if something was just about to begin.

As she was swept into the hall on the tide of people, Anna was glad of her borrowed finery. Everyone here was dressed as if at Court, in embroidered silks, fine lace ruffs and jewels. The air grew warmer as everyone pressed in around her, smelling of oiled perfumes, lavender sachets and wine. She held tightly to Rob's arm as they jostled around her, and thought Lord Edward must be popular indeed for everyone to journey to his house for a gathering when they might have stayed in London and seen the same faces any day at Whitehall.

Then they pushed their way farther into the hall and the crowd fanned out and grew thinner. She could see the musicians in the gallery, half hidden above the room. They played a lively galliard—the newest Italian version of the dance that was all the rage at Court and which Lord Henshaw's Men were attempting to learn for their next production at the White Heron. A line of couples along the centre of the hall performed it now, leaping and spinning lightly in a blur of stained-glass colours and flashing feet.

The long tables were pushed to the walls and laden with silver ewers of wine and platters of rare sweetmeats. Liveried footmen circulated among the laughing crowds with heavy trays loaded with full goblets.

Rob caught up two of them and handed one to Anna as he led her around the edge of the dance floor. She sipped at it and found it was a rich, hon-eyed punch, sweet and deceptive in its strength. It went straight to her head and made her laugh.

'I've never seen such a party before,' she said, dodging around a brocade train.

'There are revels aplenty in Southwark,' Rob said.

Anna thought of Southwark—the sounds of screams of laughter and shattering glass from taverns, the shrieks of Winchester geese in the streets. 'Aye, there is drink and noise aplenty at all times. Just not…'

'Not as well-dressed?' Rob said.

Anna laughed. 'Not quite so fine, no.'

'A rich raiment can hide so much behind its glitter,' he said, in a low, harsh, bitter tone.

Anna looked at him, startled. What did he hide behind those words, those watchful eyes?

'Robert! Mistress Barrett!' Lord Edward called. 'So you join us at last.'

Anna turned to see Edward and Elizabeth standing together near the vast fireplace, both of them garbed in exquisite blue and gold satin, like peacocks in a glorious garden. Elizabeth's hair was smoothed back and twined with a gold halolike headdress, while sapphires sparkled around her neck and on the bodice of her gown.

'Robert, you must save me,' Elizabeth said. 'Edward refuses to dance tonight, and I cannot stand still when I hear such music.'

'Refuses to dance with such beauty?' Rob said, bowing to Elizabeth and holding out his hand to her. 'His foolishness is to my gain, my lady, if you will allow me to be your partner.'

Elizabeth laughed and took his hand. 'Most

gladly I will. You're a better dancer than he is, anyway.'

Edward snorted, but Anna could see the glow of laughter in his eyes as he looked at Elizabeth. 'Go, then, minx—abandon me for a capering clown of a dancer. I will keep Mistress Barrett here with me, instead.'

Rob and Elizabeth hurried away, swallowed by the thick knots of revellers, and Anna was left with Lord Edward. He gave her another goblet of the delicious wine and took away her empty one.

'What do you think of our little gathering here, Mistress Barrett?' he asked.

'"Little," indeed, Lord Edward,' Anna said. 'I doubt there is anyone left in England outside this house tonight. You do have a great many friends.'

Edward surveyed the gathered company around him with narrowed eyes. 'It doesn't take much to lure anyone here to Hart Castle. A little wine, a little music. It is always useful to know people, Mistress Barrett, to hear their gossip and find out what is happening in their minds. To stay always a step ahead of them.'

Anna studied him over the silver rim of her goblet. There was a hardness about him as he watched his own party—a cool distance. He was there, a part of them, their leader even in fashion and courtly power, and yet he was so distant from it all.

Just as Robert was, when he thought no one watched him. When she felt that terrible longing to know what he hid in his heart.

'That does not sound like friendship, my lord,' she said.

'True friendship is a rare thing, indeed, Mistress Barrett, as I'm sure you know,' he answered. He looked at her and smiled, and those hard eyes softened. 'That is why I'm glad Rob is here tonight.'

'Is he your friend, then? Not merely your pet poet, as I hear Lord Southampton keeps?'

Edward laughed. 'I pity anyone who would attempt to keep Rob Alden as a pet anything, Mistress Barrett. He is as unpredictable and changeable as the lion in the Queen's menagerie. But as a friend he is loyal and honest. Aye, I do count him as a friend. We have known each other since we were boys.'

Anna was most intrigued by his words, by this rare glimpse of Robert before she knew him. Before he was Rob Alden, idol of the London play-houses. 'He did say he grew up in the village here.'

'His father was the local book binder and glover,

and like me Rob had no brothers near his age to make mischief with. My older brother was much older, and my younger but a babe in arms then. My parents were often gone from home to serve at Court, and I had great freedom to roam the estate and get into trouble. Rob's father was kind to me—let me hang about in his workshop when I was bored and lonely. Rob and I became friends, running wild over the countryside.'

'And you knew each other all these years?'

Edward shook his head. 'Nay. When my younger brother was in leading strings my parents sent me away to be a page in Lord Burghley's household, so I could learn courtly ways. When I returned years later, as master of Hart Castle, Rob and his family were long gone. I didn't find him again until I saw one of his plays in London. But we still have much in common.'

A lord and a player? Anna longed to know what those commonalities could be. 'A love of poetry?'

'And much else,' Edward said with a smile. 'Such as fair ladies and wild schemes to make things right again.'

Anna laughed. 'I think anyone who would befriend Robert would have to favour wild schemes, Lord Edward. Such is the life of the theatre.'

'Do you enjoy wildness, then, Mistress Barrett?'

'I certainly didn't before,' she said. 'But I am coming to see the advantage of a certain variety in life.'

Rob and Elizabeth danced past them in a peacock-blue whirl, and Elizabeth waved and laughed. Edward waved back at her, watching her as if she was the only person in the whole riotous hall.

'You're quite right, Mistress Barrett,' he said. 'There is much to be said for variety in life.'

The dancers parted into two lines with the figures of the dance, and for a moment she could see down the whole length of the room. A new guest appeared in the doorway, a burly, bearded man, red-faced and trussed in a gold-and-russet doublet, with a group of men gathered behind him. They watched the merriment with glowers on their hard faces and their hands on the daggers at their waists, while the bearded man beamed.

Edward's shoulders stiffened.

'Who is that?' Anna asked. 'Is it someone without an invitation?'

As she watched him, Edward slowly relaxed and gave her a smile. 'On the contrary, Mistress Barrett. That is my esteemed neighbour, Sir Thomas Sheldon. Perhaps you have heard of him?'

'I have, indeed,' Anna murmured. Thomas Sheldon was known in the environs of Southwark for being a cheat at cards and a rough customer in the brothels. Even by the lax standards of the neighbourhood he was a man no one liked to see coming.

Luckily for the White Heron he favoured Lord Weston's Men at another theatre, and never darkened their door. But many was the time Anna had heard Mother Nan complain of him.

She studied him now with some interest. He looked like a round, red-faced elf more than a troublemaker.

'Surely he is not your friend, Lord Edward?' she said.

'It's always wise to know what one's neighbours are about, don't you agree, Mistress Barrett?' he answered. 'Especially when they have only recently come into the estate.'

Rob and Lady Elizabeth rejoined them at that moment, both of them watching the arrival of Sir Thomas and his escorts. Rob also rested his hand on the hilt of his dagger, and though he smiled and moved with a lazy grace Anna almost feared a brawl would break out there, like a scene from one of his plays.

'My dearest Elizabeth, I should greet our new guests,' Edward said. 'I would not wish to appear inhospitable.'

Elizabeth grabbed his arm. 'Not without me, Edward. I have only recently finished the refurbishment of this hall. I don't wish to see it wrecked.'

'Whatever do you mean? I am the soul of civilisation, my love. Nothing will happen tonight.'

Elizabeth frowned up at him. 'What are you about, then?'

Edward kissed her cheek and gently loosened her hand from his arm. 'I will take Rob with me to greet Sir Thomas, Elizabeth. I don't want you subjected to his filthy nonsense. Stay here with Mistress Barrett.'

'Edward...' she began warningly.

'I promise you, love. Nothing will happen.' Edward nodded at Robert and the two of them set off across the room, threading their way through the increasingly noisy revellers. They looked as if they were entering the field of battle.

'Aye, nothing *tonight*,' Elizabeth muttered. She snatched up a goblet and drained the wine.

Anna felt chilly even in the overheated room, and she rubbed at her arms as she tried to erase that heavy disquiet. 'What is between Lord Edward and Thomas Sheldon?'

'An old enmity,' Elizabeth answered. She drew Anna to a quieter corner and whispered in her ear. 'Edward's younger brother died a few years ago—cheated of his fortune by Sheldon and then sent off to die on a ship to America. Sheldon has cheated many men of every status, but his villainy has not yet been proved to the Queen. He even tried to marry my poor niece last year—she was terrified of such a fate.'

'How awful,' Anna said. No woman should find herself married to a brute, as she herself had.

'She is happily married to a man of her own choosing now, and in a strange way it was that which brought me to Edward. But Sheldon must be stopped, one way or another.'

'You two must have great secret confidences, here in this dark corner,' Rob said as he came up behind them.

He slipped his arm around Anna's waist and tugged her close to him. Even though he smiled when she looked up at him, she could glimpse that familiar darkness lurking in his eyes.

Trouble and strife didn't live only in the narrow Southwark streets. It followed them even into grand houses. Anna had the sudden urge to grab Rob's hand and run from this place—from everything their lives held of secrets and plots and dark longings. To just—run.

But she knew running could not lead to escape.

'Where is Edward?' Elizabeth asked. 'I hope you did not leave him alone with Sheldon!'

'I'm not such a poor friend as that, Elizabeth,' Rob answered. 'We merely greeted Sheldon and found him and his men amenable dance partners among the ladies. Then your footman came to Edward with a question about the wine supplies. It seems your guests are so very greedy you are in danger of running out.'

'That is ridiculous,' Elizabeth said. 'Edward's wine is enough to last a century. Where is he now?'

'In the kitchens, I believe. And Sheldon is just there, dancing with Lady Arabella—if you dare call it dancing.' Robert waved towards Sir Thomas, weaving an unsteady path through the patterns of another galliard. Everyone else was having such a merry time they didn't seem to notice when he went the wrong way and ran into them.

Elizabeth departed to look for Edward and the wine, and Anna was left alone with Robert. She snuggled against his side and rested her head on his shoulder, suddenly weary of grand people and their parties and schemes. She felt as if a long, dark evening had just passed—one filled with matters she wasn't entirely sure she wanted to understand.

But she feared that when it came to Rob she had to know. Her life was wound around his now, for good or ill.

'Would you like to dance, Anna?' he asked quietly.

She shook her head. 'I think I grow tired of revels.'

'Then let us find somewhere quieter and make our own revels,' he whispered, and kissed her forehead.

Anna couldn't help but laugh as he took her hand and led her towards the doors. The party had grown even louder as the night went on, and Edward's generous supply of wine flowed, and more than a few of the guests seemed intent on making their own revels. They leaned on each other as they spun through the door, and couples kissed half hidden behind tapestries and in corners. Rob led her neatly around the crowds until finally they emerged into the cool quiet of the entrance hall.

There were people there, as well, but they whispered together and seemed to see nothing else around them. Anna followed Rob down a corridor, their path running beside closed doors and glowering portraits lit only by flickering torches set high in their wall sconces. The farther they went the greater the silence grew, until she could only hear their soft footsteps on the wooden floor, the swish of her skirts.

They ducked behind the shelter of a heavy velvet hanging into a small window embrasure, where moonlight streamed through the diamond-shaped panes of glass and broke into shards of light on the panelled wall. It was cool there, after the stuffy heat of the great hall, and Anna leaned back on the wall to finally take a breath.

Rob braced his hands to either side of her, his body pressed close to hers in their own little haven.

'Better now?' he asked.

'Much. I had no idea Lord Edward was such a generous host.'

'I think he would much prefer to just live quietly here at Hart Castle with Elizabeth and his studies.'

'Then why does he invite the whole county *and* all of London to a ball?' Anna thought of Sir Thomas Sheldon. 'Even those he would prefer to keep away.'

'He has his reasons—for now.'

'And you take a share in those reasons?' she asked. It was one more reminder to be cautious of Rob, that she truly knew so little of him. Not that she had heeded those cautions much of late!

Rob's eyes glittered as he stared down at her. 'Perhaps, I do. He is my friend.'

'Elizabeth said you have been friends since childhood.'

'And what else did she say?' he asked.

'She told me the tale of Sir Thomas and Lord Edward's poor brother.'

'Ah. She was talkative.'

'Does Elizabeth also work for the Queen's government?' Anna asked.

Rob laughed, but she could hear no mirth in it. 'Edward works only for himself, for his own ends—as we all do in our ways. Sometimes we use the assistance of others when it's needful.'

'And how are you assisting in this matter?'

'So many questions, fairest Anna,' he murmured, and lowered his head to kiss her ear, the curve of her neck, biting lightly at the soft skin and then blowing on it to soothe the little sting until she shivered. 'It's much too lovely a night to waste on questions.'

Anna laid her hands flat against his chest and pressed him back. 'You will not escape me forever, Robert Alden.'

'How can I escape when I can't help running straight into your arms every time you look at me?' he laughed. 'But nor can you escape *me* now, and I fear you will rue that one day very soon. Perhaps you should flee now, while you still can?'

Anna pounded her hands against him before catching his doublet in her fists and drawing him back to her. 'It's much too late to run for either of us. Oh, Rob, how you drive me to madness!'

'The feeling is quite mutual.' His mouth swooped down to cover hers, open and hot, and she met him with equal need.

She wrapped her arms around his shoulders and pressed her body against his, holding on as if he would vanish if she let go. The air around them grew hot and blurry, crackling, and she felt his touch slide over her shoulders, skimming her collarbone, her arms, until he covered her breast with a rough caress.

Anna moaned as he stroked the soft underside of her bosom through the fine, stiff fabric of her bodice and covered her hard with his palm. His fingers stroked her sensitive nipple and she cried out against his mouth. Her hands dug into his back and traced down the groove of his spine, over the shift and hardness of his lean muscles, until she cupped the taut curve of his backside through his velvet breeches. She tugged his hips closer to hers, and felt the press of his erection through her skirts.

His head arched back and he groaned. 'Anna! You're killing me.'

She reached between them and stroked the length of his penis once, twice, wanting him to feel as wild with need as she was. As desperate for connection, no matter how brief their time in each other's lives could be. She wanted to feel that he was hers—all of him, here and now—as she feared she was his.

He grabbed her wrist and held her away from him as he kissed her again, his tongue pressing deep to taste her, possess her. She felt him lift her up against him as he flipped her skirts back and she wrapped her legs tight around his waist. The fine cloth of his breeches rubbed against the sensitive skin above her garters and she moaned at the feeling of it.

He freed himself from the confines of fabric and drove into her, deep and hard. She welcomed him eagerly. The pleasure washed over her, hot and overwhelming, stealing her breath and thoughts. There was only him, only sensation—only the two of them together with everything else shut away.

He held her close against the wall, balancing her weight as he thrust again and again, deeper, wrapped all around her as they reached desperately for their release. It was a perfect moment of freedom, of soaring away, and Anna held on to him as she burst into a hundred sparkling stars.

She caught his shout of climax with her kiss, feeling his body grow taut against hers as he drove himself into her one more time. Then he let out his breath, his shoulders relaxing, and slowly lowered her to her feet.

Her legs trembled and she leaned into him, holding on until the warm weakness could pass. He held on to her, too, his forehead pressed to hers, and slowly they sank together to the floor.

They said nothing as they sat there amid the pool of her skirts, just holding on to each other as the night closed around them.

'If this is madness,' Rob said hoarsely, 'then I should be carried off to an asylum at once.'

'Oh, Robert,' Anna whispered. 'Are we not already there?'

* * *

Rob watched Anna as she slept, her face peaceful and pale in the moonlight as she drifted away in dreams. How beautiful she was. How impossible it was for him to resist her.

But he had to. He had his work to do. And when she discovered the full truth of what he was doing the desire in her eyes would die and there would be only revulsion.

Feeling hollow and cold inside, Rob drew the bedclothes around her bare shoulders. She sighed and snuggled deeper, and Rob lay down beside her again with his hands under his head to stare up sightlessly at the canopy. Aye, she would abhor him, then forget him, but he was beginning to fear *he* would never forget *her*. She would always haunt him. The one good, fine thing that had ever been his, even if it was only for one moment.

He had to be honest with her now—as honest as he could be without revealing himself too far. He owed her that much. Then perhaps one day she would look back and understand.

He would take her to meet his sister.

Chapter Eighteen

The early morning breeze was cool and crisp as Anna walked along the banks of the river, her hand in Rob's. It smelled fresh, of clean water and green growing things, the loamy sweetness of earth. Birds chattered in the treetops, and she could hear the music of the wind rustling through the leaves. She had never felt farther from London or from her real life, her everyday self.

It struck her that this was her vision come true—the image she'd had as they'd driven to Hart Castle, of herself and Rob walking by a country stream. A sylvan dream that could not last.

'Where are we going, then?' she asked, laughing.

Rob smiled back at her over his shoulder. But even though he smiled she could sense he was in a strange, distant mood. 'You asked me that before.'

'And you did not answer. I'll just keep asking until you do.'

'You'll see when we get there. 'Tis a surprise.'

'A pleasant one, I hope,' she said. 'After Thomas Sheldon's appearance last night I could do without strange surprises.'

'Ah, now, what's a day without a strange surprise?' Rob let go of her hand and looped his arm around her waist, holding her close as they walked along. 'Are you enjoying yourself here at Hart Castle? Despite Sheldon playing the dark witch at our fairy ball?'

Anna thought about his question, and all that had happened in the short time since they'd arrived at Hart Castle. It seemed as if months and not mere days had passed. So much had shifted inside her since they'd come here. She saw some things more clearly—and other things not at all.

'I have enjoyed being here very much,' she said truthfully. 'Hart Castle is beautiful, and Edward and Elizabeth have been so kind and welcoming. It's a fine life here, despite such shadows as Sheldon. I have a feeling he is not a permanent annoyance, though.'

'I have a feeling you are right about that,' Rob muttered under his breath. 'I am glad you like it here. It's been a haven of sorts to me.' There was a strange distance in his voice, a faraway look in his eye. He hadn't left behind that strange mood he had been in ever since they'd woken up.

'We should all be so lucky to have such a haven,' Anna answered. Sometimes she felt as if there was no place to hide at all. At some moments she did feel safe with Robert, safe held in his arms where nothing else could touch her.

She knew it was naught but an illusion. But she treasured it nonetheless.

They turned a bend in the footpath, and the river wound away gently down to a valley. Rob led her up the slope of a hill, away from its banks. At its crest she could see the splendid view spread before her—rolling fields, the dark mystery of the woods in the distance and a village that looked like a doll's toy of streets and houses. The pale, watery blue sky, dotted with fluffy puffs of low-hanging clouds spreading fleeting shadows on the ground below, spread over all.

'It's a beautiful prospect,' she said. 'Is this the surprise?'

Rob shook his head. 'We have a farther walk, I'm afraid. Are you up to the exercise?'

Anna laughed. 'I feel I could walk a hundred miles today! I feel so—new. It must be the fresh air.'

'Fresh air is one thing that is most plentiful here in the country,' he said as they made their way down the hill.

Even though he held on to her he didn't seem to be really with her. Was he worried about something?

The tall grass caught at Anna's hem, and she lifted her skirts up out of the way. She tried to ignore his distance and just enjoy the day, but she couldn't quite forget or cease to worry.

'Wouldn't it be lovely to have a cottage here by this very hill?' she said, determined to be cheerful. 'To wake every day to such a prospect, and to the sounds of birds singing?'

'You wouldn't miss being woken by shouts and slop buckets tossed out of windows?'

Anna wrinkled her nose. 'Who would miss that?'

'The country has its faults, as well,' Rob said. 'Perishing cold in the winter, no theatres or booksellers nearby.'

'No heads on pikes, either,' Anna said with a shiver, thinking of the boiled eyeless heads that stared down from atop London Bridge every time she walked past.

'Reminding us of the fate that awaits he who takes a misstep?' Rob lifted her over a muddy puddle and led her across a small bridge into the village. Even as they walked so close he did not seem to be entirely with her.

Unlike most rural lanes, the main street was cobbled and wide, lined with half-timbered buildings of shops and dwellings. Thatched roofs alternated with slate tiles, and at the end of the lane was a solid, square old church of faded brown stone, its churchyard of leaning grave markers enclosed in a newer-looking stone wall.

Merchants were opening up for the morning, laying out their counters spread with wares. Silvery smoke curled out of chimneys, its sweet smell blending with fresh bread from the bake shop. Women lined up with their buckets at the well, children clinging to their skirts or chasing each other about. Older boys were following a black-clad teacher into the schoolhouse.

Everyone turned to watch them as Anna and Rob walked by, a few people calling out greetings that Robert paused to answer.

'This is the village where you grew up?' she asked.

'Aye, in rooms above my father's shop just over yonder,' he said, pointing to a structure down the next lane. 'And I went to school there, as those unfortunate boys are now.'

'Learning your Latin?'

Rob laughed. 'Getting my palms whipped for being unserious, usually. And over there, in our village guildhall, I saw my first play.'

Anna looked to where he pointed—a long, low building just beyond the church. 'What was the play?'

'An allegorical tale of fortune and misfortune, presented by a ragged band of travelling players. I was five, and the hall was so crowded there was no place to sit, so my father stood at the back and held me on his shoulders so I could see. I was entranced, despite the shabby costumes and clumsy line readings. I had never known that mere words could take a person out of the everyday world and into a place that was so—magical. That they could make a person think of things in a way they had never considered before.'

'Aye,' Anna whispered. That was how watching his plays made her feel—as if she was in a new world, with thoughts and desires she had never imagined before. His plays were a part of him. Did they reveal some of the secrets she longed to know?

'From then on I wanted only to write, to watch plays,' he said. 'My father wanted me to take over his business, as sons should do, but I was no good at leather-working. I wanted fine words and poetry. I wanted to move people and make them laugh. And I wanted adventure—to see the world away from this place.'

'You could not be contained by the village any longer?'

'Nay.'

Anna nodded. 'I once thought the world I grew up in could not contain me, that I was for another sort of life far from Southwark. I used to dream and plan...'

Rob held on to her hand, surveying the streets where he had run as a child. It seemed he saw things there she could not even fathom. 'But where we come from always draws us back.'

'You left! You became what you wanted to be.'

'Aye. When I was seventeen, Lord Henshaw's Men came through here as they toured the country-side, and I persuaded them to let me leave with them as an apprentice despite my advanced age. My father was furious.'

'Did you ever reconcile with him?' Anna asked softly.

Rob didn't answer. They had reached the outskirts of the village, and he pointed at a small cottage set back in a tidy little garden. His eyes were shadowed, secret. 'This is our destination, Anna.'

'What is it?' she asked cautiously, examining the place. It looked like an ordinary cottage—painted shutters drawn back, smoke from the chimney, flowering vines curling over the doorway. But appearances, like the sweet words of a play, could deceive.

'I want you to meet my family,' he said. 'What is left of it.'

'Your family?' Anna cried, stopping abruptly on the path.

He glanced back at her, a frown on his brow. 'Is something amiss?'

'I—am not prepared to meet anyone,' she said. She smoothed her skirts and carefully touched her hair to be sure it was still tidy. 'I should have worn something finer.'

'Oh, Anna,' he said, a strange, sad note in his tone. He raised her hand to his lips and kissed it, warm and tender through the leather of her glove. 'It doesn't matter in the least what you wear—not here. And you are always lovely anyway.'

'And *you* are an unrepentant flatterer, even here,' she answered. 'Very well, then. Show me to your house.'

Rob looped her arm with his and pushed open the garden gate to lead her down the narrow front path. Though the space was small it was well kept, with neat beds lined with flat river stones and a vegetable patch around the side. It had an air of quiet, neat contentment.

Perhaps too quiet? Anna peered up at the gleaming windows but could detect no hint of life. No one peered down at them, awaiting their arrival.

Rob knocked at the door, and despite his words Anna felt herself growing nervous. She had no idea at all what to expect. And her trepidation grew as she glanced at Rob's shadowed, closed face. He seemed so different here.

There was the sound of quick footsteps from within, and the click of a latch before the door swung open. Anna's worries eased a bit as she saw the woman who greeted them—an older lady who was not in the least fearsome. She was as compact and tidy as the house itself, with a round, pink face under a white cap, and a dark blue dress covered with an apron. A smile spread across her lips as she saw them there.

'Master Robert!' she cried. 'Here you are at last.'

'I'm sorry I couldn't visit until now, Nelly,' Rob said. He stepped into the cool dimness of the small entrance hall, drawing Anna with him, and kissed Nelly on her plump cheek. 'I've missed you very much.'

'Ack, you have so much important work to do with Lord Edward you can't miss us,' Nelly said with a laugh. 'And you've picked a fine day to visit.'

'All is well, I trust?' Rob said.

'Very well. It's been quiet since the last spell—and that was days ago, as you know. Things are very tranquil today.' Nelly glanced curiously at Anna.

'Nelly, this is Mistress Barrett, who has come with me from London,' said Rob. 'I wanted her to meet you, and to see the village where I grew up.'

Nelly curtsied to Anna as Anna smiled back at her. Nelly's look was full of frank curiosity. 'We're very pleased to meet any friend of Master Alden's, mistress.'

'As am I, Mistress Nelly,' Anna answered. Any

glimpse behind Rob's ever-changing masks was to be treasured. She studied the plain, scrubbed hall of the curious little house and listened for any sounds, but there was none to hear.

'I'm just putting together a pie for dinner,' Nelly said. 'You can make your visit while I finish it up. I hope you'll stay to eat with us? There's plenty to go round.'

'Of course, Nelly. I would never miss the chance to taste your pie again,' Rob said.

He looked to the closed door at the end of the hall, and Anna glimpsed that dark shadow passing over his eyes. She tightened her hand on his arm, and he gave her a quick smile.

'Is it possible for me to go in alone, Nelly? Is that wise after last time?'

'All has been quiet of late,' Nelly answered with a smile.

She led them to the end of the hall and threw open the door. Anna followed Rob inside to find a sunny little sitting room, the window open to let in the morning air. The space was whitewashed, and laid with a dark wood floor that gleamed with polish, scattered with footstools and cushioned chairs covered with bright embroidery.

A girl sat by the window, her head bent over a

tambor frame as she worked. She wore a simple white gown covered with a loose pale blue surcoat, and her hair fell in long dark waves down her back.

She didn't look up at their entrance, until Nelly clapped her hands and said, 'Mistress Mary, your brother has come to visit you!'

The girl turned to them, and Anna almost gasped at the sight of her face. She looked like a female version of Robert, with his bright blue eyes and elegant cheekbones. Her jaw and mouth were softer, yet it was obvious they were siblings.

But the left side of her face bore a terrible scar—a faded slash across her cheek that ended at her chin and marred the peach perfection of her skin.

She gave a vague smile, as if she had no idea who it was that stood before her yet was trying to be polite.

''Tis a fine day, is it not?' she said.

'I will leave you to your visit, then, while I see to my pie,' said Nelly. She backed out of the room and closed the door softly behind her.

Mary went back to her sewing, humming a little tune under her breath.

Anna watched her in astonishment. 'This is your sister?' she whispered.

Rob gave a grim nod. 'She never knows me, though. She remembers nothing at all most days—which is surely a blessing. Sometimes she is violently upset, sometimes quiet. We must hope today is a quiet one.'

Before Anna could ask him more, he moved very slowly and cautiously to stand by Mary's chair. She merely kept sewing.

'What do you work on today, Mary?' he asked quietly. 'It's very fine.'

Mary didn't answer, and Anna edged closer to examine the half-finished cloth. It was in the same style as the cushion covers—a bright scene of flowers and leaves. The open workbox on the table beside her was filled with skeins of silk threads in all colours, even twists of gilded gold and silver. An expensive collection, and one Rob no doubt provided, along with the cottage and the nurse.

All for a sister who didn't know him.

Anna knelt down carefully next to Mary and said, 'I believe Mistress Mary is using a French satin stitch—a most complicated technique, indeed.'

Mary gave her a smile. 'Aye, it is complicated, but I have been practising it. I used a cross stitch for the border, see? And I will bead the edges when I'm done to make it shine.'

'You are very talented at the work,' Anna said. 'I can do plain mending, but I make a terrible mess of such fine work.'

Mary giggled, and Rob sat down on a chair to watch her. For the next half-hour Anna chatted with Mary about embroidery, slowly drawing Rob into the conversation. Mary seemed cautious of him, but all went well enough. She only looked truly fearful once, when a group of rowdy, loud boys dashed by outside the window, but Anna's hand on her arm seemed to steady her.

When Nelly came to summon them to dine Mary went with her, happily chattering, and Anna followed slowly with Robert.

'What is amiss here, Rob?' she whispered. 'Has she always been thus?'

He shook his head, watching his sister with hooded eyes as she fluttered down the corridor. 'Nay, not always. Only the last few years. After something—happened.'

Anna swallowed hard in sudden cold trepidation. 'Something?'

'We must go to them now,' he said. 'I will tell

you on our walk home, Anna, I promise. Though I fear it is not a pretty tale…'

Rob carefully studied Anna's face as they walked along the river away from the village. She had been quiet ever since they'd left the cottage, her face calm and expressionless, as if she pondered mysterious things.

He hadn't been sure he should take her to see Mary. Their time at Hart Castle had been precious to him—moments of passion and laughter in the midst of uncertainty and danger—and he didn't want to mar the few moments they had left.

Yet he also wanted Anna to know him, the little he could reveal, and see what drove him to his actions. Perhaps then she would not hate him quite so much when the sword that hung over them came crashing down. She would see that he had gone into this to protect the scarred and the vulnerable, like Mary and Anna herself.

Or perhaps that was a vain hope. He knew Anna was fierce in protecting herself and those she cared about, especially her father. She had a core of steel. Yet she also had a tender heart she tried to hide away, a yearning for truth and understanding that matched his own.

He'd seen that tenderness clearly as she sat by Mary and talked to her so gently and patiently. She'd coaxed Mary to peek out of the shell that protected her from the world, and even made her smile.

Rob found that he craved that tenderness for himself—that he wanted the shelter Anna offered from the past and the terrible uncertainties of the present. Shelter from himself. He wanted her goodness, her honesty, her strength.

Her beauty. The sunlight filtered through the trees above her, casting long patterns of shadows on her hair as she carried her hat. She turned her face up to its warmth and a little smile touched her lips. Her whole face softened when she smiled, and for an instant she looked free and content.

She deserved to have that all the time. He wanted to give that to her—to give her all she deserved in life, all she longed for.

She turned to him, her smile fading. 'You take such good care of your sister.'

Good care? When she shrank from the sight of him because he was a man? 'I only do what I can. I fear it is not nearly enough.'

'That can't be true. You pay for her to have a quiet home, a nurse, fine clothes and the best embroidery silks, while you live over a tavern and write plays for the amusement of the crowds. You see to it she is safe and happy. Most families would have sent her to rot in a madhouse, out of sight and mind.'

'You would not have done that,' Rob said. 'You look after your father with every bit as much care, and more so because you are with him every day. You would never abandon those you love.'

'Of course I would not. And neither do you, no matter how much you play the rakish, careless actor to the world.' She looked back to the river. 'You love your sister.'

'I love her more than life,' he said simply, truthfully. He owed his sister for not being there when she needed him. For encouraging her romantic nature with his own poetry. 'Even as she does not know me now.'

Anna stopped at a shady spot by the turn of the water, and Rob removed his short cloak to spread on the grassy ground for a seat. She put her hat and gloves down beside her and smoothed her skirts over her legs.

Rob lay down on his side next to her, propping himself up on his elbow. They were so close, close enough to touch, yet it felt as if the river flowed between them. He could see her, yearn for her, reach for her, but she couldn't fully be his. Too many secrets lay between them.

But he feared now that no matter what befell them, nor what she would come to think of him, she was *his* and always would be. Anna was like no one else he had ever known. She was more beautiful, kinder—more everything. And yet she did not know it.

'What happened to her?' Anna asked. 'You said she was not always thus.'

'Nay, she was not. Mary is many years younger than me. By the time she arrived my parents had given up hope of more children. She was such a pretty, laughing babe, always into some mischief, and we all adored her. I fear we spoiled and indulged her, and only more so after my mother died. She had a great deal of freedom, and a great imagination.'

Anna smiled down at him. 'A family trait, I see.'

Rob laughed ruefully. 'Her imaginings were always more fanciful than mine, more romantic.'

'More fanciful than running away to join a company of players?'

'She wanted to fall in love—marry a fine gentleman who would carry her off to Court to meet the Queen. She had dreams of castles and silk gowns, of a man who would always indulge her as we did and whom she could adore in return. I fear I fanned those dreams higher with my own poetry. She was always begging for a fairy story.'

Anna drew her legs up to her chest and rested her chin on her knees as she watched the water wend its way past. 'Did she find him?'

'Strangely enough, she did. Have you heard of a family called Carrington?'

She considered for a moment, and shook her head. 'I don't think so. But I don't know all the great families at Court—especially if they have no fondness for the playhouse.'

Rob plucked at the soft grass under his hand. He hated to come to this part of the tale. It sounded like a play—only far too real, with real people as its victims. And it was his fault for living in his dream world and not protecting those he cared for the most.

'They are not at Court any longer,' he said. 'Most of them are dead now. But once they owned the fine estate now possessed by Thomas Sheldon, and they had a son named William who was so handsome and wealthy he was ardently pursued by every maiden in the county.'

'And this was Mary's sweetheart?' Anna asked, drawn into the tale even as she feared the terrible ending she knew was coming.

'Well may you be astonished. The golden son of a landed family and the daughter of a leather-worker? Such wickedness! Mary and William were clever. They met in such secret even my father did not know of it, and the village gossips had no idea. I was gone on my wanderings with Lord Henshaw's Men by then, and only heard of what happened after.' He had abandoned them to their fates. Only now could he try to atone.

Anna bit her lip. 'What did happen?'

'My father became ill, and Mary and her swain grew bolder in their meetings. It seemed he declared to her he would marry her, and even gave her a ring,' Rob said, his voice flat and distant, though she could sense the terrible pain beneath. 'But there was something he did not tell her—or perhaps he did not even know himself. His father and his elder brother had joined a plot to set Mary of Scotland on the throne and depose Queen Elizabeth.'

'How terrible!' Anna cried. She well remembered what had happened to the traitors in the Babington Plot to set Queen Mary on the English throne. The stench had hung over London for days. 'Treason right here in this peaceful place.'

'Treason raises its ugly Hydra head everywhere, Anna, and especially where Queen Mary and Spain had greater room to scheme.' And Spain was not done with scheming, even with its grand Armada destroyed, as Rob knew too well. 'It destroys the innocent, as well as the guilty.'

'Innocents like your sister?'

'Aye, like Mary. She had gone to see her sweetheart when Walsingham's men raided his family's house. The tale of what happened then is a confused one, but it can easily be imagined. The servants were beaten and terrorised, Lady Carrington locked up, the house ripped apart in search of hidden priests and treasonous papers. Mary's suitor hid her in the kitchen before he went to help his family, but she was found.'

Anna's arms tightened around her legs. 'They— hurt her? Walsingham's raiders?'

'Not them. When she was dragged to the great hall of the house, she saw that her lover was dead. One of the servants who was there that day told me later Mary was hysterical at the sight, screaming and crying, trying to reach him.' Rob kept his narration carefully quiet and toneless, but the old images still made her heart ache. She could feel the pain so horribly, so clearly. What would *she* feel like if it was Rob lying there dead?

'His brother dragged her from William's body,' he continued. 'But he did not release her. He used her as a hostage to shield him as he left the house, shouting that she must be the "traitorous bitch" who had seduced his brother and set Walsingham on them all. Mary wept and protested, fought him, but he dragged her through the fields to a deserted barn where he raped her and cut her face.'

Rob's fist closed hard on the earth, and his mind clouded with hot blood and fury, as it always did when he remembered the monster who'd hurt Mary. And his own part in it all.

Anna reached out and laid her hand gently over his clenched fist. Her cool touch scattered some of the pain of the old memories, tethered him again to their present moment there under the trees.

'Was he captured?' she asked softly.

'Of course, and carried away to a traitor's death. But it was too late for Mary. Her mind had snapped and would never be repaired. My father sent for me, and I returned just before he died. He beseeched me to care for Mary, though she shrank from the sight of me as a man. I set her up with

Nelly, who had been our nurse when we were children, in that cottage, and went back to London to earn my coin.'

Anna's fingers curled tighter over his hand. 'And to work for Walsingham?'

'Aye.' Rob rubbed his other hand over his face and rolled to lie on his back. The sky arched overhead, blue and endless, and the curve of Anna's cheek was kissed by a stray curl of her dark hair. He reached up to brush that strand back, and his touch skimmed over her warm, soft skin.

'I told you I worked for Walsingham for money and advancement,' he said. 'And I do. I can't lie about that. But mostly I work for him to bring down men like the traitor who attacked my sister and who would destroy the peace of our country.'

'Oh, Robert.' Anna lay down beside him and rested her head on his shoulder. 'You do like to play the careless cynic, but now you have revealed the truth.'

'And what might the truth be?' he asked, doubt heavy in his voice.

'That you are a defender of women and the weak. A white knight.' Her hand flattened against his chest, stroking him through the thin linen of his shirt. 'With armour that is a bit rusty, perhaps...'

'Rusty?' He seized her hand and raised it to his lips for a kiss. 'I am quite ready to defeat all challengers.'

And he was. With her by his side, his secrets safe in her hands, he finally felt he could move ahead. That he could somehow make wrongs right and slay all her dragons. That he could be her protector and her love forever, be worthy of her.

If only he himself was not her greatest dragon of all.

'I know you are ever ready to charge into battle, Robert,' she said with a sigh. 'That is exactly what I'm afraid of.'

Chapter Nineteen

Anna sat on her bed, the breeze from the half-open window cool through her light chemise. From the garden below she could hear music and laughter as the other guests of Hart Castle danced in the moonlight. It sounded so light-hearted and merry, as if it all came from another world—the realm of fairies and dreams.

She knew she should go down to them, put on the fine gown spread before the fire and go dancing. But she felt frozen in place, and the silence of her chamber wrapped around her like a comforting blanket.

Her mind kept seeing Mary Alden, with her pretty blue eyes as blank and empty as a summer sky and that scar on her cheek. Lost deep in the maze of her own mind.

And Robert, who loved his sister so very much

he had given his life over to protecting innocents like her in the only way he knew how—with his pen and his sword. The servant of the great spider Walsingham.

Anna had thought she had begun to know Rob. Now she saw she knew nothing at all.

'Masks upon masks,' she whispered. She slid down from the bed and went to peer out of her window. The gardens were lit up by a multitude of torches, blazing so brightly the night itself was kept away. Everyone danced between them, like a sumptuously coloured glittering serpent, winding round and round.

She smiled to see their merriment, and wished she could revel in that one fleeting moment as they did. She wished she could feel Rob's arms around her, twirling her until the sky was a blur and all she knew was him.

She wished that life could be as a play, with heroes and villains and romances, a clear line from beginning to end and a happy jig to close all.

'But make it a comedy, please,' she said. A tale of disguises revealed, love triumphant, no tragedy or bloody revenge. No more bloodshed.

Her heart ached for Mary Alden, and for Robert. His life *was* a revenge play, and she feared there was no place in it for her. No place for tenderness and caring. He felt he did not deserve it, when she knew he was the most deserving of all. But it could never be, not now.

She heard the soft click of her door sliding open, and she turned to see Rob standing there. He wore only his breeches and shirt, the soft linen unlaced to reveal his glistening chest. His hair was tousled and he held a book in his hand. And she suddenly knew—he had been standing there waiting for her all the time.

He closed the door and leaned back against it, watching her across the room. 'You don't care to dance tonight?'

Anna shook her head. 'I am tired. It is odd, Robert—I feel as if I have passed a hundred years today, many lifetimes.'

'I wearied you with the long walk.'

'Nay. I am not weary, not now. And—and I am more grateful than I can say that you allowed me to meet your sister.'

'I could have done nothing else after you shared your own secrets with me.'

'Secrets?' she asked.

'About your marriage.'

Anna glanced back down at the party guests,

dancing on as if in giddy oblivion. 'Mine was not a secret so much as a pitiful tale I don't care to remember.'

'Then I'm doubly honoured you remembered it with me,' he said.

She heard Rob move, felt his warmth against her back as he shut the window and silence fell over the chamber.

'You'll grow cold there,' he said. 'Come, sit by me on the bed for a while.'

He took her hand in his and led her back to the bed. Anna let him help her slide beneath the bedclothes and tuck them round her before he sat beside her against the bolsters. His arm lay lightly over her shoulders and she smiled up at him. *Aye*—this was what she had waited for. To be with him, alone in the quiet.

'I'm certainly warm enough now,' she said. 'And the walk today was not too far at all.'

'Mary liked you very much, I could tell,' he said. 'You were very gentle with her.'

Anna rested her head on his shoulder with a sigh. 'That poor, sweet girl. You have made her a safe haven, Robert.'

'Whether I can keep it safe for her is less certain,' he muttered. 'I brought this for you in thanks.' He laid the book he held on her lap, and its fine red-leather cover glowed in the low firelight.

'I need no thanks,' she said. 'But I'm always willing to accept books.' She ran her palm over the soft leather and traced the title in raised gilt letters. *Demetrius and Diana*—the poem she had been reading in London, the tale of the poor shepherd and his impossible love for a goddess.

She opened it, and saw that it was not a printed book but one handwritten on vellum, as if it was the original manuscript especially bound. She knew that writing well; she saw it often on scripts at the White Heron.

'You are the author of *Demetrius and Diana!*' she whispered, astonished. How could he keep that a secret, when it was the most astonishingly wonderful thing she had ever read? 'Why did you not tell me before?'

Rob shrugged and laid his hand atop hers on the book. His fingers moved like a whispering caress over her skin. 'My plays are there for all to see, but my poems—they come from somewhere deeper, I think. Somewhere I don't want everyone to know.'

'But this work is beautiful! And very popular, too, though no one knows the real author yet,' Anna protested. 'The language and images are so vivid and real, and the emotions— This work could bring you great fame if you let it be known. They do say Queen Elizabeth rewards her favoured poets richly.'

'What would I do with more fame?' he asked with a laugh. 'Or with the Queen's rewards?'

'Do you never seek a new life, Robert?' she questioned. She remembered how he had looked as they walked by the river, so happy and carefree. Or perhaps she had only misread that, putting her own secret desires on to him, and he missed the constant movement and upheaval of London. 'You would miss having everyone hear your words onstage, I'm sure.'

'My truest words are in here, fairest Anna, for those who care to seek them.' He tapped lightly at the book's cover. 'And now I give them to you.'

'It is a very fair gift,' she said. 'I will use it to remember these days at Hart Castle, the good and bad of them alike.'

He raised her hand and pressed a warm, open-mouthed kiss to the centre of her palm. 'I hope you only ever remember the good, Anna. You deserve naught but sunshine and laughter all your days.'

She smiled at him, tenderness flooding her heart at the sight of his tousled hair and shadowed eyes.

That ice she had built around her heart in the bleak days with her husband had melted entirely away, and she felt only those sunshine wishes.

She laid her other hand against his face, cupping his cheek, and said softly, 'How dull that would be, with no poetry to fill my hours.'

Rob's arms came around her and he pulled her against his body as they both rose to their knees in the middle of the bed. His mouth came over hers in a hungry kiss, and she closed her eyes to tumble head-first into that dark, swirling, heated world she always found with him. She had never felt closer to anyone before, bound to him by desire and joy and sadness all tied into one.

She parted her lips in welcome and felt his tongue sweep against hers, tasting her just as she was hungry for him. She met his kiss with equal fervour, full of all the terrible, passionate longing she always felt with him. It was a primeval, overwhelming force she couldn't deny. She wrapped her arms around his neck, holding him so close there could be nothing separating them now. She wished she could be even closer, that she could make him entirely her own.

His lips slid to her throat, to the bare skin where her chemise fell away from her shoulder. Gently he urged her back down to the bed and drew the fabric away from her legs, up and up. He kissed her ankle, tracing his tongue over the arch of her foot. It tickled and tingled, and it made her want to laugh and cry out with need all at the same time.

He kissed the soft skin just behind her ankle. He lightly bit at it and traced his mouth up to her knee, the back of her thigh.

'Robert…' she whispered.

'Shh, just lie still,' he said against her skin. He rose up on his knees between her legs and urged her thighs farther apart as he eased her chemise up to her waist. He used the fabric to draw her closer and softly blew on the damp, sensitive curls above her womanhood.

'Robert!' she cried out. The sensation of his breath, his mouth, was almost too much. She arched her hips away but he wouldn't let her go. And she didn't really want to get away from him. She wanted to stay with him, just like this, with a desperate need she had never known before.

He leaned closer and kissed her just *there.* With one hand he held her down to the bed, and with the other he spread the wet folds of her so he could kiss her even more deeply, more intimately. His tongue plunged deep inside her, rough and delicate at the same time, tasting her, pressing at that one rough, sensitive spot. She moaned and twined her fingers in his hair to hold him with her.

It was so terribly intimate, somehow even more than when they joined together in sex, and she felt utterly open and vulnerable to him, yet also strong and powerful. She wanted to shout out at the joy of being with him!

His mouth eased away from her to kiss the inside of her thigh. He slid up along her body and caught her by the hips as he kissed her lips. He tasted of wine and mint, and also, shockingly, of her, and it made her cry out against him. She tilted her hips and felt the hardness of his own desire on her stomach.

They fell together, entwined, to the bed. She moaned again, the only sound her blurry voice could make. She could hold no thoughts now, only emotions, feelings she had pressed down inside for so long that they overwhelmed her now. Tears pierced her eyes as she turned her head away from him, and his open mouth traced her cheek, her eyelids, her temple where the pulse beat so frantically. He bit at her earlobe, his breath hot in her ear, and they shuddered together.

Her hands tunnelled under his shirt to trace the

groove of his spine, the hard muscles of his back and shoulders. His skin was taut and damp under her touch, so warm and alive it was amazing.

He reached between them to unfasten his breeches and release his erect penis. It was hard and ready, and she spread her legs wider in invitation. With a deft twist of his hips he drove into her and buried himself to the hilt.

She wrapped her legs around his waist and moved with him, hard and fast, and then even faster. She held tight to his shoulders, letting that rough, burning pleasure build inside her. Together they climbed higher and higher, until they could leap free and soar into the sky.

'Anna!' he shouted above her. 'Anna, Anna—I can't...'

'I know,' she whispered. 'I know. I'm here. I'm *here.*'

He collapsed beside her, and they held on to each other as the night closed in around them.

Chapter Twenty

'Sheldon is in debt to some very powerful people,' Rob muttered as he examined the papers spread over Edward's desk. The documents Elizabeth's bold niece had stolen from Thomas Sheldon's London home were a scattered lot, snatched up quickly and in places incomplete, but they painted a dark picture of financial desperation.

And, for a man as socially ambitious as Sheldon, desperation was not a good state.

Edward tossed down the half-finished letter he studied. 'He has made promises to the Queen's courtiers he can't keep in return for their loans. Now it seems he has turned to less exalted means of finding money.'

'Bankside moneylenders, pimps and swords for hire,' Rob said. He slumped back in his chair and propped his boots up on the table. Outside in the garden could be heard shrieks of happy laughter as Elizabeth led a game of blindman's buff, but that light-hearted scene seemed far away from the closed-in library. This was his real world, and he could never escape it for long.

'Such a man would not stop at taking Spanish or French coin, either,' said Edward. 'Treason is not so far beneath him—especially if he feels he is not getting his due attention from Queen Elizabeth.'

'Is he the one we seek?' Rob said. 'The man who used the theatre as his base of traitorous communications?'

Or was Rob searching for straw men—anyone to replace Anna's father in Walsingham's suspicions? Perhaps Sheldon was too stupid, too desperate for the patient planning of such a scheme.

But traitors were often simple-minded and over-confident—it was what got them caught in the end. Look at Babington and his friends, and their wild scheme to free Mary of Scotland.

'We must trap him well and good,' Rob said.

'I've made a fair start—inviting him here, flattering him, cajoling him, even as it has made me feel ill,' Edward said. He went to the window and watched Elizabeth as she laughed with the others. 'Elizabeth hates him for trying to wed her niece…

She doesn't see how I can stomach his presence even for our scheme. But I can invite him here again, if I must.'

'I fear our time to spring the trap grows short,' said Rob. He reached inside his doublet and withdrew the folded message that had arrived only that morning, before Anna and most of the house were even awake. 'From Seething Lane.'

Edward scowled and snatched the note from Rob's hand, reading it hastily. 'They are closing in?'

'They want this business done—one way or another,' Rob said grimly. 'We must find out if Sheldon is our man and make haste back to London with the evidence.'

'Damn it all!' Edward cursed, slamming the paper onto the desk. 'If only Lady Essex had stayed here longer, until we had more evidence for her to carry to her father.'

Rob shook his head. ''Tis better she is there, to delay them if she can. You should visit Sheldon yourself—ride over to his estate this afternoon and see what you can find. I will talk more with your other guests. They should know the latest gossip.'

Suddenly there was a shout from the garden and ladies' screams—not of joy but alarm. Edward threw open the window and leaned out to see what was happening. Rob sauntered over to peer over his shoulder.

Two of the men were arguing heatedly, it appeared over one of the sobbing ladies, and it looked as if blades were in imminent danger of being drawn.

'And now a brawl in my house, on top of all else,' Edward growled. 'Come, Rob, let's break up this dog fight before it destroys my fine garden.'

They snatched up their own swords from where they lay on the desk and ran out of the library after sweeping the papers into the drawer. Even the servants had gathered at the open front doors to watch the fight.

'Another dull country day,' Rob said with a wry laugh. Merriment could turn to violence in only a moment.

'Is anyone here?' Anna called. She made her way slowly down the corridor, peering past darkened doorways. She had slept late, and awakened to find Rob gone and her stomach grumbling with hunger, so she'd quickly dressed and ventured out to find some food.

But the house seemed eerily quiet—no guests

laughing or playing cards, not even a servant to be seen.

Anna heard a muffled shout from beyond a closed door, and tested the latch to find it unlocked. It was a small library, the panelled walls lined with shelves of valuable books and a desk piled up with blank sheets of parchment and pots of ink and quills. The window was half-open, and that was where the noise came from.

She hurried over to peer outside. When she had first awoken and looked out to the garden there had been a merry game going on—men chasing ladies between the flowerbeds as everyone shrieked with laughter. Now it seemed turned to sudden strife. Two men stared at each other in smouldering fury, blades half drawn, while one of the women sobbed.

Rob and Edward held them apart, and Rob was speaking to them in a low, quick voice. It seemed he was as good at defusing fights as he was at causing them. She learned new aspects of him every day, yet still she couldn't believe she would ever know all of him.

A cool wind rushed in from the garden and ruffled the papers on the desk, sending some of them fluttering to the floor. Anna knelt down to retrieve them before they could blow away. Most of them were blank, but one, torn in half and then quarter-wise, so only a portion remained, was covered in tiny, smudged cross-writing. As she rose to place them back on the desk, a scribbled name on the page caught her attention.

Peter Spencer. One of the Lord Henshaw's Men at the White Heron.

'Why would Lord Edward have a list of actors?' Anna whispered. For a proposed performance at Hart Castle, perhaps? Curious, she turned the fragment over and tried to read its closely writ lines.

There were more names, but not all of them were actors. She recognised a few as young, rebellious noblemen—second sons with nothing to do but get into trouble gambling and drinking, and perhaps dabbling in forbidden Catholicism. There were numbers after each name, various amounts of money, and with some there were other notes. A Spanish name—D. Felipe—and amounts in scudas plus one word—'Received.'

Had these men received Spanish money, as well as English? A double-cross scheme?

But who was being crossed? And why did Edward Hartley have such a list?

As Anna stared down at the strange document in

her hand, a terrible thought struck her. Did Edward work for Walsingham, as Rob did? Were they here to conspire on some scheme? Catching double agents and traitors? The paper looked messy, harmless, but she suddenly feared it would burn her if she held it too long.

Her fingers trembled and she felt as if the warm garden breeze had turned to freezing ice on her skin. Rob's dangerous work followed him everywhere, touched everything—now it followed her, as well.

She turned back to the desk and tried to organise the papers just as they had been, as if she could thus put the world back the way it had been. As she tugged a blank sheet over it a name scribbled in tiny letters at the bottom of the list stood out to her.

Tom Alwick—and a question mark and a star.

Her father. On an intelligencer's list.

Anna pressed her hand to her mouth to hold back a cry. Her father suspected by Walsingham? Nay, it could not be. He thought of nothing but the theatre and the tavern, his friends and his ale. He could never have the discretion and the caution needed for spying. He could never be…

A traitor.

Surely that question mark meant he was only suspected? Considered because he knew so many actors—the men Rob had said were especially sought out by Walsingham for their skills and their need of money. All people of the theatre, of Southwark's businesses, were liable to suspicion.

But mere suspicion could so easily get men tortured and killed.

Anna heard voices again outside the window. She quickly straightened the pages back into place on the desk and looked to see what was happening in the garden. The quarrelling company had dispersed, and Rob and Edward were walking back to the house. They talked together quietly, confidently, as old friends did. Anna remembered how Rob had said they'd known each other since boyhood.

Did they work together now to find traitors in the people around her?

She hastily brushed away the hot tears that prickled at her eyes and spun round to rush out of the library. She had to leave Hart Castle at once—to get back to her father in London and warn him to be on his guard. He had to look hard at his friends, be wary of what he said—and perhaps even leave London for a time.

And she had to hide from Robert the fact that she'd seen that paper. What if he was working against her? Searching for a way to trap her father while—while making love to her?

'No,' she whispered. Her whole body felt so cold and brittle, as if she would snap in two. The room turned hazy and pale at the edges, as if in a dream. Perhaps this *was* a dream, all of it, and she would soon awake in her own narrow bed in Southwark.

She hurried up the stairs, past the servants who had finally reappeared to do their morning tasks, and back to her fine borrowed chamber. She had to be gone from this place, and all its deceptive dreams.

She quickly traded her soft leather shoes for boots, and pinned her hair up under her hat. The rich costumes would have to be left behind in her haste to leave, but perhaps Elizabeth would send them on to the theatre once Anna had seen her father safe.

As she tucked her few coins into her purse, and tugged on her gloves, she saw Rob's book on the rumpled blankets of the bed. Its fine cover gleamed in the light, concealing the beautiful words of romance and longing within its pages. She remembered last night—the tender desperation of their lovemaking, the way she'd felt when Rob held her in his arms. Everything else had disappeared then—even her old self, encased in icy fear and mistrust, was gone. There had been only the new joy and freedom of being together, of sharing their secrets and coming to a true understanding.

It had *felt* so very real, she thought as she stared at that book. How could her own emotions have so deceived her?

She caught up the book and tucked it away in her purse. Somehow she could not abandon it.

She ran back down the stairs and into the bright light of the warm day. It seemed spring was truly here at last, but even that couldn't warm her heart again. Some of the guests were strolling in the gardens, the earlier quick explosion of temper just as swiftly forgotten. She could hear voices and giggles from behind the maze.

Rob and Edward were gone, but Elizabeth waved to Anna from where she sat on one of the marble benches. Anna waved back, but she didn't slow her steps. She turned away from the party and rushed around the side of the house towards the stables.

'I need as fast a horse as possible,' she told the groom.

'Are you sure of that, mistress?' he queried uncertainly.

Perhaps he remembered her lack of skill on a horse from the hunt, Anna thought. She remembered it, too, and eyed the rows of horses with some trepidation. But necessity was pressing in on her.

'I'm quite sure,' she said decisively. 'Perhaps the mount Lady Elizabeth rode?'

'If you insist, mistress,' he answered, turning towards Elizabeth's restive grey mare. 'Two of the lads can soon be ready to ride with you…'

'No,' Anna said quickly. 'I must go alone today.'

Alone—as always now. She was truly the only one she could really trust.

'Elizabeth, have you seen Anna?' Rob asked Lady Elizabeth as he came upon her where she sat in the garden. 'I have searched all over the house and she is nowhere to be found. I promised her a walk this afternoon.'

Elizabeth smiled at him and lowered the open book she read to her silk skirts. 'You are an eager swain today, Robert, setting out on a romantic stroll with your lady.'

Rob grinned. He *was* eager—ridiculously so.

He looked forward to every minute spent with Anna. Every chance to make her smile, hear the rare music of her laughter, kiss her. ''Tis a fine day to walk outdoors.'

'Edward seems to think it a fine day to visit the neighbours and leave me alone, alas,' Elizabeth said lightly. 'I'm glad *someone* thinks of romance today.'

'Yet I cannot think of romance when my lady is not here,' said Rob. 'I hope she has not abandoned me to hide in the maze with another swain.'

'I do doubt that. Anna has eyes for none but you, just as you do for her. I think she went for a ride.'

'A ride?' Rob asked in surprise. 'She doesn't much care for horses.'

'We all have to overcome our fears, I think. I saw her not an hour past, going towards the stables. She wore her hat and gloves.'

He felt a sudden touch of disquiet. It wasn't like Anna to slip away so—and to go riding of all things. Yet nothing had been missing from her chamber except the book of poetry.

'Perhaps one of the grooms saw which way she went,' he muttered. 'I'll go after her.'

Elizabeth frowned, as if she sensed his doubts. 'Shall I come with you? Help you look for her?'

She paused. 'Did you two quarrel? Is that why she left?'

'Not at all. We were getting along very well.' Rob remembered how Anna had looked as he had kissed her once more before slipping out of her chamber at dawn. Her soft, sleepy smile, the way she'd wound her arms around his neck for one more kiss before she drifted back into slumber. The way he craved so much more.

Surely it was just a simple country ride and she would soon return. Yet still that dark cloud of doubt lingered, and Rob had learned in his work to trust his instincts.

'I will go and find her now,' he said.

She could not escape him, not now. Not yet.

Chapter Twenty-One

Anna held tight to the reins as she let the horse have its head and run free down the lane. The wind rushed past her, whining in her ears and tearing at her hair, and she vowed never to go near a horse again if she could help it. But for now all she could do was cling tight and pray she arrived in London in time—and in one piece.

She met few people on the road—just some farmers with their carts, and one fine carriage that thankfully was going much too fast to take note of her. She tried not to think of what lay behind her, or what might wait in London. She could only think of what she had to do right now—get her father out of Southwark, and find out exactly what he was suspected of so he could be cleared.

If she thought of Robert, of what his part in all this might be—or what he had been doing with her—she would go mad.

She pulled up at a crossroads to rest for a moment, and peered at the sky. The sunny morning, which had seemed so ridiculously full of hope, had turned overcast and grey. Strings of clouds hid the light and cast shifting shadows over the fields.

As she tried to catch her breath she heard a rumbling sound like thunder in the distance. But it didn't fade. It just persisted and grew louder and louder. She twisted in her saddle to glance at the road behind her, but it was clear. Only as she turned back did she glimpse a horse rushing towards her from the cross lane.

It was a large black horse, a dark blur that threw up a great cloud of dust in its wake. It moved fast and with purpose. Anna turned and gathered the reins tight again, ready to flee.

'Anna!' she heard a shout. 'Wait! Don't go.'

It was Robert. She saw his face as he came ever closer, his jaw set in a hard line, tense and dark. She started to flee, yet something held her back. Something inexorable and inevitable, holding her fast where she was. She watched him come, anger and hope and fear all boiling inside her. She couldn't run from him any longer.

He reined in his horse just in front of her, dirt and gravel flying. His boots were splashed with dust, his doublet unfastened to show his loosely laced shirt and the gleam of sweat on his bare skin. He had ridden hard indeed to catch her, and Anna sat tense in her saddle, unsure of what he would do.

'Where the hell are you going?' he demanded roughly.

'To London,' she said. She tightened her hold on the reins as the horse shifted restively under her.

'Now? Alone?'

He looked at her as if she had suddenly gone mad and he couldn't fathom her, and that made her angry all over again. *She* was not the mad one here—not the double-deceiver. *He* was the one who owed her an explanation.

'I must see to my father,' she said. 'Unless you and Lord Edward have already seen him arrested.'

Rob's eyes narrowed at her words, and she rued the way her anger and confusion made her so rash. If he did suspect her father, she had revealed her discovery. And if he did not she had landed him in greater danger than he had been in before.

Either alternative felt intolerable to her.

Rob suddenly moved his horse closer to hers and reached out to grab her bridle. 'What do you mean?' he drilled out in a voice made all the worse by its quiet calm. A hot-tempered Rob was bad enough, but Anna had seen how his temper was changeable and quickly cooled. This darkly intense Robert...

'Is my father in danger?' she asked, holding her head high. She had to be strong now—to find the truth and face it, no matter what. It was the only chance she had to save the ones she loved. 'Did Walsingham set you to spy on him?'

'What do you know, Anna?' he demanded, his grasp firm on her bridle. He held her fast.

'I found a torn list in Lord Edward's library. A list of purported traitors. In your writing.'

Rob's jaw tightened. 'Did you keep it? Do you know what would happen if you were found with such a thing?'

'Nay, I did not keep it! I put it back on the desk where it came from. But I remember what it said—that my father's name was on it,' she said. 'What is that list, exactly, and why is he on it?'

He shook his head. 'I wanted to protect you from all this, Anna. To keep you safe.'

'To be ignorant of the danger around us is not to be safe,' she protested. 'Tell me! Is my father suspected of something? Is he...?'

A traitor. She could not even say the words aloud.

Rob raked his fingers through his hair, and she could see the tension of his muscles, the rigid way he held himself, as if he had to restrain his temper.

'Someone connected to Lord Henshaw's Men is taking Spanish bribes,' he said at last. 'For what exactly we do not yet know, but Walsingham and his men will soon find out. And anyone involved will pay dearly.'

'They think it is my father?' Anna squeezed out, her throat tight.

'He is only one possibility,' Rob answered, his voice tense, as if he held a hard leash on his emotions. As if he didn't want to tell her anything at all.

'And how many *possibilities* have been tortured and killed?' she asked. She closed her eyes, but the terrible images were still there. The taste of fear in her mouth.

'Walsingham will not act without some kind of proof,' Rob said quickly. 'He knows the cost of moving too quickly and losing evidence of a wider plot. Your father is safe for now. The information Lady Essex brought to Hart Castle shows that.'

Anna shook her head. 'But for how long?'

'I am working fast, Anna, I promise you. I will find the villain.'

She heard him slide down from his horse and come to her side. She opened her eyes to stare down at him, and he reached for her hand. She let him take it, and she tried to read the truth in his eyes, feel it in his touch. She wanted to trust him so desperately.

'Who do you really work for, Robert?' she said. 'What do you really know?'

'Anna, I—' he began, and suddenly broke off with a frown. He looked back over his shoulder as his hand tightened on hers.

'What is it?' she said, but then she heard it, too. Hoofbeats, coming swiftly closer along the road from London.

A cloud of dust in the distance suddenly revealed five black-clad horsemen, moving towards them.

'Alden!' one of them shouted. 'We have been searching for you.'

Rob slapped Anna's horse on its flank and called, 'Run, Anna—now!'

'Nay, not without you,' she cried out, but the horse had already taken off across the field. She could only halt it at a distance, and she twisted around in her saddle just in time to see the riders overtake Rob as he climbed back into his saddle.

One of the men leaped from his horse, and there was the heavy, metallic clang of steel as he and Rob both drew their swords.

It was a quick and furious fight, a confusion of clashing blades and whirling dust. The two men grappled closely, viciously, and Rob managed to kick out at his opponent's leg and land him in the dust.

But Rob was outnumbered. Before he could lunge forward with his blade he was set upon by the other men. When the dirt cleared and they backed away Anna saw him lying still in the road, his leg bleeding.

Anna couldn't hold back her scream at the shocking sight. Her horse, already panic-stricken at the rush of noise and violence, wheeled around and Anna lost her grip on the reins. She felt herself falling, falling, the sky wheeling above her in a grey-blue blur.

Then she hit the ground, and pain shot through her body like a hundred knives. Her head struck something hard and everything went dim and hot.

She heard a man say, 'And who might this be?

Our little lamb, dropped right at our feet? Good fortune, lads.'

Someone touched her shoulder, and fiery agony shot down her side. She couldn't breathe through it, couldn't hold on to the light. She tried to gasp Rob's name—and then all went black.

Chapter Twenty-Two

The first thing Anna knew was the sound, faint and fuzzy, of blurry voices and the patter of wheels over gravel. She tried to reach out for it, hold on to it, but the noise kept fading in and out.

She slowly prised open her gritty eyes and saw what looked like wooden slats turned askew. Her head pounded, as if it would split open at the slightest movement, and her whole body ached. She struggled to remember where she was, what had happened, but all was blank. A sudden coarse, loud laugh from somewhere above her was as piercing as an arrow to her skull.

She closed her eyes again and tried with all her strength to move her limbs. Her legs were so heavy, every movement painful, but she managed to wriggle them around against her skirts. Gradually she felt other things—her hair fallen loose on her neck, the cool air on her arm where her sleeve was torn, the prickle of straw under her cheek.

She seemed to lie on her stomach in a cart of some sort, jolting as it moved along. She struggled to open her eyes again and saw the blur of green hedges beyond the wooden slats, and a figure in black on horseback that rode alongside and led Anna's horse.

And then she remembered all too clearly, as in a great flash of light. The men galloping towards them on the road. Rob shouting at her to run.

Rob falling, set upon by those men with their swords. She had tried to run to him, but she too had been brought low as she struggled to reach Robert. To see if he was alive or—or not.

No! No, he could not be dead—not Rob. He was the most burningly alive person she had ever beheld. Surely she would feel it, deep in her heart, if he was dead. She would sense if he was no longer in the world.

Yet when she took in a deep breath and quieted her mind to try and search in her heart for him she could feel nothing. She could see nothing but his handsome, strong body crumpled on the road, so far away from her.

But he had to be *somewhere.* She had to find him, to be with him no matter what.

Anna summoned every bit of her strength and slowly pushed herself up to a sitting position. Her head spun, and pain shot up her arms as she used them to brace herself. But she kept breathing, and gradually the world righted itself. She opened her eyes to see two men on the cart's seat above her, one holding the reins and the other watching her. His eyes were bright and beady above his thickly bearded jaw.

It was the same man who had leaned over her when she'd tumbled from her horse. She remembered it all now—every terrible, vivid detail.

'Well, well, it seems our lamb is awake,' he said, as cheerful and affable as if he greeted her in a tavern. 'And just in time, as we grow near our destination.'

Anna pushed her tangled hair back from her face. 'Where are you taking me? Who are you? I demand to know what is happening!'

The man smiled. 'I hardly think you are in a position to demand anything, Mistress Barrett.'

'You know who I am?' she asked, trying to remain calm and not give in to hysterics. That would help no one. Not herself, her father, nor Robert. But the uncertainty, the not knowing, was terrible.

'Of course I do. I was sent to find you. Someone is eager to speak with you. It was very kind of you to meet us halfway as you did.'

'Then may I not have the courtesy of knowing your name in turn?' she demanded, struggling to hold on to cold, unrevealing politeness. To keep her distance from the whole scene.

'I am called Smythe. But that hardly matters. My part in this assignment is nearly complete.'

Anna turned away from his piercing stare to study her surroundings. Perhaps she could leap off the cart as it slowed and run into the woods? But there was that horseman close beside them, with his hard face and shining sword.

'I wouldn't try to leave us if I were you, Mistress Barrett,' Smythe said. 'It would only go the worse for you when you are caught.'

'I doubt I am in any condition to run,' Anna murmured. She had hoped to see another cart, one carrying Rob, but they were alone on the road. The fields to either side grew narrower, and in the distance there was a grey cloud of hovering smoke. It seemed they neared London.

'Where is Master Alden?' she demanded. 'Did you murder him?'

The man suddenly climbed over the back of the seat and dropped down beside her in the straw. He no longer smiled.

'Master Alden should not be your concern, mistress,' he said. 'You must look to yourself.'

'How can I do that when I do not know what is happening?' she ground out. 'I have done no wrong.'

'Have you not? Then you need have no fear.' He leaned closer and whispered, 'Yet I think the same cannot be said of Master Alden. You should have a greater care of those with whom you associate.'

Anna bit her lip and said nothing. It was clear she would learn nothing else here. She'd have to wait until they reached wherever they were going. And she refused to show even a hint of fear.

Smythe reached for her hands and bound them tightly with a coarse length of rope. As they sat there in silence, the cart slowly joined the stream of people passing through London's gates and into the city itself. The silence of the country gave way to the clang of shouts and cries, the shrill call of merchants selling pies and ale and broadsheets of all the day's scandals. The fresh green air became thick with smoke and humanity, and the buildings grew closer and closer together until their eaves nearly blotted out the sky.

Anna was back in London, her home, yet she had never felt so strange before, so cut off from all that was familiar.

So very alone.

The cart halted by the riverside. In the distance along the crowded ribbon of water she glimpsed the edifice of London Bridge, its decoration of traitors' heads mere black dots against the gray sky. Beyond that somewhere was the round wooden O of the White Heron, and her father's house tucked behind it.

Smythe took her arm and helped her to stumble down from the cart. She was quickly surrounded by the other guards, their tall frames blocking her view, and they hurried her into a waiting boat. As they were rowed across the river she glimpsed the impenetrable stone walls of the Tower, and she remembered the day she had followed Robert there. They had taken much the same path then—across the river, beyond the Tower.

Had that been the first step that had led her here?

Once on the other side she half feared she would be led into the Tower itself, but she was hurried past its silent bulk and into the narrow lanes just past. Then she did see where they were going. The house in Seething Lane.

Smythe held her arm in a hard grasp as he rushed her down the narrow street, almost lifting her from her feet. They went not to the front door, but to a half-hidden entrance at the back of the garden. She was borne down a narrow staircase, dim and dusty, and along a silent corridor. The house seemed like a maze, one where a person could wander lost forever.

Smythe unlocked a door at the end of the hall and pushed her inside. 'Please wait here, Mistress Barrett,' he said, with another of those terrible smiles, before he untied her hands and shut the door behind him.

Anna heard the grate of the lock turning, trapping her there. The man's footsteps retreated and she was truly alone.

The chamber was cold, and Anna rubbed her hands over her arms as she studied this new prison. It was a small, grey space, far away from the luxuries of Hart Castle, with plain whitewashed walls and only one tiny window high up for light. There was a fireplace, but no blaze lit within it, and only one backless chair and rough table. An ewer of wine and a plate of bread sat on it.

Anna dared drink nothing here. She needed to think, and what if it was drugged or—or poisoned? She slowly sat down on the chair and rubbed her fingers over her aching temples.

She felt the weight of her purse still tied around her waist, and quickly pulled it open. Her coins were gone, but they had left her the book of Rob's poetry. It gleamed ruby red in the murky light, a precious jewel to sustain her. She raised it to her face and inhaled deeply, as if somehow his essence would still be in those pages.

'Where are you, Robert?' she whispered, pressing the book to her heart. 'Oh, my love, where are you?'

Chapter Twenty-Three

Rob paced the length of his gaol, ten steps one way, ten the other, prowling like the caged lion in the Queen's menagerie. He knew now how those creatures felt, burning with the need to run, to howl with fury and frustration. He had pounded on the stout, iron-bound door until his fists bled, but he was no closer to freedom.

And no closer to knowing where he was—or where Anna was. Was she even still alive? Had she escaped?

He braced himself against the cold stone wall and stared up at the beamed ceiling as if he could peer into the building above him and know what was happening. The room was very small, like an underground dungeon lined with stone. The packed-earth floor was covered with straw, and there was a low cot and a slop bucket in one corner. A small table was set against the wall, where a rush light cast a precious warm glow. It was a much cleaner prison than others he had found himself in before. There were no rats.

But there was also no Anna.

Rob slid down to sit on the floor and rubbed at the hard knot at the back of his head. It still burned like hellfire, and he cursed the man who had knocked him unconscious from behind. They had also left him with a wound on his thigh, but he had given as good as he had got. He had stabbed one in the shoulder and hit one on the head before they had taken him down, still struggling to give Anna time to flee.

After they had beaten him down onto the road he remembered nothing more until he had woken here. Had she got away? Was she safe? If she was safe, they could do with him what they would.

His heart had never felt heavier, darker. He had taken on this work to protect the vulnerable, like his sister and Anna, to try and make their lives safer. All he had done was expose them to greater danger. He was cursed, and he had brought the curse upon them, as well. He had to get out of there, to make things right somehow and let Anna go free again.

Rob carefully stretched his leg out before him to examine the wound on his thigh. Someone had roughly bound it up with a cloth, but blood had seeped through and dried so it clung to his skin. He set his jaw and carefully prised it free. The cut was not very deep, but it needed to be cleaned and tended to.

He shrugged out of his torn and dusty doublet and tore a strip from the bottom of his shirt for a makeshift bandage. As he bound it carefully, he remembered Anna's soft, cool hands as she mended his wounds, the warm rose scent of her hair as she leaned close to him.

He had so many scars, she had said. And now he had one more. But it was nothing to the scar of remorse on his soul. He had wanted to keep Anna safe, and instead he had driven her right into danger. He was worse than her brute of a husband.

'I will find you,' he vowed. 'No matter what, I will find you.'

He heard the sudden rusty scrape of a bar being drawn back from the door, and he stood up to face whomever was coming. He had no weapons, only his determination to find and protect Anna however he could.

Only one man appeared in the doorway, thin

and bent, swathed in a black cloak and shadowed by flickering torchlight from the corridor outside. The only things that stood out from the darkness were his grey-flecked beard and waxen skin.

'Walsingham,' Rob said tightly. *Of course*—who else had the resources to snatch a man from the public road and make him vanish?

A faint smile whispered over the Secretary's gaunt face. 'Were you expecting someone else, Master Alden? We had an appointment, you and I.' He shut the door behind him and slowly crossed the small room with his walking stick before lowering himself onto the cot.

'Where is Mistress Barrett?' Rob demanded.

'Is that your only concern now? The theatre owner's daughter?'

'She has naught to do with any of this,' Rob insisted, struggling to hold back the primitive urge to shout, to fight, to find his way to Anna however he could. Only a coldness to equal Walsingham's own could save them now.

'Does she not? Yet she was with you at Hart Castle. Does she know nothing of what her father does?' Walsingham demanded.

Rob watched Walsingham warily, feeling as if

he walked a sword's blade. Which way to jump? Which way lay safety for Anna? 'She is innocent.'

'Innocents are caught up in plots all the time, I fear. As you well know, Master Alden. Her father has a finger in many pies—not all of them to Her Majesty's advantage.'

'It is Thomas Sheldon you want in this plot.'

'So you and Lord Edward say—and so say the documents you kindly sent via my daughter. But we must find his conduit in Lord Henshaw's Men before we can move. Mistress Barrett can surely help us with more information concerning that.'

'So you *do* have her,' Rob said, cold fury pounding at his heart as he thought of her locked in a dungeon like this one. His sweet, fair Anna. Surely she was in fear and pain because of what he had done.

'She is in a comfortable place, never fear. We seek only to speak with her. Often people know more than they realise they do.'

And torture was used to help them 'remember.' 'I wish to see her.'

'Of course you do. But I don't see how you can help us in these circumstances, Master Alden. You are much too—engaged. Perhaps closer to the scheme than you should be?'

Rob froze. Walsingham's calm words were filled with menace. Was this the end, then? How could he save Anna if he was dead? 'Am I accused of treason?'

Walsingham studied him closely for a long, silent moment, his thin face giving away not a flicker of his thoughts. 'We have been speaking to someone else inside Lord Henshaw's Men. He makes certain claims, but I do have my suspicions of him. He is not entirely what he claims, and he is much too emotional—like all you actors.'

'If this man accuses me, I have the right to refute him, surely?' Rob demanded.

'You have only the rights the Queen chooses to bestow upon you,' Walsingham said. He waved his stick around the cell. 'And you should think of yourself now. Will you help me bring this to a conclusion? To save yourself and Mistress Barrett—if you are not lying to me?'

Rob crossed his arms over his chest. He felt a faint glow of hope, which he pressed down under cold calculation. 'You know that I will.'

Walsingham seemed to consider this. Finally, he nodded. 'You have served us well in the past. And I am in need of a fresh scheme to close in on our quarry. Very well. The young man who has been speaking to us of you and Mistress Barrett and her father is an actor by the name of Henry Ennis. I am sure you know him.'

'Ennis,' Rob muttered. It *would* be him— he followed Anna about like a besotted puppy, and picked quarrels with Rob in the middle of the White Heron when he only saw Anna smile at Rob. Rob remembered the burning hatred in Ennis's eyes as he had swung his sword at Rob's head.

'Yes. You do know him, then? He certainly seems to have taken against *you*,' Walsingham said.

'I believe he is in love with Mistress Barrett and she spurned him,' Rob said slowly.

Walsingham's eyes widened with interest. 'Is he, indeed? Men are so foolish in love. That is certainly a bit of information we can use to our greater advantage...'

Chapter Twenty-Four

Anna reached up as high as she could and tried to grab the ledge of the window with her finger-tips. She had pushed the table up against the wall and climbed atop it in the hope she could peer outside. Maybe if she could see what lay outside Walsingham's house she could plan some sort of escape.

But that was a vain hope. The tiny window was too far above her head, and she could hear almost nothing beyond her room. She wasn't even sure how much time had passed since she had been carried here. Was it another day now?

'Z'wounds,' she cursed. 'Robert, where are you?'

She scrambled down from the table and sat back on the chair to stare into the empty fireplace. She reached for the book again and held it tightly in her hands, as if it was a talisman against fear.

She couldn't afford fear. Not now.

Suddenly the silence was shattered by the faint click of the key at the door. Anna jumped to her feet, the book held before her like a shield against whatever was coming.

The entrance slid open, creaking on its heavy hinges. Anna blinked at the sudden rush of torch-light, dazzling after the dimness of the room. When the glare cleared, she looked again—and beheld the most welcome of sights.

It was Robert who stood before her, alive and whole. He braced his hands on the doorframe, studying her in turn just as greedily as she watched him.

'Are you real?' she whispered. 'Or am I merely dreaming?'

'If you are, I hope it is a dream from which we never wake,' he answered hoarsely. He rushed across the room to snatch her into his arms and pull her close, his arms around her.

Anna held on to him desperately, as if she would never let him go, never let him be snatched from her again. She felt the heat of his skin, the pounding of his heart, and sighed a deep prayer of thanksgiving that he was *alive*—here, now, with her. Even if they were prisoners together, she could fear nothing with him.

'You are alive,' she whispered. 'But what happened there on the road? Are you Walsingham's prisoner, as well?'

'So many questions, fairest Anna,' he said, pressing a kiss to her hair. 'I would have thought you would be waiting here to kill me yourself for getting you into this.'

'Were you the one who landed us here in this gaol?' she asked. 'It seems strange you would contrive to have *yourself* locked up thus. Unless…'

She drew back to look up at him. She had thought him unable to hurt her, but she wanted to see the truth of that in his eyes. 'Unless this is some sort of twisted scheme to coax confessions out of me? Is my father here?'

'Oh, Anna. You do have every right to distrust me,' he said sadly, wearily. He held tight to her hands, not letting her pull away from him. She didn't want to leave him, though; she wanted only to know the truth. 'But I fear I am bound here as you are, and I need your help now to discover the truth.'

Anna shook her head in confusion. 'What truth

do you seek? I know my father is on your list, but I also know he can be no traitor.'

'And I know that, as well. But someone in Lord Henshaw's Men has been taking Spanish coin, and we must find out who and for what purpose. Then we will be truly free.'

Her head spun and she struggled to bring her thoughts together. 'There are so many people around the theatre, and as you said yourself they are all constantly low on funds. And there are so many grudges and quarrels—it could be any one of the actors. They are as adept at hiding their true selves as…'

His hands held even closer to hers. 'As I am?' he hinted, a tiny flicker of emotion finally there, deep in his voice.

'Aye, Robert, as you are. At Hart Castle I thought I could see you at last, but now I fear I know so little.'

'You *do* know me, Anna, and I swear to you now I want only to help you.' He raised her hands to his lips for a kiss, and inhaled deeply of the soft turning of her wrist, as if he tried to memorise her, savour her and this moment together no matter how fraught it was with fear and uncertainty.

Anna swayed towards him, a heavy longing for

so many things sweeping over her. She wanted to believe him, to be close to him, to have all this vanish and life be as it was in those too-brief moments at Hart Castle. But she couldn't let herself fall. Too much depended on it.

'Let me show you,' he said urgently. 'Give me a chance to set all this right before you refuse me.'

'Refuse you what?'

He shook his head with a frown, as if he felt confused and desperate, just as she did. But that couldn't be—not for Robert Alden. 'The chance to see you. To touch you as I do now. To be near you.'

'How?' she demanded. 'How will this be set right? How can we be free?'

'I have a suspicion who our villain is—or at least who is in the pay of the villain,' Rob said. 'Come, sit, and I will tell you of my scheme. I fear it is a wild one, but for all that I think we can succeed.'

Anna let him lead her back to her chair and help her to sit. As he knelt beside her, he glimpsed the book where she had dropped it at the sight of him.

'You were reading *Demetrius and Diana*,' he said.

'Aye,' she answered softly. 'It has kept me from going mad today, I confess.'

'Then I am glad I could help you in some way.'

His tone said clearly he could help her in no other way.

'I think you can help me in other ways, as well,' she said. 'Tell me your suspicions.'

Rob pressed the book into her hand and closed her fingers around it. 'You know Edward and I have been working to trap Thomas Sheldon in one of his schemes? We have known for some time that he is in the pay of the Spanish, and possibly of the French, as well—he is in very deep debt and has made many errors. He grows desperate and careless now. And he uses equally desperate men to help him.'

'Actors?' she cried, her heart freezing. It was someone near to them who had betrayed them?

'One in particular, who passes messages between Sheldon and his contacts in verses and takes their coin, while also claiming to inform on others to Walsingham. He is a double agent, but his desperation makes him a good one no longer.'

Anna closed the clasp on the book as if it was this double agent's neck. 'Who is it?'

'You know him well, I think. And now he tries to turn on *me,* since fighting me did not work. It is Henry Ennis.'

'Henry!' Anna cried, shocked. Henry Ennis?

Who had declared his love for her? Who tried to kiss her in her father's garden? Could it be true? She had seen there was something obsessive and strange in him, but being so hopelessly passionate and unrealistic was often a stock in trade for actors. It shouldn't make a man turn to treason.

She looked deeply into Rob's eyes and studied the steady glow of truth she found there. Any person was capable of anything when pushed far enough. She saw that around her all the time. If Henry Ennis had been insulted by her refusal and was jealous of Robert—if he needed money or revenge—aye, it *could* be him. It could be anyone.

And she needed to know. She needed to reclaim her life and move forward once again, to examine her feelings for Rob and discover the truth of his for her. But before she could do that she had one single imperative—to save all their lives.

'Tell me how I can help you,' she said.

Chapter Twenty-Five

Anna took a deep breath and carefully folded her hands in her lap. The soft silence around her made the waiting feel interminable, and she had to press down the urge to cry out and run about in futile circles.

Could this scheme of Robert's and Walsingham's work? She wasn't sure her meagre acting skills were up to the task. But it had to be worth a try. She had to do what she could, before Walsingham and his men resorted to Tower torture threats. If Henry Ennis had truly joined forces with Sheldon in treasonous schemes, he had to be brought to justice and her father cleared.

Anna sat back in her chair and listened carefully for any approach that signalled her waiting was over. She had been moved from her small, cold gaol to this sitting room, where there was a fire in the grate and fine tapestries on the walls. Refreshments had been laid out, but she couldn't eat or drink. She couldn't do anything but think.

She refused to consider what would happen if this scheme failed and the villains escaped. But what would happen *after,* when Sheldon and Henry and their cohorts were gone and she was back home with her father? Would Rob vanish and she would never see him again? Would she have only the memories of those days at Hart Castle to remind her of him and what they had been to each other?

And yet—could she forget all the danger and the lies?

Anna shook her head. Her feelings for Rob Alden could not be fathomed now. They were all too tied up in emotion, in hope and fear all tangled together. She had to concentrate first on this one task.

At last she heard footsteps outside her room, and jumped to her feet as the door opened. A tall, thin man clad in the black they all wore in that house appeared there, and gave her a short bow.

'Secretary Walsingham is ready to see you, mistress. If you will follow me?' he said.

Anna nodded and followed him along the corridor and down a flight of stone steps that led back to the damp lower floors where she had been kept before. There was a row of stout closed doors and all was quiet behind them, but a cluster of men waited at the far end.

It is just a play, she told herself as she followed her escort. *Imagine it is the stage at the White Heron.*

But the solemn cluster of men who watched her approach seemed all too real.

Two of them bore swords, and Anna's escort said quietly, 'Those men will act as your guards. The ones who are being questioned have been searched for weapons, of course, but it would be best if you stayed close to the guards.'

Anna nodded, and as he opened the door the guards stepped in behind her. They walked in together—a small, curious procession. Anna clasped her hands before her to keep them from trembling.

To her surprise, it was not a dark, cramped cell, but a large, panelled room lit by several lamps and torches that showed every detail of the careful stage set. Walsingham and two other men sat at a long table at the far end of the room, papers scattered before them. Henry Ennis sat to one side, slumped on a stool, his fine clothes torn and dishevelled, his handsome face sunken and grey. He looked up as she entered the room.

And stared at her as if a ghost had just glided into his presence. His skin turned pale, his eyes growing wide. One hand lifted as if he would reach out for her, but then it dropped back to his side.

Anna's guard pushed her down into a chair, and she noticed a small gap in the dark panelling behind Walsingham. She glimpsed a flash of white cloth, and realised that was Rob's hiding place. He was with her in this strange play-acting.

She stiffened her back and looked straight ahead, refusing to acknowledge Henry even as he couldn't cease staring at her.

'Thanks to your excellent work, Master Ennis, we have been collecting Her Majesty's enemies in this case,' Walsingham said, calmly sorting through the papers before him, as if bringing down traitors were an everyday chore in his life—too close to the truth for Anna's liking. 'We have already been questioning Sir Thomas Sheldon, and now Lord Henshaw's Men are being cleaned out. Mistress Barrett here and her father have much to answer for.'

'Nay, she is not involved in this matter!' Henry cried, his face growing even whiter.

'But we have evidence of her father's schemes, thanks to you,' Walsingham said coolly. 'And we know Mistress Barrett keeps her father's business ledgers and runs most of his concerns. She is the one able to send information to any foreign contacts. Is that not so, Mistress Barrett?'

Anna kept staring straight ahead. Despite the fact that this was all meant to be a play, she couldn't help shivering. No wonder Walsingham had captured so many over the years—the very calm ordinariness of his demeanour was chilling. 'I have nothing to reply to that. I have declared my innocence.'

'So you have. But we all know the truth, do we not, Mistress Barrett?' Walsingham queried grimly. 'As does Master Ennis, who has been of such help in this matter. Perhaps Lord Henshaw should make you a sharer in his company now, Master Ennis? He will be in need of them once we are finished here.'

'I told you—Robert Alden is the traitor in the company,' Henry cried. 'I was wrong before. Mistress Barrett has nothing to do with it.'

'Ah, but Mistress Barrett is Master Alden's

lover,' Walsingham said. 'Surely she has some interesting information to share.' He studied Anna and added, 'Is that not so, Mistress Barrett?'

'A woman can take a lover as she chooses,' Anna answered. 'It does not make her a criminal.'

'It depends on who that lover might be,' one of Walsingham's men said with a coarse laugh.

Henry's face shaded from white to deep red as he stared at Anna. 'So it *is* true?' he whispered. 'You *are* with him?'

Anna looked to him, careful to keep her expression smooth and cool. 'Is what true, Master Ennis?'

'You spurned my honourable offer to whore for *him*,' Henry said. 'I suspected, but I never...'

'Why should I not choose him?' said Anna. 'He is handsome and dashing. He is a skilful lover. And he is not the one whose accusations have led me to this place. I could never have been your wife, Henry. Or even your whore.'

'I would have given you everything! A respectable life, my name, my love.' His voice grew hotter and wilder as he spoke.

'Love?' Anna rose to her feet and stalked towards him, a wave of disgust washing over her as she looked at his face. He was a weak man, acting like a cruel, spoiled child denied the toy he de-sired. He had tried to destroy her father with these lies and secrets, and thus destroy her.

'Love would never have brought me here,' she said. 'You wanted to possess me, or at least the woman you thought I was. You did not even know me, and when I refused you I was arrested as a traitor.'

She stopped mere inches from him and stared up at him steadily. 'As I die on the scaffold, Henry Ennis, brought low by *your* revenge, I will curse your name to eternal damnation. And I will take my love for Robert Alden with me into eternity. Nothing you have done can erase that. He is a hun-dred times the man you could ever be.'

She started to turn away, but Henry suddenly grabbed her arm and dragged her back to him, nearly pulling her arm from its socket. His clasp was bruisingly painful, and Anna cried out.

'I loved you—I worshipped you as a gentle god-dess,' Henry shouted, as if years of frustration and anger were falling out. 'And all along you were an-other one of Alden's bawds, wallowing in the dirt.'

'Let go of me!' Anna demanded, a bolt of fear running through her as she remembered her hus-band's beatings.

The other men clambered to their feet, her guards drawing their swords, but Henry's blind fury made him faster than them. He wrapped his arm around Anna's waist and dragged her against him, her back to his chest, and snatched a sharp letter opener from the table. It was a small but lethal-looking object, and he held it right at the pulse pounding in her neck.

She felt a sharp prick on her skin, the warm trickle of blood, and Henry cried, 'Stay back, or I will rob the hangman of his victim!'

The panelling where Rob hid crashed open, and he leaped out with his dagger in hand. 'Let her go now, Ennis,' he said roughly. 'I am the one on whom you seek revenge, not her.'

Henry laughed wildly. 'So you are here with her. You scheme against me.'

'You have trapped yourself,' Rob said. 'But no one else needs to be hurt. She never meant to wound you.'

'Ah, but she did. She did it most deliberately.' Henry's voice was suddenly terribly calm. 'As did you, Alden.'

Henry kissed Anna's cheek tenderly—and plunged the dagger into her side.

He let her go and she slid to the floor. For an

instant she felt searing pain, burning down her ribs and through her legs, an agony that stole her breath and left her unable even to cry out. Then there was only numb ice, closing in around her.

She lay on her side on the flagstone floor, vaguely aware of shouts and metallic clashes, pandemonium in that cold, cold room. Yet it all seemed to be happening far away, in a soft bubble of silence.

She forced herself to move, to push herself up on her elbow and try to call out Rob's name. Only a strangled gasp escaped as she watched him grapple with Henry Ennis.

In a strange, sparkling haze she saw Rob's dagger plunge into Henry's shoulder, and Henry fell to the floor as the guards closed in around him. His threat was done. Anna let herself collapse. The darkness was closing around her, and even as she fought it with all her fading strength she felt its grip tightening.

'Anna,' Rob said, and in his voice she heard anger and horror—and stark fear.

Rob fearful? How could that be? She had to be worse off than she feared.

She felt his arms go around her, lifting her up against him. She tried to hold on to him, to use his great strength as her own, but her hands felt so numb.

'Robert,' she whispered.

'Don't talk,' he said. 'Rest now. You're safe. I have you.'

Anna nodded, but she could hold back the darkness no longer. She closed her eyes and it covered her in its thick, icy oblivion.

Chapter Twenty-Six

Rob hummed a soft tune to Anna as he bathed her shoulders and arms with a cool cloth. She didn't wake at the sound of his voice, but murmured and frowned in her sleep. Her head tossed on the pillow.

He laid another cloth, freshly rinsed with cool water and essence of lavender, on her brow. She was still warm with fever, her body fighting off infection. Two days she had lain there in the bed at Walsingham's house, tossing in restless dreams only she could see. She would cry out incoherent words or clutch his hand weakly.

Rob smoothed the tangled hair back from her face and softly kissed her brow. 'Anna,' he whispered. 'My beautiful Anna, please don't leave me now, I beg you. I can't live without you. Anna, please.'

He had never begged before in his life, but he would now if it would bring her back to him. He would do anything at all to save her, and the realisation of that, the primitive fear and fury at the thought of losing her, hit him like a sizzling lightning bolt. He, who had never needed anyone in his life, who fought his battles alone, needed Anna.

He loved her. He couldn't deny his burning, raw feelings for her any longer, but now she was slipping away from him. All her goodness and beauty was tumbling further and further from him, and without her the world would be cold and cruel again.

'Anna, fight with me!' he called out fiercely. 'Stay with me. Let me show you that I can be a better man. That I can be worthy of you. Or stay just to fight me, to despise me. Just don't go.'

She turned away from him on the pillows, whispering incoherently. Rob held on to her hand, drawing her back. He kissed her palm and held it against his cheek. Her pulse still beat, just under her pale, fragile skin. She was still alive. There was still a chance.

'Just hold on to me, Anna,' he said. 'I won't let you go.'

Anna grew quieter, as if she could hear him. Her fierce frown eased and her hand relaxed in his.

'Aye,' he said. 'Sleep will help you find your strength again.' And when she was strong again he would leave her, as he should have long ago. He had hurt her, and he could not bear to do that again. He had failed her as he had Mary.

The bedchamber door opened and Rob glanced back, expecting one of the maids again, or perhaps the doctor he had already tossed out once. But it was Lady Essex who stood there, a tray in her hands.

'Is Mistress Barrett better?' she asked.

'I think she is resting now, Lady Essex,' he said wearily, rubbing at the back of his stiff neck.

'That is good. My mother says a fever will never break without quiet. She sent some of her own herbal mixture for Mistress Barrett to drink, and more salve for the wound.' She put the tray down on the table by the bed, and her jewelled hands quickly set about mixing the sweet-scented herbs into a goblet of wine. She moved with brisk efficiency, but Rob could see the deep-set lines of sadness and weariness on her pale face.

'It is very kind of Lady Walsingham,' he said.

'And kind of you to bring it yourself, Lady Essex. You must have many duties at Essex House.'

A bitter smile touched her lips. 'My duties are here at the moment, with my father ill. And my husband rarely misses me. He is much too—occupied.' She stirred the wine mixture and held it out to him. 'This will help ease her.'

'Thank you, Lady Essex,' Rob said as he took it from her.

'Let me help you give it to her,' she said. 'I am very good at dispensing medicine to the reluctant patient by now.' She slipped behind Anna on the bed and lifted her to a half-sitting position as she steadied Anna's head on her satin-covered shoulder.

Rob poured the wine past Anna's white lips, drop by precious drop, until it was gone and she lay back down among the pillows. She did seem to rest easier with the herbs, not tossing or crying out.

Lady Essex smoothed the sheets and tucked the blankets closer around Anna's shoulders. 'My father still thinks the doctor should be brought back.'

'Your father is a wise man in many ways,' Rob said. 'But the doctor has already bled her twice, and it only seemed to weaken her more. I won't have him do it again—or feed her powdered uni-corn horn or lamb dung mixed with pearls.'

Lady Essex chuckled. 'Indeed such things have not helped my father very much. I'm sure rest will do her more good.' She paused, and then went on, 'My father does want to make amends for what happened to Mistress Barrett.'

'Does he?' Rob muttered. He doubted Walsingham regretted anything that gained him his goals. Not even the pain of an innocent woman. But wasn't Rob himself just the same? That was what had brought Anna to this bed.

'I know it does not always appear so, but he has a heart in his way.'

Rob just nodded and reached for the basin of water to bathe Anna's fevered skin again. He had no time for Walsingham's complexities now, or to think of the future at all. He could only think of Anna.

'You do care for her very much, don't you, Master Alden?' Lady Essex said questioningly, as she watched him.

'I love her,' he said simply. And somehow merely saying those words aloud made him feel free. He had been a fool to think anything mattered but the people he loved. And that was why he would leave her. He had to be unselfish for the first time in his life and think about her first.

'Do you?' she asked sadly. 'What must that feel like?'

Rob heard her move away across the room, the click of the door closing behind her.

What did love feel like? He had thought he knew the answer to that before. He made his living by his pen, creating words of love and desire, but he saw now that had all been counterfeit—a pale reflection of real love. He had lived all his life thinking only of himself, but that was impossible now. He must think only of Anna.

'Anna, you must live,' he said. 'And I swear to you I will not put you in any more danger. I will leave you to live your life in peace, as you deserve.'

She deserved a man of kindness and tranquillity after all she had been through. A man not like her boar-pig of a husband, nor a man with a twisted life and past like himself. It would be the hardest thing he had ever done, but he would give her that.

'I will do anything for you, Anna, if you will fight to live,' he said.

As if she could hear him, Anna shuddered. The chills were returning, hard behind the hot fever.

Rob climbed onto the bed beside her and took her into his arms to hold her close to the warmth of his body. She trembled and shivered, as if buffeted by icy winds, and he held her even tighter.

He would hold her tethered to earth, to life, no matter what.

The softness of a feather bed under her was the first thing Anna felt as she slowly swam up from the hot, smothering folds of dark sleep. It felt smooth and cool against her body, so fluffy she could sink back into it and let it surround her.

But then—then there was pain. It swept over her from her scalp to her toes, a deep, raw aching feeling that held her pinned down and wouldn't let her move. Her mind went blank and white. She could remember nothing but the ache.

I must cease these adventures, she thought. Too often of late she had woken in such a state. But where was she now?

With all her strength, Anna prised open her eyes and focused them until she saw the pleated folds of dark blue bed-hangings high above her. She could smell smoke from a fire and hear its crackle, and soft pillows were piled behind her head. She was not in some bare prison, but neither was she in her own bed at her father's house.

She tried to move, but a sharper pain shot up her side beneath the folds of her chemise. She carefully laid her hand over her ribs and felt the lump of a bandage there.

Then she remembered. Henry Ennis grabbing her, driving his blade into her side. Rob falling onto him. The whole violent, chaotic scene came crashing back over her and she bit her lip to keep from crying out.

But Robert! Where was he now? Had he been hurt in that fight?

She gritted her teeth together and levered herself up on her elbow to try and rise from the bed and call for help. Surely someone was nearby?

That was when she saw him. Rob slept in a chair by her bed, slumped over with his head cradled in his arms at the edge of her mattress. His wrinkled shirtsleeves were pushed back from his bronzed forearms, his hair was rumpled, and dark purple circles were etched under his eyes. He was the most beautiful sight she had ever seen.

Cursing the weakness that made her move as slowly as an old woman, Anna gently shook his arm. 'Robert,' she whispered.

He leaped awake, his hand flying to his hip as if he would draw a sword that was not there. For a second he looked baffled, but then his gaze focused on her and a brilliant smile broke across his face.

'You're awake!' he shouted jubilantly. 'Anna, you're awake.'

'Am I?' she said. It felt as if she still dreamed—a wondrous vision of being with Rob, the two of them alone together, safe at last.

He gently cradled her face between his hands, his touch cool on her skin. He kissed her brow, her cheek, and smoothed her tangled hair back from her temples. 'The fever has gone,' he said. 'How do you feel?'

'Battered and sore, and rather tired, but alive,' she answered. She covered his hands with hers, holding him to her as if he would fly away like one of those dreams. 'What happened? I remember Henry and that dungeon, but nothing after. Where are we?'

'In a chamber at Walsingham's house. We've been here three days now.'

'Three days?' Anna stared at him and saw that his face was drawn, his eyes hollow, as if he too had been ill. 'Have you been here with me all that time?'

He kissed her hand. 'Someone had to drive away that clownish doctor before he bled you dry.'

'Oh, Robert.' She almost cried at the realisation that he had stayed with her in her fever, that he had nursed her. 'Are we safe, then? Or are we prisoners still?'

'Safe? Your fever has broken. Surely you will recover your strength now.' His voice was low and terribly gentle, as if to hold her at a distance.

'Nay, I mean—you are not under arrest? My father is not suspected?' she asked, desperate to know.

Rob laughed wryly. 'The last we heard of your father he was drinking ale at the Three Bells. It was thought better not to tell him of your illness until you were improved. And Sheldon has given up all his allies under Walsingham's questioning. The mere sight of the torture implements made him tell all. It was only Ennis and two other actors, as well as another disgruntled man in Sheldon's circle. Not the most organised conspiracy Walsingham has ever faced.'

Anna nodded, feeling the deepest sense of relief—and a deeper wave of exhaustion. Rob and her father were safe—for now, anyway. Rob was with her. She was alive.

But she was also so very tired. 'I think I need to sleep now,' she murmured.

'Of course,' Rob said quickly. He helped her lie back down on her soft pillows and drew the bed-clothes around her. 'You need to be strong again, and rest will make you well.'

Anna held on to his hand as she drifted back into sleep. Surely she had all she needed to make her well now.

Just before the darkness claimed her, she felt his kiss on her brow and heard him whisper, 'Sleep now. I will see you well and happy before I go…'

Chapter Twenty-Seven

'I cannot *wait* to leave this place,' Anna whispered as she tucked her meagre belongings into a travel case. The Walsingham house was a silent, dark edifice that seemed to press in around her with the terrible weight of all that had happened there, and Secretary Walsingham's illness. The very walls seemed to hold on to Anna's own pain and fear, and even though Lady Essex and her mother had been very kind Anna wanted nothing more than to go home.

Wherever 'home' was.

She paused in folding a chemise to consider that word *home*. She would go back to her father's house behind the White Heron, of course, for there was nowhere else to go. Back to the bustle and noise of the Southwark streets, ledger books and collecting rents, and keeping her father from drinking too much.

Yet in her illness she had had such dreams—a tantalising glimpse of other possibilities. A place of her own, quiet and peaceful, with her own garden, her own books of poetry to read, her own hearth to sit by in the evenings. And Robert sitting there with her, talking and laughing about the day they had just passed and their hopes for tomorrow.

Anna reached for *Demetrius and Diana,* cradling its soft cover in her hands. It was already worn with all her reading. Could Robert ever leave his London house of adventure and danger, his adoring audiences and tumultuous street brawls, to write poetry in the country with her? Could he be happy there?

She thought of how he had sat by her in her illness, bathing her fevered skin, holding her hand. How tender and careful he was—and how close they were bound by all that had happened. Surely there was hope in that? Surely he cared for her, and one day might…?

Might come to love her as she loved him?

Did she even dare to hope?

There was a knock at the door, and Lady Essex

peered inside. 'Mistress Barrett, I came to see if you needed any assistance in packing, but I see you are nearly done. I hope you haven't tired yourself too much.'

Anna smiled at her. She had come to like Lady Essex in the time she had spent sitting by Anna's bed while Rob rested, reading to her or talking of Court fashions and gossip. There was a kindness to her, but also a great sadness that showed how even the greatest nobility were not excluded from the troubles of the world. The pains of love.

'I have so little to pack I could hardly grow tired from it,' Anna said. 'I needed to move about before I became too accustomed to sitting by the fire being waited on. You and your mother have been the most excellent of hostesses.'

'Although the circumstances have been deplorable, we've been glad you're here. You've given my mother a welcome distraction when she most needs it.' Lady Essex carefully folded a pile of snowy handkerchiefs. 'Now I suppose you will go back to your theatre?'

'Yes. My own father needs me, as yours needs you.'

'My father does not need anyone—not really,'

Lady Essex said. 'Nor does my husband. Not as Master Alden needs you.'

'Rob doesn't need me. He only…' Anna suddenly heard a noise from the courtyard below her window, and she hurried over to investigate. A groom had led a horse onto the cobblestones and was settling a saddle on its back. It was an unusual sight, for it seemed no one had come or gone from the house since Sheldon and Ennis had been hauled to the Tower.

'Does your father have an errand today?' Anna asked.

Lady Essex peered over Anna's shoulder and shook her head. 'My father hasn't ridden in a long time. Everyone comes here to him now.'

As they watched, it was Rob who emerged from the house with a leather messenger bag slung over his back. He spoke to the groom and glanced up at Anna's window. She instinctively shrank back behind the curtain, where she could not be seen, and saw him climb up into the saddle.

He looked grim and sad, and very determined, and that look on his face planted a touch of chilly disquiet in Anna's heart.

'Is your father sending him on another mission?'

Anna asked Lady Essex, who shrugged and looked just as confused as Anna felt.

'My father sometimes lets me deliver messages for him, as lately I did to Hart Castle,' she said, 'but he seldom talks to anyone about his work, or about the people he employs. I would have thought Master Alden would be of no use to him now, after this escapade.'

'Why is that?' Anna asked in alarm. To be 'of no use' to Walsingham sounded like a dangerous thing.

'It has gained attention, and Master Alden has worked for my father for a long while now. Such people are usually given a pension and retired.' Lady Essex took Anna's hand and said soothingly, 'I am sure he is only on an errand of his own and will soon return.'

Anna was not so sure as she studied Rob's solemn face through the windowpane. She knew him well by now, and had learned his expressions and gestures—the way he tried to hide his darker side from her and protect her. Something told her something was amiss now.

She lifted the hem of her skirts and ran from the chamber and down the stairs, ignoring the pain in her side from the bandaged, healing wound. She took a couple of wrong turns, but finally tumbled out into the courtyard as Rob gathered the reins in his gloved hands.

'Where are you going?' she demanded.

He looked at her calmly, as if he had been expecting her, but his face was cool and polite. So very different from when she'd been ill and he had never left her side. 'I have a new task to perform for Secretary Walsingham, since my old one is now concluded. Clumsily so, I admit, but I have been given another chance.'

'Another chance to risk your life among villains?' Anna demanded, fear rising up in her.

'To do my work,' he said impatiently, and Anna felt she had never known him at all. Never sighed in passion in his arms, never felt his tenderness. He was a stranger.

'And where might this work be?' she countered tightly.

'In France,' he said, as lightly as he might have said *in Spitalfields.*

'France!' she cried. He was going away to France—across the sea, to hunt down England's enemies and perhaps die—and he had not even said farewell? After everything they had done together?

After—after she had thought herself in love with him, and even dared think he might come to love her, too?

She felt as if she was sinking into the ground, her heart like a stone in her chest, and a loud buzzing grew in her ears. She grabbed on to his saddle to keep from falling.

'Why didn't you come to tell me? To say goodbye?' she asked, a feeling of numbness spreading over her body.

'I left a letter with Lady Walsingham to be given to you,' he answered.

He swung down from the horse to land lightly beside her. He took her hands in his, but Anna could hardly feel it. She stared down at their joined fingers and felt as if she watched from a great distance.

'What does the letter say?' she said. 'That we had a merry time together but now you are off to France and adventures new?'

'Anna, I would hardly call our time together *merry*,' he said, his hands still tight on hers. 'Kidnappings, fights, imprisonments, wounds— you deserve much better than what I brought you.'

'Is that why you are leaving? Because we are a curse on each other?' she cried.

'It's for the best. I must do this if I am to hold my promise to you,' he said, his voice cold and distant, as if he was already gone from her.

Anna shook her head. 'And what promise is that?'

'To protect you. I failed in that before. I will hold to it now.'

'How can you protect me if you are in France?' she whispered in confusion.

'Men like Sheldon and Ennis will have no need to hurt you if I am not here,' he said. 'You can find a better man—a man with no secrets. A country squire who can give you the peaceful home you want, children, quiet days.'

That had long been her dream. But now she found those dreams were as nothing beside her feelings for Robert. She had come to crave his fire and passion, the passion that ignited something long frozen in her own soul and brought her to life again.

'You deserve a life, as well,' she said. 'Please, Robert, don't go now. Stay here in England.'

He raised her hands to his lips and kissed them with a lingering caress, as he had so many times. She tried to study him, to memorise the way he felt and looked, but it all seemed too unreal. He was leaving, their affair was over, and she couldn't quite hold on to that terrible knowledge.

'I must go, fairest Anna,' he said. 'Please—don't forget me.'

He pressed a soft kiss to her brow and set her away from him. As Anna watched, rubbing her arms against the cold inside her, he swung back into the saddle and led the horse through the court-yard gates and out into the lane.

She hurried after him, but she didn't call his name or try to bring him back. She knew that would be futile, and now she could only hold on to the tattered remains of her pride.

But she watched him until his horse turned the corner and he was gone from her sight. Gone from her life as suddenly as he had landed in it. She felt hollow inside.

'Godspeed you, Robert, and keep you safe,' she whispered. If only she could have done the same. If only—if only he could have loved her as she did him.

Rob stood on the crowded, bustling docks, watching as the ship that would carry him to France was loaded. Yet he truly saw none of it—

didn't hear the shouts and cries around him, the shove and clamour of the crowd.

He could only see Anna's face as he had told her goodbye—how pale she'd been, her eyes huge and dark with pain. An echo of the same pain he felt in his own heart, sharp and more cruel than any dagger. That pain had grown and grown ever since he'd made his decision to leave her, and he knew it would never be gone from him. The loss of Anna was a mortal wound.

He gave a bitter, self-mocking laugh at the thought. He had spent his career creating the illusion of passionate, tragic love while keeping himself at a distance from such tumult. He had never really believed it—not until Anna.

She had slipped into his soul before he knew it, and she was there forever. No matter how many seas and mountains there were between them.

He turned away from the ship, telling himself he had to follow his chosen path alone. He had left Walsingham's service. He was of no use to the Secretary now. He could carry on with such work no longer—not after it had injured Anna. But Walsingham had found him a place with a troupe of players connected to the Queen's ambassador in Paris, and Rob had chosen to take it.

If he was in Paris, Anna could move on with her life, free of him.

But, z'wounds, he did not *want* her to move on without him! He could still feel the touch of her hands, trying to hold on to him, still see the hurt and love in her eyes. She was his, just as he was hers. She had stood with him in the darkest moments, believed in him.

How could he ever do less for her?

Rob was suddenly filled with the burning, urgent need to find Anna, to beg her to give him a chance to prove himself to her. To spend his life trying to make her happy.

He would do anything at all just to stay with her.

Chapter Twenty-Eight

'So you are home at last, Anna!' she heard her father call from the sitting room as she stepped into the house behind the White Heron.

She put down her case on the floor and looked around her. The house looked so much the same she might never have left. There was more dust, and the smell of old food and spilled wine in the air without her housekeeping, but otherwise the days seemed to have stood still. Yet she felt so much older.

'Aye, I've come back, Father,' she answered. She took off the hooded cloak she had borrowed from Lady Essex and went to greet her father.

He embraced her and gave her cheek a hearty kiss, squeezing her until her side hurt and she had to suppress a gasp. 'I've missed you, daughter,' he declared.

'So I see,' Anna said with a laugh, extracting herself from his arms to sit down in her usual chair. She suddenly felt very tired. 'I don't think the hearth has been swept since I left.'

'You haven't been here to keep an eye on Old Madge, and it's been busy,' Tom said. 'We've started rehearsals at the White Heron! So I have kept myself occupied while you were on your grand travels.'

'Rehearsals for what? I thought you were reviving old productions for the time being.'

'Why, Master Alden's new play, of course. It is sure to be a great success.'

Anna sat up straighter in her chair. It was as if someone she'd thought dead—someone she mourned fiercely—had suddenly appeared before her at the mention of his name, and her emotions ran hot. 'He sent you a new play?'

'Certainly. It was delivered here only a few days ago, and then this morning another package arrived. The messenger said it was a gift for you.'

As Anna watched in puzzlement and confusion, her father fetched a small wooden chest from the desk and laid it on her lap. It was heavy and solid.

'Have you opened this, Father?' she asked.

'Certainly not! It is for you.' He gave a sheepish

smile. 'I may have given it a shake or two, though. Go on and open it.'

Anna slowly turned the little key in the lock and eased back the lid. It felt so strange to find a gift from Rob after their parting—as if a conversation she'd thought abruptly over still went on.

And what a conversation it was. Before her lay a pile of gold and silver coins, along with a smaller box and a note.

She unfolded the paper and read Rob's bold, slashing hand: *For your peaceful country cottage, fairest Anna. Don't forget me.* That was all. But when she opened the little box she found a ring— a band of small pearls set in gold. Another note, a mere sliver of parchment, told her this had once been his mother's but now was hers, if she cared to wear it.

Cared to wear it? Anna pressed her hand to her mouth to keep from crying as she looked down at the ring. She felt doubly foolish now—first for letting Rob leave, and then for believing he cared nothing for her when her instincts had told her that he did. Their time together had not been a lie. It could not be.

'Father,' she said in a choked voice. 'What is this new play about?'

'It's quite splendid—exactly what an audience could desire,' Tom answered. 'A faraway kingdom where a princess falls in love with an assassin who saves her from a murderer, and she in turn saves him and redeems his soul from damnation. But they are parted, and he dies of love for her. Most moving, and several good fights, as well.'

'What else does a story need?' Anna murmured. She slid the ring onto her finger and locked up the chest of coins. It would not be for a country cottage where she would live alone, but for one to be shared. The princess had to fight for her assassin and his soul. She had to fight for her love. Rob had given her that strength, that belief in herself, and now she had to use it to bring him back to her.

'I must leave again, Father,' she said. 'But I will return soon.' And hopefully not alone.

The docks were crowded and chaotic as Anna pushed her way through, past sailors and confused passengers, stacks of crates waiting to be loaded. The salt-fish smell of the water and the hot tang of tar was thick there, and she was elbowed and jostled as she struggled to find her way.

Lady Essex had found the name of Rob's France-bound ship for her—the *Royal Henry*—and it was to depart on the evening tide. But there were so many ships being boarded for just such voyages, and Anna could not tell them apart.

She was determined to find him, though, and to learn the truth once and for all. If he preferred his work—a life of danger and excitement—to a life with her, then she would have to let him go, no matter how hard that would be.

But if he did leave because he thought it was best for her—because he thought to protect her as his assassin could not protect the princess—then she would have to gather her courage and tell him her own truth. She would rather face any danger with him than a hundred quiet years without him. She had found life again with him—life and hope and passion. If there was any chance at all that he felt the same, she had to seize it.

She stood up on tiptoe and strained to see past the people pressed in all around her. Time grew shorter. Soon all these vessels would slip their moorings and head one by one to the sea, and Rob would be on one of them.

'Where are you?' she whispered.

Then, as if to answer her, the crowd before her parted for an instant. In that space she caught a glimpse of Rob, clad in his black leather doublet and breeches and purple short cloak, hurrying past. It looked as if he, too, searched for something, with a fierce frown on his face.

'Robert!' she called. 'Robert, wait for me. I beg you!'

She pushed the people out of her way and ran towards him, dodging around crates and coils of rope. *Don't let him vanish,* she thought frantically. *Don't let him be my imagination.*

Her prayers were answered when she saw him again. He was hurrying towards her, and she dashed to him to throw herself into his arms. His embrace came around her, hard and fierce, and he lifted her from her feet.

She wound her arms around his neck and held on tightly, relieved he had not pushed her away or run from her. She—*they*—had this one chance.

'Anna, why are you here?' he demanded. 'Did you come alone?'

'Lady Essex wanted to send a footman with me, but there was no time to wait.'

'Lady Essex?'

'I was at Seething Lane, looking for you, and she found the name of your ship.' He slowly lowered her to her feet but they still held on to each other. 'I had to find you before you left—to ask you...'

Anna swallowed hard before she plunged forward. This was no time to hesitate, no time to be scared.

'To ask you to stay,' she said quickly. 'Or to beg you to take me with you. Either way, Robert, let me be with you.'

He stared down at her for a long, silent moment and her heart began slowly to sink. Then he laughed, and lifted her from her feet again to twirl her around.

'Anna, you have read my mind,' he said. 'I had come to the ship only to turn back again. I tried to be noble, to leave you—but I cannot. I'm too selfish. I need you too much.'

Anna laughed in giddy, heady relief. All her fears vanished like a spring storm banished by the sun. 'Then we are both selfish creatures, for I couldn't let you go. I had to know how you truly felt—if these days together meant anything to you.'

'Fairest Anna, they meant everything. All is changed for me—*you* have changed it. I never thought to know joy or peace again, and you brought them to me.' He kissed her tenderly, and in that soft touch of his lips on hers she tasted the truth of what he said.

All was changed for both of them. They had found the whole world with each other, and that was all that mattered.

'I love you, Anna,' Rob said. 'And if you will let me I will spend all my life striving to be worthy of you.'

'Robert Alden, I believe you have not said anything so poetical before,' Anna said with a happy laugh. 'I love you, too, and I promise you I will follow you wherever you go. To Paris, or Turkey, or an island jungle—you will never be rid of me.'

Rob grinned and kissed her again as they clung together against the world. 'That is a promise I will assuredly hold you to, my fairest Anna.'

Epilogue

'I will race you to the top, Mistress Alden!' Rob called.

Anna laughed and tugged on her horse's reins as she followed Rob up the slope of the grassy country hill. She had lost her hat, and her hair whipped around her shoulders, but she didn't care. It was a glorious high summer day, the sun warm and golden in the cloudless sky, bright green fields spread around them as far as could be seen. Hart Castle, which Elizabeth and Edward had loaned them for their honeymoon, loomed in the distance—their own private sanctuary for this precious time.

And she was on her way to a picnic with her new husband. She glanced at Rob as they galloped along the path, dirt and grass flying with their speed. He looked more handsome than ever,

his skin darkened by the country sun, his hair tousled and waving over his brow, his leather doublet
open over his unlaced shirt. He laughed with her,
light-hearted and happy.

Since he had left Walsingham's service and they
had married, it seemed as if a great burden was
lifted from them—a rock rolled away to let light
and fresh air stream in. Living in the Southwark
house behind the theatre was not ideal, but Rob
was writing his poetry and they were together.

It was wondrous to Anna—the way the more
they were together, the more she learned about
him, the more she loved him and wanted to be
with him.

They drew in their horses at the crest of the hill,
and as Anna caught her breath she studied the
landscape before them. The summer fields were
as rich and green as a velvet counterpane, promis-
ing a good harvest in the autumn. Off in the distance one way was the little village, where they
often walked to visit Mary Alden. Anna could see
the church spire there, the curl of smoke from the
bake-shop chimney.

And the other way lay the old Carrington estate—empty and abandoned since Thomas
Sheldon had been arrested and his lands seized by

the Queen. The gates were closed and padlocked, but she could make out the tall brick chimneys of the grand house, the rich gardens and groves of trees.

'It's a pretty prospect, is it not?' Rob asked.

'Very pretty, indeed,' Anna answered. 'I think it will be hard to go back to the soot and stink of London.'

'What if we did not have to?'

'Did not have to?' she said in surprise. She twisted in her saddle to look at her husband, who gave her a mischievous grin. 'What do you mean, Robert?'

'I have a surprise for you, wife. I received confirmation of it today, when the messenger came from London.' He swung down from his horse and reached up to take her by the waist and lift her to the ground beside him. 'Walk with me for a moment.'

Anna looped her arm through his and let him lead her down the other side of the hill. 'I'm not sure I can bear any more surprises.'

'I think you might like this one.'

'Tell me, then, before I burst from curiosity!' she demanded. He had already given her so, so much. What else was there in the world she could want?

'Walsingham has been persuaded that I should be rewarded for my good work,' he said. 'And he has at last agreed—I am to be given a portion of the Carrington estate.'

'The Carrington estate!' Anna stopped suddenly, staring down at the abandoned woods behind the locked gates.

'Not the house, of course,' said Rob. 'Not that we would want the cursed place. That's to go to some crony of the Queen's. We are to have the hunting lodge, along with a caretaker's cottage for your father and a portion of the farm. If we can learn to be farmers, there should be a fine living in it. And I can finish my new sonnets.'

'This is ours? Our home?' she whispered. 'Is this some sort of dream?'

Rob laughed. 'No dream, Anna dearest, and no trick, either. This is our home now, if you wish it to be. I will show you the letter for proof.'

'I need no proof, Robert, for I feel it in my heart. This *is* our home,' Anna said, her throat heavy with happy tears. She twirled round to her husband and rested her head on his shoulder as the fresh, sweet air of their new home wrapped around them. A beloved husband, a home, a place for them—it was all she had once thought could never be hers, and her heart was bursting with it all.

'And we will be happy here together for always?' she said.

Rob laughed and held her close. 'Yes, my love. For always.'

* * * * *

Author Note

In so many ways, writing historical romance is the perfect job for a 'nerd' like me! I can bring in many of my history obsessions and apply them to my characters, spend hours reading history books, and watch *Shakespeare in Love* over and over and call it 'Important Research.' What could be better?

Anna and Rob's story was inspired by a wonderful evening at the new Globe Theatre in London, watching a production of *A Midsummer Night's Dream*. I had long been obsessed with the Elizabethan theatre, and this trip was a dream come true—the closest I could come to experiencing a play the way sixteenth century audiences did. I knew I had to write a story set in the thrilling, dangerous environs of the Elizabethan underworld, and Robert, the writer/spy—inspired in part by the brilliant Christopher Marlowe, and by the famous actor Edward Alleyn, who married the daughter of theatre impresario Philip Henslowe—jumped into my mind right away. He was so dashing, and I fell a bit in love with him myself. Sadly, I had to relinquish him to Anna…

I was able to research several aspects of Elizabethan life for Rob and Anna's story—theatre, Sir Francis Walsingham and his espionage work, life in Southwark and other suburban—and lawless!—neighbourhoods, and the relations between the different classes of Elizabethan London. A backstage tour of the Globe and some books purchased in their shop gave me a very good start.

I also loved looking more deeply into the life of Spymaster Walsingham—one of the many fascinating characters of the Elizabethan era. He spent his life corralling information in a time when such an endeavour seemed impossible, managing a vast network of informants and agents in an effort to keep the Queen safe. He liked to use actors—such as the ill-fated Marlowe—due to their literacy, their powers of observation, their fluid movements, both geographically and socially, and the fact they always needed money.

Walsingham died in 1590, soon after the action of this story, but I enjoyed giving him a role in this tale, as well as his daughter Frances, Lady Essex—who, despite reputedly being rather plain, married first the famous poet Sir Philip Sidney and then the Court heartthrob the Earl of Essex.

And I also loved seeing what happened to Edward and Elizabeth, whom I first met in my *Undone* short story, *To Court, Capture, and Conquer!* They set me on this journey in the first place, and I'm glad to see they are still happily in love and having adventures.

Please visit my website—http://ammandamccabe. com—for more behind-the-book history!